He Fixed The Match
She Fixed Him

Shikha

Vitasta

Let Knowledge Spread

Published by
Vitasta Publishing Pvt Ltd
2/15, Ansari Road, Daryaganj,
New Delhi - 110 002
info@vitastapublishing.com

ISBN 978-93-82711-50-6
© Shikha 2015

All Rights Reserved.
No part of this publication may be reproduced, stored in a retrieval system, or transmitted, in any form, or by any means—electronic, mechanical, photocopying, recording or otherwise—without the prior permission of the publisher.
All the names and the characters in this book are fictitious. Resemblance to anyone, living or dead, is purely coincidental.

Typeset by Vitasta Publishing Pvt Ltd
Printed by Vits Press, New Delhi

Dedicated to my parents, Shobha and Vipin Mehra—who never preached the righteous way of life. They lived it flawlessly and I simply followed.

I could have never ever made it without you two.

My 'Love ki factory' & 'Life ki Battery'—My husband Suman & our son Parth.

Contents

1. A Heaven-sent Phone Call — 1
2. A Man With A Past — 8
3. The First Conversation — 18
4. The Kohli Men In Mumbai — 25
5. Did Kunal Meet Shreya? — 34
6. Preparations, Operation And An Unexpected Guest — 42
7. Seven Vows Of Marriage — 51
8. The Veil Is Lifted — 57
9. The Grand Reception — 63
10. Another Seven Vows Of Marriage — 68
11. Jab They Met — 73
12. Shreya's Revenge — 78
13. Life Moves On — 85
14. The Match Begins — 88
15. When The Going Gets Tough, The Tough Get Going — 96
16. What's Cooking? — 101
17. Horror Date — 109
18. Accident At The Factory — 112
19. Quality Testing? — 117

20.	Delhi and London	127
21.	The Joy Of Giving	134
22.	Fasting Time	140
23.	Mumma Finds Out	146
24.	Attack—The Siege Begins!	163
25.	Mid-Anniversary	178
26.	Happy Diwali Indeed	186
27.	A Divine Evening	192
28.	Kunal's Ma-in-law	206
29.	Final Bastion	216
30.	One Two, Mumma Loves You	226
31.	A Dirty Secret	235
32.	Love Expressed	248
33.	Happy Trip to Jeju	257
34.	Together We Stand	264
35.	To sum it Up	278

Acknowledgements

Kumar Suman, my husband, is the first one to thank for standing by me through an array of emotions—excitement, hesitation, rejection, acceptance, fear, confusion and craziness. But for such tremendous in-house support, my world would have appeared unstable.

My parents, for always motivating and believing in me and for filling me with faith, self-confidence, happiness and positivity.

My brother Vishal Mehra and his wife Jisha Mehra, with whom I shared every crazy idea that crossed my mind. For their unconditional love, even when oceans apart.

The families who surround me—the Mehras, Wahis, Kumars, Tanejas and Nirulas. I've always learnt a lot from them.

Swati Aggarwal and Deepa Wahi, my friends to whom I can make the most honest confessions without ever being judged. For their friendship, without any strings attached.

Nidhi Arora, my cousin, for walking with me through the entire journey of the book.

Manish Pathak, a friend and a guide to the marketing world, for bringing great publicity ideas. I just knew how to write but very little about how to sell. (He's CEO at Nokooda, a social enterprise working in the field of Environment and sustainable development.) Renu Rao, my first editor, who reminded me of my class sixth English teacher by painting my manuscript red. But was far more pleasant. She was the first ever to make me believe that my script was 'good stuff'.

Veena Batra, my editor at Vitasta Publishing, who gave it the required shape. Renu Kaul Verma, my publisher, for accepting my book and giving me wings. I will always be grateful to her for believing in me.

My nutty friends who went to Bal Bharti Public School, Brij Vihar with me. We all are rockstars in our own sense. Thanks for being a part of my fondest childhood memories.

My friends—Khanna Aunty, Tanurima and Anuj Aggarwal, for sharing my enthusiasm.

Last but not the least, my son Parth for being someone I needed to make proud. Mumma loves you.

Thanks to Nitin Grover, Managing Director and Nikhil Grover, Director at *Scavin International Exim Pvt Ltd* for co-branding my book. It's an absolute delight for a first time author to receive such marvellous support from an established business house.

Special thanks to *Happytrips.com* for giving me the opportunity to be associated with them. I have always been an avid visitor to their website. It's an honour to be associated with the prestigious banner.

Thanks to *Bharatmatrimony.com* team for joining as promotional partners and for their generous support and encouragement. It's an honour to be associated with this esteemed banner.

A Heaven-sent Phone Call

It's advisable to be careful about what you wish for; a cold breeze could be a tornado approaching.

"Delhi is very soothing at this time of the year," Mahesh said appreciatively, as he sat down on his rocking chair, sipping his third cup of tea, watching his wife Sandhya shelling peas effortlessly. Not being able to stand the fact of peas gaining more attention than him, Mahesh made another attempt.

"You are perhaps the best tea-maker of the country, Sandhya." She looked up, blushing at the out-of-the-blue compliment.

"Mr Kohli, I'm so glad that now that you're retired you can manage to take out time to appreciate small things."

Mr Kohli smiled back flirtatiously. "Retirement is great, you get to be your own boss and tell yourself to do nothing all day." They chortled together.

"So what next?" Sandhya teased.

"World Tour, let's start finding interesting places on HappyTrips.com."

"I see you stuck to that site all day." Sandhya raised a brow.

"Yes, so much information, so much fun." He grinned.

"By the way is Madhav travelling to Pune tomorrow?" He asked; she nodded.

Madhav Kohli is the elder son of the couple. He's thirty years old, an MBA from FMS, Manager with a leading computer manufacturing company in a demanding job that calls for a lot of travel. Madhav is married to his childhood love Aastha for about eight months now. Aastha is a computer engineer working with a software consultancy firm.

"I really like Aastha's idea of a full-time domestic help," Mahesh said thoughtfully. "It would be a help to you."

Sandhya smiled back. "Not at all; I've been doing this for years now. Just one more family member isn't really extra work. However, when Aastha gives me an additional family member, I swear I'll take her opinion without a second thought."

Mahesh shook his head, "You're being pushy here; it's just been eight months." Their eyes locked and Sandhya laughingly admitted to being impatient to be a grandma.

The smiles shrank noticeably as they contemplated the problem that had caused them sleepless nights for months now. "I know she's at a marriageable age now. And you know it's really tough to find a match for a girl like ours. She earns more than double the guys of her age do. All discussion just ends as soon as the groom's side hears about her pay package."

Sandhya put her hand on his shoulder. "What about the *Bharat Matrimony* site? Did any good match respond?"

Mahesh looked at her with a little disappointment. "No, Sandhya. There were a few queries over her profile, but no one reverted back."

Sandhya made a face, "...And then our kids are always bragging about e-age."

Before the discussion could move forward, the phone in the living room burst into shrill peals. Mahesh walked swiftly to answer. He cleared his voice before picking up the receiver, "Hello."

"Namaste. Am I speaking to Mr Mahesh Kohli?" A middle-aged female voice asked.

"Oh yes, it's me. Namaste. May I know who's calling?"

"Well, I'm Anuradha Kharbanda calling from Mumbai," the lady answered. "And this is with regard to your daughter's profile on the *Bharat Matrimony* portal. Is it a good time to talk?"

Mahesh charged up to sing his usual anthem. "Yes. Yes, please. Of course, it's always a good time to talk about good things. Well, my daughter works with a leading audit company, and she earns…" Mahesh was interrupted abruptly yet politely.

"Mr Kohli, I did read the details about her work and qualifications on her profile. I know all that."

"Oh! Of course you must have, ma'am. I was just trying to provide a brief introduction." He hoped he didn't overdo it.

"Yes, I do understand. But I am totally disinterested in her income. I am really happy with the fact that my son liked her picture. I have been trying hard for about a year to get him interested in any girl's profile. Your daughter's face has caught his attention. And that means more than anything to me."

Mahesh gulped turning his head towards Sandhya, standing near the kitchen door. She registered the context of the call and wanted to play a constructive role. She whispered, "Ask about the guy's qualifications." Mahesh nodded and spoke.

"Well ma'am, that's really a good thing to know. May I please know something about your son's occupation?"

"Of course, you must. We live in Mumbai, and my son is 29 years old and an MBA from Oxford. We are the owners of

Kharbanda Textiles. Have you heard of it?" Her pride chimed in her voice.

"I am sorry, ma'am. I don't know much about clothes. In fact, I have never been to the market to even buy clothes for myself. My wife does that for me."

"It's okay. My husband, when he was alive, never went shopping with me too. Do you want to know more about our firm?"

Mahesh was bewildered, and also distracted by Sandhya's constant gestures to put the phone on speaker so that she could hear the conversation, too.

"Can you hear me, Mr. Kohli?" Mumbai questioned.

"Of course I can, ma'am. I am sorry for not being so well-informed about textiles." Mahesh frowned at his wife and put his finger to his lips to quieten her.

"Let's meet then," Mrs Kharbanda was saying. "Is travelling to Mumbai alright with you?" The enthusiasm from the other side was well-matched with the Kohli's.

"Sure, ma'am. My younger brother lives in Mumbai. Can I ask him to come over, before I travel to Mumbai?" He asked hesitatingly.

"That's really a great idea. I will have my address and phone number mailed over to you right away," Anuradha replied. "But, hmmm…."

Mahesh detected a little discomfort in her tone, and enquired immediately, "What happened, ma'am?"

"Well, nothing as such. But I would really like you to meet my son, personally, before we talk any further. I would really appreciate it if you judge him first hand for his qualities," Anuradha said assertively.

"Sure, ma'am. And I wish the same treatment from you for my daughter. She's a jewel of a person; I hope you like her for what she is." The father's eyes filled with tears as he said that.

Sandhya shook his shoulders while murmuring, "Name?" Mahesh realised she had a very valid question. "Ma'am, can I have your son's name?"

"Kunal Kharbanda," the proud mother replied. "He's a very nice, affectionate and intelligent boy whom I am very proud of. But don't believe me. Come over, meet him and find out for yourself."

Mahesh smiled and his joy could be felt in his voice too. "Sure, ma'am. I look forward to that." He smiled at Sandhya expressing his triumph. She smiled back.

"I'll hang up now. It was really nice talking to you. Kunal was very excited to see your girl's picture and profile. He said it'd be great to have someone so qualified to join our family business too. I hope to meet you soon. Namaste."

"Namasteji. Namaste," Mahesh said respectfully. He hung up the phone and Sandhya started darting questions at him.

Mahesh flopped down into a chair and took his time to let the discussion sink in. Sandhya chose silence finally and sat next to her husband. Somehow she waited a few minutes for him to compose his emotions. He then looked at her and said, "If all goes well, it could be the best match we can ever find for her." Sandhya was elated. The couple held hands and he narrated the entire conversation to his wife.

Later that evening the entire family sat down for dinner. Next to Sandhya sat the most beloved member of the family: the darling daughter of the Kohli couple, the adorable little sister of Madhav and the childhood best friend of Aastha: Shreya.

Shreya Kohli is about 5 feet 6 inches tall. She's fair and has beautiful black eyes. There's a spark in her eyes; eyes you can't ignore unless she's wearing her black-rimmed spectacles. She has a pointed nose and naturally pink lips. Her hair falls halfway to her waist; she's slim but the kind of girl who doesn't have an agenda of working on her curves.

One thing everyone surely notices about her is the calmness on her face, evidence of her maturity and intelligence. For a 27 year old to attain that is really remarkable in the corporate world. Shreya for some reason is far more mature for her age. She's a B Com (Hons) from SRCC, Delhi University, followed by an MBA from IIM, Lucknow. And it's because of these credentials of hers that today's phone call was no less than heaven-sent for her parents.

Shreya noticed her parents looking at her more emotionally than usual. "Is everything okay?" she asked. To ward off any suspicion Mahesh said, "Oh yes, of course. Can't I look at my daughter? God knows how many more dinners she can share with us before she leaves for her final home." Madhav's ears perked up—something unusual had obviously happened today. This thought had never been served with dinner before.

Later that night, after Shreya went to her room, Mahesh asked the rest of the family to stay back.

"Yes Dad, what is it? I can make out something's happened," Madhav said.

"Oh yes, it was a good day for us. But before that, have you heard of Kharbanda Textiles of Mumbai?" Mahesh enquired.

Madhav pulled out his smartphone and read out the information. "They are one of the major garment manufacturers in India; they have a good reputation." He paused. "The owner is 29 years old, an Oxford guy. That's impressive. No picture though." He suddenly stopped. "Dad, I am sure that this family discussion has nothing to do with how they run their business."

Mahesh looked at Shreya's room to confirm that the door was shut. "We had a call from them this morning offering their son's alliance for Shreya." Madhav's eyes widened and so did Aastha's.

"Are you sure, Dad?" Aastha asked excitedly.

"What next, Dad?" Madhav asked.

"Akash will visit them after two days, and he'll call us up and then we both shall visit them," Mahesh suggested.

"Yes, that's a great plan, Dad. We mustn't delay it and also make sure Shreya doesn't hear about it until it's nearly *pucca*," Aastha said softly to ensure that her voice didn't reach Shreya's door.

"You know her very well, Aastha," Sandhya smiled fondly at her daughter-in-law.

"And we hope it works out well." Mahesh heaved a sigh of relief. Everyone smiled. Somehow they all felt that their search was over.

As Aastha left the room, Madhav turned to his parents. "Dad, don't you think we must be honest with them about Shreya's past in the initial discussion itself?"

Sandhya's smile vanished and worry took over. "What past? It's an old story now. Why are you bringing it up when there's some hope of happiness in her life?" Mahesh gestured helplessly to Sandhya to stop.

"Mom, you know I'm the biggest well-wisher Shreya can ever have. But I know Shreya. If you don't tell that guy, Shreya will surely do that first thing," Madhav said giving a hug to her. "Don't worry, Mom. I know Shreya will be the most valued possession of her husband."

A Man With A Past

Two days later, Mahesh was literally hovering around his phone; picking up the receiver every two minutes to check that the line was working. Madhav had also returned a night earlier from his official trip and decided to take the day off to hear the entire conversation.

The phone finally rang!

Mahesh almost jumped towards his phone but Madhav was far quicker. He put the phone on speaker, as he knew that later he may have to depend on his father's selective account of the conversation.

They all shared namastes and formal how-are-you-doing queries.

"Well, Akash. How did you like him?" Mahesh asked curiously.

"What should I say, *Bhaisahab*? I am not sure what your stand will be on this. After all Shreya too has a past," Akash replied honestly.

Madhav got impatient. "Uncle, please can you elaborate? This vague information doesn't really help."

"Well, son, Kunal's mother was very welcoming and is really looking forward to her son settling down. The house is big and spacious, and I noticed at least four servants. And since the house is in Juhu, I am sure they are making very good money." Akash sounded no less than a news reporter.

"What about the guy, Uncle? I am much more interested there," Madhav asked assertively.

"Well...." And there was a big pause. "The guy is very good looking. In fact, he looks like a hero. Also, he is nice and the only successor of the family. After his father's demise about three years back he runs the entire business, and they are doing very well. "

Madhav was relieved by his uncle's answer. He suddenly recalled Akash mentioning the past. But before he could frame his question, his mother asked, "What is this past thing?"

A big pause again.

"Well, *Bhabhi,* it's not actually your fault if sometimes things don't work out."

"You are making me curious, Akash," Mahesh said.

"Well, *Bhaisahab.* About two years back Kunal was married for four months. His ex-wife was a supermodel and the marriage failed miserably since she chose her career over her family life. My son Prateek has a friend who knows Kunal and I verified these details from him," Akash said.

Everyone at the other end was dead silent, staring blankly at each other. A silence of a few seconds had the gravity of hours.

"Yes, Uncle. Anything else?" Madhav still wanted to know about the situation. Both his parents gave him a furious look. "Well, that's pretty much it, my boy. Mrs. Kharbanda really insisted on meeting face to face." He added, "And one more thing."

"What, Uncle?" Madhav asked.

Akash said, "Kunal insisted he wants to speak to Shreya before she takes any decision. He said, 'I can't force someone to marry me, but I would like a reason other than my divorce from the girl. If my past is a big deal then it's me who should be answering her questions'."

"Leave it, Akash *bhai*. We are wasting our time here now," Sandhya said with irritation. "Why the hell do I need to marry my daughter to a divorcee?"

"Well, *Bhabhi,* this could happen to anybody. It almost did happen to Shreya herself." Akash regretted the words as soon as they left his mouth. However, the damage was done. Sandhya was furious.

"Well, in that case let me tell you that calling off an engagement is a far minor issue than dissolving a marriage. You should know to equate things properly."

Madhav gestured to his mother to cool down.

"I'm sorry if I hurt you, *Bhabhi*. Shreya is like a daughter to me and I want the best for her. And if you can really overlook this petty divorce issue, Shreya will live like a queen. He's well-settled, belongs to a good family, is well-educated, liberal in his thinking and is very affectionate. He has a younger sister too, who's married in London. Every *Rakshabandhan* he visits her personally to make her day. But then Shreya is your daughter; your decision has to be final." Akash paused again. "And, I repeat, he wants to speak to Shreya."

Mahesh interrupted before Sandhya could charge at him again. "We heard you, Akash. Thanks for taking out time and doing this for us. We really need to talk this over."

The call finally concluded leaving the entire Kohli family at Delhi dumbfounded.

"So much work pending. I wasted so much time uselessly the past two days." Sandhya's disappointment and irritation were very clear.

"Yes, I too need to go for my evening walk," Mahesh responded in the same mood and both left the living room the next moment.

Madhav stayed back, sitting quietly staring at the phone. He was thinking.

There was a brooding silence at the dinner table and the elder Kohli couple, particularly, were in an extremely bad mood. Shreya came in smiling. "Hey guys, I have an announcement to make."

"What is it dear?" Aastha asked smiling.

"I quit my present job. The new company has offered me a 30 percent hike and an even better job profile," Shreya replied with excitement.

"Wow! You need to treat us for that," Aastha replied.

"Take it easy, Shreya. You were so well-settled in your present company. And what is this hike again? Soon, your annual income in lakhs will match your age." Mahesh's words confused Shreya, but before she could speak, Madhav interrupted.

"And what is wrong with that?" He smiled at Shreya to provide her the encouragement she was hoping for.

"Well, Shreya's ambition is understandable," Mahesh said. "But she needs to know that family is important too."

"Hang on!" Shreya interrupted. "How's my changing companies linked to not giving importance to family? You guys are my world."

"We aren't talking about us, Shreya," Sandhya raised her voice a little. "And I don't understand how all three of you, such geniuses at your workplaces, raise the most childish questions possible when it comes to family matters." Sandhya stared at Shreya. "Do you even know how much trouble we are facing to find a suitable boy for you? Then you come here raising the bar even more. Why is it so difficult for you to read your parents' minds?"

Shreya was shocked at this unexpected objection. "Everyone is looking for better opportunities, and there will be many guys who are so well-settled too. It's just a matter of time when things click. As I always said, I just want him to understand my passion for work and not be more than 30 years of age. Besides that I don't even care. You know I agreed to get married just to make you happy; I won't mind being single all my life otherwise."

Madhav was uncomfortable at seeing Shreya having to give justifications on a trivial issue. "Mummy, I really like the fact that Aastha loves her job. And Shreya is also the same. This is how the modern Indian woman is." Madhav's voice now showed restrained anger. "And, if asking for some understanding is really asking too much, then so be it. It should have been a time of celebration that she is moving to a better job; it's so unfortunate that we ended up with a discussion like this."

"It's okay. Let's just cut it short," Mahesh took control, turning to Shreya. "My child, I know there are many successful guys too. But most of them are either committed, or don't support an ambitious wife or are not really nice guys. So, it's actually not that easy as you think." His smile broadened, "Also dear, I won't make any compromise when it comes to finding a perfect match for you."

Shreya replied, "Talking about compromises, it's a fast moving world; we all have a past and shortcomings. There's nothing called a perfect match anymore; it's all a matter of how you can carve your relationship to perfection."

Madhav looked at Shreya with immense pride and knew deep down that his sister was very mature, and for her, values and abilities mattered more than the thoughts his parents were pondering over.

Later that night Madhav was not able to sleep. He raised his pillow against the headboard and sat up. Aastha finally asked him, "Are you still thinking about that Mumbai call?"

He caressed her hair. "How do you always manage to read me?"

Aastha raised her head a little and replied, "Bad childhood habits die hard." Both laughed lightly.

"Yes, dear," Madhav spoke soberly now. "For some reason, I see him as a prospective match for Shreya. And if he's as capable as he sounds, then surely Shreya won't be bothered about his divorce, since the marriage lasted just four months, and none of it was his fault. Uncle investigated."

Aastha replied, "Do you think we should speak to Shreya?"

Madhav sighed, "Mom-Dad won't appreciate that. But it's a good match. They look forward to her joining their family business. It can really do wonders for Shreya's life."

Aastha nodded. "Shreya is extremely sensible for her age. But when her engagement was called off five years back, she kind of lost any enthusiasm to be in a relationship again." Her voice got heavy. "I would love to see her being in love again. It's her stubbornness to not pay attention to this matter that keeps her so busy with work."

Madhav held Aastha's hand. "I wish the same for her. And the only thing I pray for is that the guy she marries doesn't get insecure with her capabilities, but loves her for her qualities and has plenty of his own. This Kharbanda guy would have no reason to be insecure of a highly talented wife, and she can in fact be a big asset for him." He looked at his wife for an answer.

"Absolutely, my dear," Aastha said giving him a warm hug.

The next morning everyone prepared to leave for office. He waited for Shreya to leave to speak to his parents. He requested his father not to give any negative answer if they got a call from the Kharbandas.

A couple of hours later, Mrs Kharbanda did call. Mahesh explained that their elder son was out of the city and assured her they would get back to them by Monday.

Friday evening is blissful for everyone in the corporate world. All three children of the Kohli house returned in the evening in a jovial mood and unanimously decide to order pizza for dinner. It was a fun-filled evening with the whole family and they also celebrated Shreya's new job, which she was scheduled to join after four weeks. After dinner, Aastha and Madhav waited for their parents' room light to go off before speaking to Shreya.

"Shreya, Mom and Dad may kill me for this, but I want you to know." Madhav spoke softly. "Well, there's a reason they were so irritated yesterday."

Shreya nodded, "I guessed so. It was really very unlike them to react in that manner."

"Is it something I've done?"

"Not at all, dear. It's just a potential alliance for you, which went sour," Aastha replied, patting Shreya's shoulder.

"Can I have the entire story, please?" Shreya was curious.

"Well, you've heard about Kharbanda Textiles? There was a proposal for their only son. He kind of really liked your picture,"

Madhav answered smiling.

"What?!" Shreya fluttered. "My picture?" She paused. "Are you guys sure? I haven't heard anything like that in years now!"

"Why? What's wrong with your picture? You have such a pretty face, especially those big black eyes. What kind of useless question is that?" Aastha really loved her and didn't appreciate Shreya belittling herself in this way.

Madhav looked at his wife lovingly. "Well said, Aastha."

Aastha continued. "And the picture on the matrimonial website is the one taken at our wedding. You looked stunning that day. Anyone who'd see you like that would jump from a building for you."

Shreya suddenly homed in on two words. "Wait a minute. What is this matrimonial website?" Aastha bit her tongue, realizing she'd given out a secret.

"You mean my picture is all over the internet saying "PLEASE MARRY ME?" How could you guys do that? I don't even like to have a Facebook account and you put me on display on a matrimonial website," Shreya was really upset.

"Relax. You've got to leave it to us to find a good match," Madhav tried to calm her down. "And we have an even more important thing to talk about right now."

"Anyway, what more about the guy?" Shreya said and was smouldering.

"He's 29 years old and from Mumbai. Oxford graduate. Very good looking, according to Akash Uncle," Madhav narrated.

"Akash Uncle? You guys have really done good homework. I'm really the last one to know," she blasted again.

"Shreya, can you please hear me out without reacting?" Madhav was now getting a little irritated.

"Fine. Yes, so he's from Mumbai, 29 years old, Oxford graduate. Very good looking but he still liked my picture!" Shreya was rueful. "And yet it went sour?" She looked at Madhav in confusion.

"Well, it's only one single fact about this guy. It's his past," he said.

"We all have a past. I too have a past. But I don't want it to eclipse my entire life. It's not worth it," Shreya said sympathetically.

"See, Shreya. I know you are a very positive person and a liberal thinker. And that's the only reason we decided to talk this over with you. Because when Akash Uncle met the guy, he said some very impressive things. He said that he'd like to talk to the girl and know a reason for turning down the proposal other than his past," Madhav said.

Shreya grew more curious. "What exactly is wrong with his past? Was he a criminal?"

Madhav moved closer to Shreya to answer. "No, dear. It's just that he was married for four months about two years back. And his ex-wife moved out of the marriage to pursue her modelling career."

Shreya looked up at them blankly and paused briefly before speaking anything. "Does he have a child out of that marriage?"

Aastha replied instantly, "No. If you are moving out of marriage to pursue a glamorous profession, a child would be out of the question."

Madhav added, "I googled this guy today; all his credentials are genuine. But he seems to be like you; there was no picture of him anywhere." He paused. "I think we should leave now and let you think it over."

Shreya was quiet and just gently nodded back. Aastha left the room first and just when Madhav was about to close the door,

Shreya spoke. "Maddy," he turned immediately.

"Yes, Shreya?"

Shreya spoke with a little hesitation "Name please?"

Madhav smiled back at his little sister, "Kunal Kharbanda."

The First Conversation

It was raining the next morning. Everyone had gathered for breakfast. Madhav and Aastha looked at Shreya keenly, wondering how she was feeling after their conversation the night before, but she returned their looks with a blank face. Suddenly the phone disturbed their slient interaction.

Madhav answered. It was Akash uncle from Mumbai enquiring whether he needed to pay the Kharbandas another visit. "Well Uncle, it's top on our agenda to talk it out today. We'll get back to you by evening."

As Madhav took his seat again at the dining table, Sandhya gave him an angry look. "Madhav, we don't have anything to talk, I hope I am making myself clear?" Shreya quietly continued to eat, pretending not to listen.

"Mom! You really need to think again. Such proposals don't come everyday," Aastha supported her husband, winning Sandhya's annoyed look.

Mahesh jumped in, "Why are you so insistent, Madhav?"

"Well, I think people do deserve a second chance. And apart from that one issue, everything does appear picture perfect to me," Madhav spoke affirmatively.

"Whatever, Madhav. The topic stands closed. He can have his second chance with anyone else on this planet," Sandhya said thumping the table. She turned to move away but was stopped by Shreya's gentle grip on her wrist.

"Mom! Five years back you taught me life is beautiful and we must always work to make it better every day," she spoke gently. "And for you calling off an engagement might be a minor thing but, maybe someone I get married to, may taunt me my entire life for this."

Sandhya put her hand on Shreya's head, "I can make out that you know what we are talking about. We are not in a hurry; we can really wait for a better match."

"No, Mom! It's not an issue about a good match or a better match. My concern is that you are being unfair to someone for his past." Sandhya looked at Madhav and Aastha accusingly. She figured the two of them had spoken to Shreya. "If you look forward to some compassion for your own child in this regard, you should also be open-hearted to someone else's child as well." Shreya paused to clear her throat. "Still, I maintain that for me the credentials and personal qualities come first. And I would like to evaluate the match on those criteria."

She looked at her father. "So if I have your permission, I too would like to speak to the guy." She continued, "Let's see whether we are really two well-educated and liberal individuals or just hapless victims of our past."

Shreya left the dining table. The elder Kohli couple looked at each other blankly and the junior one joyfully.

A few hours later Madhav walked up to his father in the balcony. "Dad, what's the delay all about now? You are not getting married. So you don't have to think so much." Mahesh finally surrendered to Madhav. He moved to the living room and did the needful. Delhi called Mumbai.

"Namasteji. This is Mahesh Kohli."

"So nice to hear from you." There was a delighted note in Mrs Kharbanda's voice.

"Well, my son returned yesterday. And we spoke about your proposal. He had a suggestion about the situation at your end," Mahesh said.

"What is that, Mr Kohli?"

Mahesh said, "We should let Kunal and Shreya talk and decide what they think about it. After all, it's their life. And if she's fine with Kunal's past then we certainly have no issue with the alliance. Similarly, Shreya may also have something to talk to Kunal before things move further." Madhav kissed his father's cheek gratefully as he said these words.

"You took the words out of my mouth, *Bhaisahab*. I am so much of the same opinion. These days kids think differently than we used to. We should let them take the world forward," the happy note continued. "I will have Kunal call Shreya today itself. Please message me her number."

It was about 10 pm that evening Shreya was reading a suspense thriller when her phone buzzed. She almost screamed in fright; she was so engrossed in the story. She took a few seconds to collect herself and took a deep breath before answering. "Hello."

"Hello," a very clear and deep masculine voice hit Shreya's ear. "Am I speaking to Shreya?" Shreya was impressed with the voice.

"Yes, it's me. May I know who's calling?"

"This is Kunal Kharbanda. Is it a good time to talk?" Shreya was stunned; Madhav hadn't told her Kunal would be calling so soon. "Oh, hello. Yes. We can talk right now," she managed to say.

"Well, I am not sure how to start." Kunal paused. "I hope that you know what this is all about?"

Shreya had a big smile on her face, realizing the awkwardness of the situation. "Well, yes, I know."

"Thank God you do. At least I know that I don't have to formally introduce myself." Kunal sounded relieved. "How's the weather in Delhi?"

"Well, winter is on its way back to the Himalayas and summer should be moving up from Chennai soon," Shreya said teasingly.

"Ahaa. Good that Delhi people have guests that leave in due time. We here in Mumbai don't even get the good fortune to offer hospitality to anyone from the Himalayas," Kunal replied wittily. "I saw your credentials. I hope you are not a nerd?" Kunal teased.

Shreya smiled. "Well, it's a matter of perception. Even an Oxford pass-out could be posed the same question."

"Well, I am not. In fact, I didn't even deserve to go to Oxford. But my dad thought I was a bright student," Kunal replied, laughing.

"Well, what does that mean, 'your dad thought'?"

"As you said, it's a matter of perception. I think I was just a better student than he was." They both laugh out aloud.

Kunal's voice became serious. "Shreya, I have something important to talk about before we go any further. See, I need you to know a few things, since it might come up later if I don't address it right now."

"Yes, sure. If that makes you feel better, please go ahead. But you need to hear me out as well once you're done," Shreya said.

"Well, Saloni and I dated for about one year before I proposed.

She wanted to postpone it for a few more years, but I really wanted it to happen. She finally did succumb to my wish, but half-heartedly. I kind of take the blame for forcing her into the marriage. On her insistence, though, we had a simple court marriage.

"She started feeling within the first two months of marriage that it was the end of her career. Then she spread the word around that we hadn't really got married and that she was very much single. However, we did have to get legally divorced for her to be free and so we did go that route. We were married not even four months."

Shreya sympathized with him. "I'm sorry to hear that. I too had a broken engagement five years back. Is that a concern to you?"

"Absolutely not. Since I look forward to a life where the present and future matter, I should be wise enough to offer you the same," Kunal instantly replied.

Shreya was moved. "I must say, I like the way you think."

"Then shall we bury the topic of the past and can we talk more about each other?" Kunal sounded positive.

"That's really a good idea," Shreya smiled.

"Well, I know my mother is not very good at keeping secrets. She must have expressed my opinion on your profile," Kunal's voice became soft again.

"You know, it's just last night that I discovered that I have a profile on a matrimonial website. It's so embarrassing to be put on display," Shreya said hesitatingly.

"Oh no, it's a requirement today. How else will Mumbai and Delhi connect otherwise?"

"Yes, right, e-age!" Shreya laughed.

"By the way, did anyone tell you that you have beautiful eyes?" Shreya turned pink at the unexpected compliment.

"Well, hmmm…I don't know. I mean, I think they're very average," Shreya failed to find any other answer.

"No, I think they really are beautiful." Shreya chose to be silent rather than give a stupid answer.

"Also, we have a vacancy on our board of directors. I think your qualifications can be really instrumental there. Would you also like to join our company, and not just the family?" Kunal asked without hesitation.

He waited for over 30 seconds, but didn't hear anything back.

"Does Delhi usually sleep while on a call, or is this just an exception?"

"Well, Kunal, we've just talked about 15 minutes," Shreya answered shyly. "I think, let's meet once in person before we take a final call. And I think our families should also meet personally before they can take that call."

Kunal took a few seconds before speaking. "I respect your opinion. I think you make complete sense, and it's a better approach to any alliance. I will have my mother invite your family to our home." Kunal continued, "Does that suit you?"

Shreya was completely clueless on what to say next. All she knew was that Kunal was impressively eloquent and an honest person.

"Well, absolutely. I would like to leave it to them to make the next move. But all I can say is that it was really nice talking to you." Shreya almost blushed as she said so.

"Same here, Shreya. It's one of the most wonderful conversations I've ever had." Joy ringed clearly in his voice too.

"Can I ask one more question?" she said.

"Please do. Most welcome."

"Do...do you smoke?" Shreya asked hesitatingly. This was one habit she couldn't stand.

"No, I don't. In fact, I hate smoking." Kunal replied calmly. Shreya was relieved.

They ended the conversation with good night and, more importantly, "Catch you later."

The Kohli Men In Mumbai

It was raining the next morning too. Shreya stood at the open window of her room. It had been a long time since she had admired the rain and its accompanying breeze. She was more in the habit of complaining of the effect untimely rains have on the roads and the worsening traffic jams in Delhi.

Today was different; the rain appeared beautiful and the wet soil fragrant. The wind from the window ruffled her hair and she started to enjoy the sensation, shaking her head to let the wind play around easily. There was a smile on her face as if she was rediscovering herself. The wind got stronger and she shut the window. She now saw a weak reflection of her face in the window, and she smiled as she remembered the words: *"By the way, did anyone tell you that you have beautiful eyes?"*

It was the usual breakfast time, with a little discussion on miscellaneous topics. Just when everyone was about to leave the table, Shreya cleared her throat. "Dad, that Kunal called up last night."

Madhav and Aastha were very interested. "Well, so?" Aastha teased. Shreya got even more self-conscious.

"Well, I think you may want to visit Mumbai." Shreya blushed and fled to her room. She could hear Madhav and Aastha laughing at her embarrassing performance.

Mahesh was still unsure and Sandhya was adamant about letting go of the proposal. Madhav, however, was in no mood to entertain their concerns any further. He called his boss to make sure he could take a day off the next week. While all these preparations were being made, the phone made its presence felt loudly.

"Well, *Bhaisahab*! When can I have the privilege of hosting you and your family at our residence?" Anuradha Kharbanda's excited voice came over the wire.

"That's exactly what my son is working on. I retired last month, so I'm free any time, but he needs to check his schedule." Mahesh now saw that Madhav had finalised the tickets on his laptop. "Well, ma'am, is Wednesday good for you? We could block the tickets for Tuesday night."

"My pleasure," Anuradha said.

The call ended with formal namastes.

Mahesh looked at Sandhya as soon as he finished the call. She was still against the whole idea.

On Wednesday, at 4:00 pm, Mahesh Kohli and Madhav Kohli were standing in front of a big black gate with a name plate carved in stone on the lower right which said, "Kharbandas".

A watchman opened the gate with a bow—he had been informed about important guests coming over. The house was a bungalow built on about 500 yards. There was a garden at the entrance and a driveway on the left, with a BMW parked there. The house was two-storeyed, painted beige on the outside, with wooden windows and doors. Mahesh and Madhav crossed the driveway to the main door of the house. It was already being held open by a servant who yelled, "*Maaji*, here they come."

A lady in her early fifties came almost running to the door.

"Namaste, Sir. Please come in. I am Anuradha Kharbanda. It's my immense pleasure to see you here." The joy in her eyes matched her warm words.

Anuradha Kharbanda was a woman of average height. She was pretty for her age—it was apparent she had taken good care of her hair and skin all her life. She wore a light blue silk saree and was very soft-spoken. She ushered them into the living room.

This was a very spacious room, with a sofa kept some steps from the entrance to the room and the dining area on the other side. From the left of the dining area there was a staircase climbing up to the upper storey. The doors of the rooms on the first floor were visible from the living room itself. The expensive interior reflected the standard of life of the Kharbandas.

"We are extremely sorry to be late. We should have been here by 3 pm but there was a terrible traffic jam," Mahesh said apologetically.

"You don't have to be sorry. Even Kunal is stuck in traffic," Anuradha replied.

While they spoke, the servants were arranging food on the table. Anuradha offered Mahesh and Madhav plates even as she chattered on. "Well, just to let you know a little more about our family. My husband passed away three years back after a sudden heart attack. The entire responsibility fell on Kunal's shoulders to run the business. After a few initial hiccups, my son has managed to do justice to his father's name. He has tremendous support from my sister's son. My daughter Ridhima married and settled in London four years ago. She's three years younger than Kunal."

Anuradha's eyes showed mixed feelings of loss and pride as she said so.

"Kunal's struggles didn't end there. Two years back his life hit the rocks again." Madhav interrupted her, "Ma'am, you don't have to mention that; we heard that from Shreya. And as long as she understands, it's not at all an issue with us." Anuradha smiled at Madhav. "God bless you!"

And before the discussion could move further, they heard a car stopping in the driveway. Seconds later they could hear footsteps moving quickly towards the main entrance. And Kunal Kharbanda walked in.

Madhav's jaw almost dropped on seeing Kunal. He was indeed one of the most handsome men he had ever seen.

He was about 6 feet tall, with a light wheatish complexion. He was in great shape and it was evident that he hit the gym regularly. He had a long face and black eyes. As he walked towards them, even the walk was very elegant. The guy certainly looks like a hero, Madhav thought and felt his sister was very careless in this regard. She too was one of the most beautiful creations of God but she had neither time nor the will to acknowledge that. *Sis, you have a big task at hand,* he thought.

Kunal very gently took out his *Scavin Aviator* sunglasses and hung them down the neck of his shirt. He then shook hands warmly with the guests.

"I am extremely sorry to keep you waiting. Mumbai traffic gets pretty ruthless at times," Kunal said shaking his head. Madhav admired his voice too. *Shreya was right.*

"Not at all; we too had a similar experience today. And, trust me, Delhi has the same story every day," Madhav replied.

"Thank you so much for your understanding. Can I please borrow five more minutes? I'm stinking," Kunal smiled. Madhav nodded.

Kunal sped upstairs and entered the central big room on the first floor.

"Well, that's Kunal's room. There are two more relatively smaller bedrooms on that floor," Anuradha informed them. "My room is on this floor. I have a heart problem, so the doctors suggested I avoid the stairs."

Kunal returned soon, dressed casually in a t-shirt and a pair of jeans. His good physique was now even more defined. Madhav was already getting inspired by Kunal to get into shape.

"Well, here he is. Please feel free to bombard him with questions." Anuradha smiled.

"Kunal, what kind of textiles do you deal with?" Madhav asked.

"Well, we have a factory set up on the Mumbai-Pune highway, closer to Pune. We have retail and wholesale customers in over six states, some export houses as well," Kunal answered with absolute confidence.

"I see. Then you must be spending time in Pune too?" Mahesh asked.

"No, I don't go to the factory that often. In fact, my mother's sister lives in Pune. Her husband is the manager there. His son Vineet travels there about twice a month to ensure smooth functioning of the Pune unit. The rest of the time he helps me out here with other operations and marketing."

Madhav smiled. "You must have a good-sized team for yourself."

Kunal turned to Madhav. "Yes, at the next level and ground level we have trained staff. But to oversee everything, it's mostly me and Vineet. It was pretty manageable until six months back but now the workload is really mounting. With the growing business we need more people at all levels, especially someone who can work at the top level with us."

Madhav was impressed. "You must be on the lookout for good resumes in that case."

Kunal nodded. "Yes. And I personally liked the one from Delhi." He smiled broadly as he said that. Everyone laughed.

The Kohli men spent a few more minutes at the Kharbanda residence before they took their leave. While everyone was walking towards the main entrance, Madhav purposely slowed down, forcing Kunal to slow down, too, till they were at a distance from other two. Madhav spoke softly. "Kunal, if it's okay with you, can I ask one last question? It's a personal one though."

Kunal nodded, "Yes, please feel free."

Madhav hesitated for a while, but then asked since it was important for him to know that. "Are you truly emotionally over your first marriage?"

Kunal replied, smiling spiritedly, "Yes, that is one thing I am very sure of as I am making a new beginning of my life. You can take my word there." He paused. "Trust me, there's nothing worth remembering about it."

Madhav smiled back.

"And can I have a photo of yours? Maybe Shreya would like to see it?"

"Let me know when she wants to see me. I look better in person than in a picture. Tell her, I hope to meet her soon," Kunal replied with a sweet smile.

They exchanged a warm handshake.

The Kohli men reached home on Thursday morning. Shreya was working from home although Aastha had already left for work. Madhav also logged onto his official laptop so as to report working from home.

"Well!" said Mahesh happily, "I'm extremely satisfied to have met the Kharbanda family. They are very well-to-do, yet very down-to-earth. I think we should take it forward." Sandhya was crestfallen. Shreya however wore a shy smile.

"Kunal especially was very impressive. He's really intelligent, good looking and a responsible man. I see him as the only perfect match I've come across for Shreya," Madhav said firmly. Shreya's smile turned into a blush.

Sandhya, by now, had realised that it was useless to stick to her point anymore. "What next?"

"Let's call them tomorrow morning, and invite them over to Delhi so that Shreya and Kunal can meet." Mahesh said.

Later that night when Madhav and Aastha were in Shreya's room, he gave more details about the visit, and especially of Kunal.

"Well, Shreya, you need to start paying attention to your appearance. You should look more like your profile picture. You should make sure not to disappoint Kunal, as he seemed to be particular on that front."

Shreya smiled. "You seem really impressed!"

Madhav nodded. "And if I have to define Kunal in one word…" Shreya's eyebrows rose. "My dear sister, he's very classy!"

They all laughed out loud.

In the next room, Sandhya lay tossing on the bed adjusting the blanket repeatedly. Mahesh got irked with her restlessness. "What is it, Sandhya? You know I've been travelling the last two nights. I'm really looking forward to some good sleep."

"Well, you chose to travel. I didn't ask you to." Sandhya was visibly unfriendly.

"What is it, dear? You need to trust my decision."

"I'm expected to trust your decision but you have no faith in my intuition," Sandhya's voice was sour.

"What's bothering you so much?"

"For some reason, I am not getting good vibes about this alliance. There's something wrong somewhere, my lord is hinting to me time and again." Sandhya started crying. "I have a feeling that my darling daughter has a tough road ahead."

Mahesh patted his wife's back. "Dear, it's a very common worry for every mother when her daughter's getting hitched. But trust me, things are really great. As far as I can judge Anuradhaji, Shreya is not even going to miss you." He realised that his words may not have helped when her shoulders shook with sobs. "Trust me, dear. Madhav is right. He's a perfect match for Shreya. You need to stop being so apprehensive and start thinking about preparations. From what I have gathered, they will not give us much more time with our daughter. They are going to be quick to fly her away to Mumbai."

Sandhya gave a wan smile. Mahesh stroked her shoulder affectionately. "You being a mother must have noticed what I did."

She looked up in confusion. "What?"

"Your daughter's eyes. Your most cherished asset," he said.

"That worries me the most. I can see her being emotionally involved in the alliance. That Kunal must be a magician with words to have such an influence on her just with a phone call."

Mahesh laughed lightly. "Or, it's your lord's wish. But her eyes are twinkling these days. She's really looking forward to meeting him before she gives a final answer."

It was then that Sandhya surrendered her resistance. She rested her head on her husband's shoulder, "I pray to my lord that you're proven right."

Did Kunal Meet Shreya?

The next morning Mahesh called up Anuradha and introduced Sandhya to Anuradha for the first time.

"Anuradhaji, when can we have the good fortune of meeting you and Kunal?" Sandhya asked.

"I am so glad you said what my ears really wanted to hear," Anuradha was unable to contain her joy. "How about tomorrow evening?"

Sandhya was dumbfounded. She gestured to her husband that they wanted to come the next day; Mahesh nodded his approval.

"You are most welcome tomorrow evening. It's an honour for us," Sandhya said respectfully.

The conversation ended with formal namastes.

"Oh God! Tomorrow is too early!" Sandhya frowned. "I'm going to faint now. These *Mumbaiwalas* are moving at supersonic speed."

"Take it easy; we'll work it out. Tell me what needs to be done," Mahesh replied calmly.

A few minutes later the two domestic helps in the house were cleaning every possible corner. Sandhya had the fans, tubelights, wall-hangings etc, all cleaned up. After three hours the house was shining, as bright as a miniature Taj Mahal.

Sandhya had already called up all three children to come home soon. Aastha and Shreya drove out to find a "classy" dress for Shreya. In the midst of all these busy preparations, the phone rang again at 9 pm.

Madhav kept the phone on speaker. Anuradha was sounding hesitant. "I am extremely sorry to inform you this late, but Kunal informed me of this just a minute ago."

"Well, what is it Anuradhaji?" Sandhya's worry grew.

"Kunal needs to attend a friend's wedding in Jaipur tomorrow. He said it would be too much travel to reach your home in East Delhi from the airport and then go to Jaipur. The Jaipur Highway is actually closer to the airport," Anuradha said with some hesitation. "Kunal has this plan. Can Shreya drive to some coffee shop near the airport area and the two can meet up there? However, I will take a taxi from the airport to reach your residence." At the ensuing silence, Anuradha mumbled in embarrassment, "Please say something."

Mahesh came to her rescue. "Well, it's a very small adjustment. Please feel easy." Anuradha sighed in relief. "But more than Shreya, my wife and daughter-in-law will be disappointed at missing Kunal," Mahesh said humorously.

"I will make sure he meets them before D-day." Anuradha said, smiling.

Later at night around 10:30 pm, Shreya got an STD call.

"Hello!" Shreya was half-asleep by then.

"I hate to wake someone up this late, but I thought I owe you an apology."

Shreya sat up at once, recognizing the voice instantly.

"Oh, hello. No, it's not late," Shreya replied.

"Well, your voice doesn't suggest that," Kunal smiled while saying that.

Shreya cleared her throat to fake sounding awake.

"Well, does that sound better?"

Kunal had a little laugh, "If you really insist."

They both laughed.

"I'm sorry for the last-minute change in plan; my darling cousin Vineet messed up the dates," Kunal explained.

"Hmmm."

"What does 'hmmm' mean?" Kunal joked.

Shreya replied in the same tone, "Well, it doesn't mean anything. It's used as filler when you have nothing to say."

"I know. I know," Kunal agreed laughing. "I've been to Delhi several times. I have this favourite coffee shop near the airport and that's exactly where we're meeting tomorrow," Kunal said. "And once again, I'm sorry for this last-minute change."

"It's really okay. Your mother has already committed that you'll come over to my place soon, so you don't have to worry about it," Shreya replied.

"She did? When? Oh God! She never asks me anything!" He snapped.

"Well, all I hope is you've not been 'asked' to get married," Shreya retorted.

They laughed together.

'Good nights' were followed by 'See you tomorrow'.

A minute later Shreya had a message on her phone with details of the coffee shop and the flight timing.

Shreya was wearing the dress Aastha had chosen for her, a sleeveless white long *kurti* with elegant red embroidery, with a tight red *pajami*, picked up from a top-notch designer shop. Shreya also wore white high-heeled sandals and long earrings for the first time. Aastha insisted that Shreya keep her hair open. She'd also done a reasonably light make-up for her. Shreya looked very pretty indeed for the date—nearly a blind-date.

She looked around the coffee shop but couldn't find anyone who matched Madhav's description. Suddenly a voice came from behind, "Hello. Are you looking for me?"

Shreya slowly turned around, to see somebody resembling Madhav's description standing there wearing a trendy *Scavin Wayfarer*. She smiled, hoping that would answer the question.

Shreya looked at Kunal scrutinizingly; he was not six feet tall but then she remembered Madhav mentioning "about six feet tall." Madhav, who was 5 feet 10 inches also used that phrase for himself. So Shreya kind of ignored that miscalculation.

Next, Shreya noticed that the guy was indeed handsome and in good shape, but "being a hero" was an overstatement.

They walked closer to each other, and then suddenly Kunal was pushed by a Sardarji wearing a bright yellow t-shirt and turban. He caught their attention for a while and then Kunal pointed to a table seat and ordered two cups of cappuccino. Coincidentally, the Sardarji also found a seat just adjacent to them.

Shreya stared at the Sardarji for a while until Kunal interrupted, "Well, I can come later, if you are more interested in meeting him right now." She burst out laughing.

Kunal cleared his throat and it was then Shreya noticed that his voice didn't sound as clear as on the phone. "Something seems to be wrong with your throat," Shreya showed concern.

"I hate having such a sensitive throat. It's just been this little variation in weather from Mumbai to Delhi, and my throat couldn't even handle that tiny bit." Kunal's voice was really hoarse.

"Oh, it's okay. Don't bother yourself too much with it," Shreya replied.

"Your brother told me that you wear specs," Kunal said.

"Well, I wear contact lenses at work, and specs at home," Shreya replied.

"Really?" Kunal didn't sound happy. "Hmmm…."

"What does 'hmmm' mean?" Shreya asked teasingly, remembering the banter last night.

"That's news to me," Kunal replied bluntly.

Shreya's face fell at his response. But maybe her specs were a real concern for a "classy" guy.

"Why don't you consider lasik surgery?" he said. "And you can get rid of this trouble forever."

"Sure. I'll give it a thought," Shreya replied.

"You know what, I would really like you do that," Kunal was being adamant.

His voice was getting worse now. Coffee arrived just at the right time.

"So, Kunal you've always been in Mumbai?" Shreya took the conversation further.

"Yes, born and brought up in Mumbai." Kunal kept it simple.

"How's your sister doing? Does she have any children?" Shreya made another move.

"Not yet."

"What are your hobbies?" she asked.

"Travelling."

"Oh! Then just like Papa and Madhav, you must be a frequent visitor too to *HappyTrips.com*."

"I love the site. It's my favourite."

Shreya felt a little better, but still not up to the mark. She was still irritated with the way the conversation was going, noticing Kunal making no effort to take it forward.

"How's your darling cousin Vineet?" Shreya made yet another attempt.

"Vineet! He's a darling for sure. He's the most precious element of my life. He's a wonderful guy. Intelligent, good looking and what not. He's simply amazing." Kunal finally showed enthusiasm.

Shreya's attention was again diverted as the Sardarji got up swiftly, almost hitting their table.

Kunal's phone rang. "Yes, leaving right now? Fine, then I'll be at the airport in a few minutes." Kunal looked at her. "Shreya, I need to go now. My friends are waiting. I'm sure you must be disappointed today. But I promise to make it up very soon." He had an apologetic smile on his face.

"It's alright. Please carry on." Shreya smiled back sportingly.

They said goodbye at the coffee shop door and Kunal walked on to get a taxi while Shreya went to the car park. As she was unlocking the car, she saw the Sardarji almost bumping into Kunal again. Then she saw Kunal speak angrily to the Sardarji. Shreya was worried there would be a fight, but smiled in relief when she saw Kunal finally walk away. She got into her car and drove back home. She was hoping to reach in time to meet Kunal's mother.

Shreya drove really fast and was home in less than 45 minutes. Aastha opened the door and was confused to see Shreya. "That was quick!"

"Well, his friends were waiting and then he had this terribly bad throat." Shreya looked disappointed.

Aastha tidied up Shreya's hair quickly before she walked in.

Shreya's eyes met those of the special guest at her home and both smiled warmly at each other. Anuradha stood up as she saw Shreya walking towards her.

She was very emotional on seeing Shreya; with her experience she could make out the calmness and maturity of the young girl. Shreya offered a very formal namaste, and suddenly noticed her mother moving her eyes towards Anuradha's, feet.

Shreya, quick to realize what her mother meant, bowed down to touch Anuradha's feet.

"No, no, my child, it's okay. It's really an old fashion. Kunal in fact never does that even to his uncles and aunts." Anuradha smiled. "I would prefer a warm hug."

She embraced Shreya and then put her hand on Shreya's face gently. "You truly have the most beautiful eyes!" Shreya averted her eyes, floored by the warmth of this lady who could become her mother-in-law.

Anuradha's phone rang. She moved towards the balcony to take her call. She returned in less than two minutes almost jumping with joy.

"*Bhaisahab*, it was Kunal." Anuradha was as happy as a five-year-old who had just got hold of the latest video game. "If Shreya too is in agreement, I would like to leave your house with a box of sweets."

Shreya turned pink, and then red and then hid her face behind Aastha shyly. Everyone looked at Shreya fondly.

"Well, what's your favourite sweet Anuradhaji?" Sandhya asked.

Preparations, Operation And An Unexpected Guest

In the midst of all these discussions Anuradha's phone rang again. It was Kunal again insisting on Shreya's lasik surgery.

"Is that a big deal, *Bhaisahab*? Kunal doesn't like specs," Anuradha asserted.

Madhav replied. "No way, in fact even I was thinking of suggesting that to Shreya." He turned to Shreya. "Should be more than okay." Shreya nodded.

"You know, Kunal has even booked an appointment for you with the best eye surgeon of Delhi for the day after tomorrow. You can get the initial tests done and then book a surgery date. He will message you the details soon," Anuradha informed.

"That was lightning fast," Aastha joked. Everyone had a laugh.

Anuradha insisted on looking for an appropriate and early date for the marriage. She suggested a simple affair with just the immediate family, followed by a grand reception.

The marriage and reception had to take place in Mumbai; the Kohlis didn't have many relatives in Delhi, so arranging for their own relatives as well as of the groom's side in Delhi would have been a real tough task for them. So, they agreed to have the functions in Mumbai; with Akash's help they could manage their guests and need not be worried about the groom's guests.

Anuradha was handed over a few boxes of sweets. Before she left, she turned to Shreya once again. She took off a gold bangle from her wrist and pulled Shreya's hand towards her. Shreya looked at her mother, mulling over what to say.

"Anuradhaji, please don't be so formal," Sandhya said. "You'll have a lifetime to give Shreya whatever you feel like." Shreya nodded in agreement.

"Please, Sandhyaji, I have already waited a lifetime for this." Anuradha put the bangle on Shreya's wrist and then touched Shreya's face again. "You have no idea of what she means to me." Her eyes were moist. The love in her eyes reached Shreya's heart instantly, and she bowed down again to touch her feet. Anuradha smiled. "God bless you, dear. Come home soon!"

Later that night around 11 pm Shreya's phone rang again. To her surprise, it wasn't Kunal; in fact it was an ISD phone call.

"Hi, I'm Ridhima, Kunal's younger sister. I hope I didn't wake you up," a sweet excited voice spoke.

"Of course not, it's a pleasure to speak with you." Shreya was really touched to hear from Ridhima.

"I'm just so excited that my brother is finally getting married. We were after his life for this for about a year now. He rejected girls left and right. You must be very special to catch his attention. My brother is really hard to please," Ridhima said laughing.

"I'm really curious to know why," Shreya replied.

"Oh please, you don't have to dig deeper into that. Good that it happened. Let's all thank the Almighty and take it easy." They both laughed. They shared a few more minutes, speaking about each other's lives. Ridhima talked about her life in London, her husband Rohan, and a little about his perfume business.

"Well, I think you must catch some sleep now. Good night, *Bhabhi!*"

Shreya's ears tickled on hearing Ridhima's last word. She kept smiling all night, tossing and turning. A certain IIM graduate didn't sleep that night for a reason other than her career.

The next morning Anuradha called the Kohli residence while she was still in Delhi at her cousin's place. She informed them that she had visited a priest that morning. "There's an auspicious date after four weeks," she said excitedly and even before the Kohlis could voice their concerns, she had all the answers. Kunal had made all the calculations. Shreya could take a week's time for her shopping before the surgery, since the rest could be done by others; and anyway she didn't need to go for card distribution or other errands like that. She could rest for two weeks, or that would bring nearly an end to the third week. She would still have three more days before leaving for Mumbai to make any arrangements if she wanted to.

Anuradha added that Shreya's dress for the reception would be designed by a renowned designer and the Kharbandas would be taking care of that.

Mahesh insisted that Kunal's outfit for the wedding would be from their side.

Anuradha assured that when Shreya got her surgery done, Kunal would pay her a visit.

Everyone at the Kohlis residence was spellbound with Kunal's efficiency. It was clear the Kharbandas were looking for an early wedding. It was to happen on April 13, 2009.

Late that night, Shreya was sitting alone in her room, a little unhappy about her life being arranged so quickly. The phone buzzed.

"Hello."

"Hello," Kunal's voice sounded better than the day before.

"Hope you and your mother reached Mumbai safely?" Shreya asked.

"Yes, we're safe thankfully, and so are the co-passengers," Kunal replied.

Shreya got concerned. "Was there a problem with your flight?"

Kunal pretended to sound serious. "No, it's just my mother. She was so excited that she wanted to fly the aircraft."

It took Shreya a few moments to register the joke and laugh out.

"You're slow at catching a joke," Kunal teased.

"I was not prepared for this one," she said. "And how's your throat?"

"Leave it. I've given up. It always refuses to cooperate." Kunal sounded irritated. "Hey," he exclaimed. "I called for something important."

"Tell me."

Kunal cleared his voice. "I heard you're getting married. Congratulations."

Shreya took a while to control her joy, and replied, "The same to you."

Kunal smiled, "I hope you're okay with the date. I know it's a bit early. But Mom is superstitious about the date. I want her to be happy. She's really looking forward to it."

All the concerns that Shreya had had a few minutes earlier

suddenly vanished. "No, it's fine. And she's right. Apart from some shopping what else do I really need to do?"

"That's exactly what I thought. I remember Ridhima's marriage; she was the most relaxed person while everyone else in the house was running around. It's your chance now, so just sit back and relax," Kunal explained. "And that eye surgery thing. Please make sure you take all necessary precautions for two weeks. No TV, no laptop."

Shreya smiled. "Sure, I'll do that."

Kunal realised Shreya wasn't sounding her usual self. "All fine?"

"Yah."

"Sure?"

"Well just that it's too quick. We don't even know each other enough."

"You know I recently came across an interesting thought about marriage. It said that successful marriages are always between deaf husbands and blind wives. I promise to be deaf."

Shreya was thoroughly amused,"Yes and I'm anyway actually going blind temporarily with surgery soon."

"Works perfect. I'll hang up for now. I'll call you up in two-three days when I sound more like myself. Enjoy yourself. Good night and take care.'

The next two days were filled with shopping and other arrangements like getting cards printed, finalizing guest-lists and travel arrangements. Shreya also went to her prospective employers and told them she would not be able to accept the post now.

On Day 4, at about 11 am Shreya got her eye surgery done. She was helped back home by Madhav and taken straight to her room where she could lie down and rest. At about 4 pm Shreya's phone rang. Madhav helped her find her phone and put it to her ears.

"Hello," Shreya was in pain.

"Ouch! Someone really sounds hurt," Kunal teased.

"Thanks to you," Shreya pretended anger.

Madhav smiled at Shreya's tone, happy to see Shreya getting comfortable with Kunal. He thought it would be a good idea to leave Shreya's room then.

Kunal laughed, "You'll really thank me for this one day."

Shreya managed to smile somehow.

"Is it really hurting bad?" Kunal asked.

"I can't even open my eyes." Shreya complained.

"It's just a matter of one or two days, then it's just a few days of precautions." Kunal tried to soothe her.

"Well, your mom promised that you would pay me a visit when I got it done. When shall I expect you here?"

"No way. That's not happening. You shouldn't even be opening your eyes, and if I come over you definitely will and make it worse."

Shreya was a little disappointed. "Well, I know it will be bad on my part to do so."

"If I were you, I would cheat," Kunal was assertive.

"If I assure you I won't cheat, I mean it. I always keep my word. I can swear by it."

"So, promise, rather swear you won't cheat," Kunal said.

"I swear I won't cheat."

"Well, in that case I can think about it."

"When?"

"Bye."

Ting-Tong!!

Aastha opened the door to see a good-looking young man

standing there wearing stylish *Scavin Aviator* sunglasses.

"Hello."

"Hello, whom do want to meet?" Aastha asked.

"Well, all of you, maybe."

"Do we know you?" Aastha got curious.

"Perhaps yes." After a pause, "I am Kunal."

She welcomed Kunal inside the home, and everyone greeted him. After paying his respects to everyone Kunal looked around. Sandhya ran to the kitchen to prepare tea; Madhav signalled to Aastha to show Kunal to Shreya's room.

Shreya's room was almost totally dark that day. So as to ensure that the bright sunlight didn't hurt her eyes, the curtains had all been drawn. It was hard to see anything.

Aastha opened her door a little. "Shreya?"

"Yes, I am okay. The pain is coming down. But this watery thing is continuously flowing from my eyes." Shreya assumed she had come to ask about her health.

Kunal spoke immediately from behind Aastha, "Well, you have to keep them closed properly."

Shreya shrieked, "What?"

Aastha rushed inside and whispered, "Just be calm, Shreya. He's here to keep his promise. Make sure that he doesn't regret it."

Aastha got Kunal a chair, and left the door ajar.

"Travelling twice to Delhi in a single week must be so much trouble." Shreya said.

Kunal smiled back, "Well, less trouble than what I see you are experiencing."

"And I'm really glad that it didn't hurt your throat this time."

Kunal laughed lightly, "I didn't inform it about my travel this time."

Shreya laughed out too. "Yeah, last time you weren't even talking. The only time I heard you being excited was when I mentioned Vineet."

Kunal pretended to be offended. "I hope you aren't doubting my orientation?"

They both laughed at his happy joke.

"Yeah, so I think I can answer your questions now," Kunal said. "Yes, Mumbai has been my only home. Though we've moved a lot within the city. We have seen the times of struggle of my father, and then his journey to success. I myself moved to many schools as his life events changed. Finally, I did my engineering from Pune. At 22, I started working with my dad, but by 24 he fired me. He asked me to get an Oxford degree if I wanted my job." Shreya laughed.

"Then when I returned after a year, and just when I was getting better with the nitty-gritty of the business, he left me, completely devastated."

"Kunal, I'm sorry to hear that. But a few things are beyond our control."

Aastha entered the room with tea and plates full of snacks. Kunal just took tea and a small bite.

"I agree. But at times, things very dear to you are taken away due to the evil of a few frustrated souls. And that doesn't deserve my forgiveness." Kunal now sounded harsh. Shreya related this to Kunal's trauma that he must have experienced during his divorce.

"Leave it, Kunal. The past really needs to be buried," Shreya tried to soothe him.

"Talking of the past, Shreya, have you ever been evil to someone?"

Shreya took a few seconds to reply. "Not really. But I did settle a score with someone. My way may not have been fundamentally correct, but then how else do you really teach someone a lesson? How else does someone really know how deeply it hurts?"

Madhav now entered the room and requested Kunal to accompany them to the market to help choose his wedding outfit. He smiled. "We want you to spend some time with us, too."

Kunal instructed Shreya to take care of her eyes, and that he'd see her next on the wedding day and left.

For the next three weeks before the wedding, Kunal called every night at 10 p.m. They would talk at length; Kunal once even interviewed her for the job opening in good humour. She found his voice hypnotic and his words magical.

And Sandhya's misgivings faded away as she saw Shreya getting close to Kunal. She was now hopeful that her daughter would have a happy married life.

Seven Vows Of Marriage

The *mandap* was decorated in a temple in the Juhu area close to the Kharbanda residence. The weather was also pleasant on that evening of 13 April. Kunal was seated at the *mandap*, his face covered with a *sehra*. Both families were there in full attendance—the Kohlis, Anuradha and Ridhima and her husband Rohan.

Shreya was brought to the *mandap* a few minutes later. She wore a red saree with a red *dupatta* covering her head, and she looked beautiful. Her face was reflecting her joy and her eyes were cast down while she was walking towards the *mandap*.

As she came and sat down next to Kunal, he requested the *panditji* to conduct the wedding without the fire in the middle. Anuradha was shocked and tried to reason with Kunal.

"How can the holy ritual be completed without the holy *agni?*" she asked him.

But Kunal said the flames and smoke could harm Shreya's eyes. The Kohli family were touched by Kunal's concern for her newly-operated eyes. Aastha lowered Shreya's *dupatta* to ensure that it covered her eyes completely, teasing Kunal not to worry, since her eyes were well-protected now. But Shreya couldn't see a thing through her veil.

The marriage rituals began. The priests now started pronouncing the vows of marriage.

Shreya listened carefully, committing herself to each one of them.

The First Vow

"Om esha ekapadi bhava iti prathaman"
The Groom promises to provide his wife with all her needs, to take care of her in every season, and in all phases of life. When children follow, the Groom is committed to extend his support to his entire family.

"Dhanam dhanyam pade vadet"
The Bride promises to support her husband and share all his responsibilities. She commits herself to household duties, children and welfare of the family.

The Bride and Bridegroom now stood up to take the first circumlocution around the holy fire; keeping their right feet forward. The Groom leads the first *phera* and the Bride follows holding his hand.

The Second Vow

"Om oorje jara dastayaha"
The Groom commits to protecting his wife forever. Her security and well-being are now his responsibility. He promises to defend her, their children and their home till eternity.

"Kutumburn rakshayishyammi sa aravindharam"

The Bride vows to support her husband in every possible way. She's committed to provide strength to her husband.

The next circle around the holy fire was led by the Groom; a vow promising to be each other's physical, mental and spiritual strength for life.

The Third Vow

"Om rayas Santu joradastayaha"

The Groom promises to work towards the prosperity of the family. He offers his honesty to his wife with this vow. He commits to be truthful in every way. He seeks spiritual blessings to strengthen their relationship.

"Tava bhakti as vadedvachacha"

The Bride too prays to the almighty to bless their nuptial bond with understanding, trust and compassion. She also promises to be faithful to her husband lifelong. Every other man is secondary to her; she just belongs to her husband now.

Another circle around the holy fire, the Bride following in the Groom's footsteps.

The Fourth Vow

"Om mayo bhavyas jaradastaya ha"

The Groom declares himself fortunate for marrying his wife. He promises to offer his accommodation and understanding forever. He prays for a peaceful and harmonious life and to set an example for his children.

"Lalayami cha pade vadet"
The Bride promises to make every possible attempt to keep her husband happy. She assures to take care of all his needs and wishes; and to offer her understanding in all phases of life.

The Groom leads another circle around the holy fire.

The Fifth Vow

"Om prajabhyaha Santu jaradastayaha"
The Groom and Bride pray together to be blessed with noble and obedient children. They pray for a harmonious household, and respect in society. They wish their children to grow up as righteous adults and have a long life.

"Arte arba sapade vadet"
The Bride reinforces her commitment to stand by her husband. She vows to be a good mother and caretaker of the household. she will ensure that happiness and laughter are always around.

After the fifth Vow the Bride takes the lead. Shreya now led Kunal around the holy fire, signifying that she holds the prime responsibility for grooming their children and taking care of the home. The Groom needs to trust her decisions, and be supportive of her in every possible way.

The Sixth Vow

"Yajne home shashthe vacho vadet"
The Couple commit to stand together through all seasons. Sailing through turbulent phases, their relationship must emerge stronger and they promise to share all their joys and sorrows.

Shreya again led, signifying that the Bride will stand between her husband and bad fate if need be. Bad luck has to fight her first, before striking her husband.

The Seventh and Final Vow

"Om sakhi jaradastayahga"
With this final vow, the Groom accepts his wife as his friend for life. There will never be any secrets and lies in their married life. He promises to be faithful, understanding and committed to her always. And as friends they will sail through all phases of life harmoniously, holding hands.

"Attramshe sakshino vadet pade"
The Bride expresses her pleasure to be married to the man of her dreams. She seeks heavenly blessing for her married life. She promises to stand by her husband at all times, offering fidelity and maturity. Her husband is the most important person to her in the universe, and she will always put him first. She prays to be united till eternity.

The Bride leads the final circle around the holy fire with her right foot first. She promises to keep her deeds righteous, and keep right conduct; so that she keeps earning her husband's friendship lifelong.

The priest now gave them his blessing. "In the holy name of God, your angels and fore-fathers; you both now stand as husband and wife. May you respect the seven vows of marriage; may love and harmony be a synonym of your married life always."

Shreya's eyes filled with tears at the priest's blessing. She bent to touch his feet; Kunal joined his hands in a formal Namaste.

Shreya now sought the blessings of her mother-in-law. Anuradha gave a warm hug to the newlyweds, her eyes filled with tears of joy. The couple then received a delighted hugs from Ridhima and Rohan.

The Kohli family stood by with mixed emotions. They had waited so long for this moment, only to see their beloved daughter being taken away. Madhav was the first one to burst out crying; Aastha too lost control over her emotions as everyone embraced Shreya.

Saying good-bye to their loving daughter is the most difficult task for parents. They are happy at her starting a new life but sad about her leaving their home.

Aastha was now about to raise the *dupatta* from Shreya's eyes, but Ridhima almost screamed, "No, let it be."

Everyone turned to look at her. "My brother will do the needful when we reach home." Ridhima's teasing lightened the mood; everyone laughed out loud.

The *doli* reached the Kharbanda residence in less than ten minutes.

The Veil Is Lifted

Shreya received a grand welcome at the Kharbanda residence. All the traditional ceremonies of welcoming a daughter-in-law were conducted in full. The house was decorated with flowers, lights and glittering fabrics draped over pillars and the banister of the staircase. Every corner of the house was illuminated. All the servants came running for a glance of their new mistress.

Shreya too was very excited to see her new home. It was indeed very close to what Madhav had narrated to her. As the clock struck 10, Ridhima escorted Shreya to Kunal's room on the first floor. She helped Shreya to sit comfortably on the bed, and drew all the curtains of the room.

"Well, I'll just ask *Bhai* to come over," Ridhima teased.

Shreya kept looking down, not saying anything. Ridhima laughed and left the room.

Shreya then raised her head to look around the room. It was very spacious and painted in light green. Next to the bed was a small side table and some steps away was the door to a balcony which was directly opposite the main door of the room. Adjacent to the balcony door was a wall, which had two paintings. Further down the wall was the bathroom. Right in front of her about a few feet away the wall was covered with a big red cloth. *How come repair work was still being done in the groom's room?* She thought.

On the left of the room, starting from the farthest end was a dressing table. Next, there was an open door which led to another small room, a walk-in closet. On the other wall was a 52-inch TV and a sofa set with a stylish centre table facing the TV. Then there was a rocking chair and a small bookshelf at the end of the room. Shreya was very impressed with Kunal's taste.

She heard footsteps coming up the stairs. She felt shy and quickly pulled her *dupatta* down to cover her eyes.

The sound of footsteps grew louder. Shreya could feel Kunal approaching. The footsteps stopped near the door and then Shreya heard the sound of a latch. She was nervous and excited at the same time, her heart beating fast and her face flushing pink. The footsteps came closer, and finally halted as he sat right in front of her.

He held the edges of Shreya's *dupatta* between his fingers, and very delicately raised it. Shreya however continued to look down.

He then placed his index finger on Shreya's chin and lifted it up. Shreya raised her eyes shyly to have a look at her groom.

And as she did, her pink tinged face turned crimson and the expression of shyness changed to horror. Shreya screamed, "WHAT THE HELL ARE YOU DOING HERE?"

She got up from the bed, extremely agitated. "I beg you, please leave immediately. What is wrong with you? Who the hell are you?"

He too stood up from the bed, looking right into her eyes.

"See, you really need to leave. My husband could be here any moment. I've already had much pain and trouble because of you; I beg you not to repeat it." Shreya was almost pleading.

He, however continued gazing at Shreya. She realised that her words had had no effect on him.

She ran towards the bedroom door, opened the latch and rushed down the stairs. Ridhima and Anuradha were still sitting in the living room.

They were shocked to see Shreya hurrying down. They stood up to know what the matter was. Shreya was breathing very fast, and ran straight into Anuradha's arms for comfort. Anuradha stroked her back. A minute later, he had also come down. Shreya was pointing to him, still stammering out of shock. Anuradha looked at him and asked, "What's the matter, Kunal? What did you say which was so frightening to Shreya?"

Ridhima added, "What's wrong, guys? It's your first night, what kind of fireworks is this?"

"Trust me! I just showed my face."

Shreya's heart almost missed a beat. The voice was Kunal's. But the face...!

Shreya, however, unconsciously did point to him, and looked at Ridhima, "Kunal?" she stammered.

Ridhima jokingly answered, "Why, *Bhabhi*? Is he not Kunal? Were you expecting some other Kunal?"

Anuradha held Ridhima's hand and laughed too. "Shreya, what happened, dear?" Shreya stood gaping. And then she somehow managed to gain some strength, "Nothing, Mom, I was just hoping I could get a medicine for a headache?"

Ridhima quickly pulled out some tablets from a nearby shelf, while Kunal turned and went back to his room.

Ridhima again escorted Shreya to the room, and then closed the door as she left.

Kunal was now standing near the balcony door facing outside, but he turned when he heard the door closing.

They looked at each other, the words they had said echoing in their minds.

But at times, very dear things are taken away from us due to the evil of a few frustrated souls. And that doesn't deserve my forgiveness.

I did settle a score with someone. My way may not have been fundamentally correct, but then how else do you really teach a lesson? How else does someone really know how deeply it hurts?

Shreya glared furiously at Kunal. He was exactly as Madhav had described, but she knew he was no hero. Rather, he was a villain.

Kunal moved few steps closer to her, staring hard. "I hope today was the first and last day that such an unwanted reaction came from you."

"How can someone stoop so low?" She said whimpering.

"Really !! Well, I give you all credit there, my dear wife. You taught me that."

"Don't you dare call me your wife," she shrieked.

"I repeat; I don't want any unwanted reaction or nuisance. You need to learn to keep your voice down."

Shreya also moved a few steps closer to Kunal.

"Shut up! I am leaving right now."

As Shreya turned to walk towards the main door, a strong grip clutched her arm. "Not so soon, my dear. You'd been really hard to find."

"Let go of my arm right now," Shreya said in a tight voice twirling her wrist.

"Well, on second thoughts, you are more than welcome to leave." Kunal's tone changed dramatically. "Please go ahead, and tell them who I am and what this is all about." He scowled harder.

"I must say, you are not only a great planner; but actually a schemer. Now I realize why you asked me to come over to the coffee shop, all alone. And the next time you actually met me as yourself, you ensured my eyes were shut!"

"See, even I can be a schemer." Kunal narrowed his eyes. "I am indebted to your parents for putting your picture on the web. And my mother for discovering it accidentally and suggesting you as a potential daughter-in-law."

"And marriage is the only revenge you could think of?" She said fuming.

"Yes, indeed. The best way to ensure that you cry all your life. To ensure that you live a life without love, like me." Kunal pushed Shreya's arm away in anger.

"Oh really! Only you had a heart full of feelings? I too had a beautiful life until your curse struck me." Shreya blasted. "God dammit. You STARTED it!"

"You deserved it!"

They were glaring at each other like a bull and a matador.

"So !" Kunal said folding his arms and wearing a crooked smile. "So, Mrs Shreya Kunal Kharbanda. What are your options now? Number One. Leave right away, and let's clean our dirty linen in public. And give pain to your parents, too. Number two. Stay and Suffer. I leave you to choose—your suffering or your parents'. Let's check how much your small world really matters to you."

Shreya's expression changed as she inferred the gravity of the matter. She was now thinking, and not just reacting.

"Well, I guess I need to give you time to reflect on the matter." Kunal smiled harshly. "Be my guest for today, and I hope you have a comfortable night in my room." Kunal bent to pick up a pillow and bedsheet, and walked towards the sofa.

"I have a lot in store for you tomorrow." He smiled devilishly. "And most importantly, I hope for better behaviour tomorrow onwards. I hope the Kohlis taught their daughter to be respectful towards her husband. And if not, be mentally prepared to learn the hard way." Kunal lay down on the sofa.

Shreya stood in the middle of the room completely immobile and dumbfounded. *What joke is fate playing on me?*

The Grand Reception

Shreya did manage to get some sleep as the medicine made her drowsy. She didn't change though and got up the next morning in her wedding saree. She looked at her hands, patterned with mehndi and adorned with the wedding *chudas*.

What a mockery of the ceremony! She thought

Kunal walked out of the bathroom.

"Good morning, Mrs Shreya Kunal Kharbanda. I hope you had a comfortable sleep."

Shreya looked down and didn't answer.

"I would consider that rude and disrespectful", Kunal smiled grimly.

Shreya took a deep breath. "Good morning," she said.

"That's better. Please get ready. My family must be waiting anxiously for the new bride downstairs."

Shreya's bags from Delhi had been moved to Kunal's room. She did a reasonably good job of draping a saree by herself for the first time. Breakfast was hell, with Kunal chatting on and ignoring her throughout. Anuradha and Ridhima welcomed her to the table with broad smiles.

"How's your headache now, *bhabhi*?" Ridhima giggled, but as they were busy planning the reception, she was basically left alone with her turbulent thoughts tumbling all over her mind.

What should I do? Should I get out of this marriage? How? Mumma and Dad would be so unhappy. Mumma was right, she'd been suspicious of the whole arrangement from the beginning. What can I do? What?

The only relief came later in the afternoon, with two make-up artists who arrived to help Shreya and Ridhima dress up for the reception.

Shreya was dressed in a violet-coloured silk *lehenga-choli*. It was the most magnificent outfit she had ever seen. It was obvious that it was a very expensive designer outfit. The embroidery on the *lehenga* was elegant and traditional, although the *choli* was deeply cut, a factor that made Shreya a little uncomfortable. She'd never worn anything so revealing before, but Ridhima dismissed her fears saying this was the fashion.

About three hours later, Ridhima declared herself satisfied and asked Shreya to look at herself in the mirror. Shreya stood wonderstruck at the sight—she looked like a princess!

Shreya arrived at the venue and found her family already present there. She got emotional seeing them and moved forward to embrace them. Ridhima however playfully prevented everyone from hugging Shreya.

"No hugging and kissing please," she laughed. "We have to be careful not to smudge *bhabhi's* makeup or mess up the *lehenga*! Isn't she looking lovely?" No one was offended. The Kohlis smiled indulgently at Ridhima's enthusiasm.

Shreya was in full control of her emotions, and made sure she didn't send out wrong vibes to anyone. She was terrified of Kunal, not sure of what he had in store for her next.

'Maybe a legal action! Was I caught on camera?' The thoughts were hovering over her mind.

Kunal and Anuradha had gone ahead to check the arrangements and he now joined them. He was wearing a jet black suit with a violet tie to match Shreya's *lehenga*. He looked strikingly handsome and extremely happy. He offered his arm to Shreya, signalling her to hold it. She hesitated and then heard Aastha and Ridhima cheering on Kunal's gesture. She put her hand through his arm and held it lightly, so as to avoid any scene.

Kunal smiled at Shreya. "Good!"

Only she knew how much it had cost her to touch him.

Close family members from both sides started arriving. Kunal was very warm while meeting Shreya's extended family. Shreya also made sure to show respect to every guest.

Then arrived the Kharbandas' favourite guests. "So late!" Anuradha scolded. "How could you guys do that?"

"Please forgive us, *Didi*. We had this serious issue at the factory." It was Ramesh Talwar, the husband of Anuradha's sister, Anita.

Shreya touched their feet and Kunal was hugged by them both. "I hope your devil is not here today. I am going to kill him otherwise." Kunal laughed.

"That's why I am hiding right behind you. I deserve to be assassinated," a voice answered.

When he emerged from behind Kunal, Shreya was flabbergasted. It was the guy who had met her at the coffee shop!

Kunal was speaking as she looked at him in a daze. "Shreya, this is Vineet. My friend, my brother and my right hand at work too. Like him or hate him, but being my wife, you can't ignore him!"

Everyone around had a big laugh. Shreya was still staggered.

Vineet noticed Shreya's expression. "What happened, *bhabhi*? I hope you are not mad at me for that day. It wasn't my idea. You must know, Kunal has always been the family prankster."

"Yes, I know he's a merciless prankster." Shreya smiled at Kunal sarcastically. He faked a smile back.

The number of guests was increasing very rapidly. Within a couple of hours, there were over a thousand guests at the reception.

Kunal ensured Shreya stayed by his side the entire evening, while he introduced her to all his friends, relatives and business associates. Anuradha and Ridhima were sitting at some distance, watching the new couple.

"Mom, I agree, Shreya is beautiful, and sweet to talk to. However, I don't find her beautiful enough for Kunal to almost go down on his knees to marry her. Although I am extremely happy for my brother, I am still not able to find an answer to that."

Anuradha turned to her daughter. "Dear, he's already been stung by beauty. What made you think that he would consider Shreya's beauty as a criterion?" She looked at Shreya smiling at the arriving guests. "I am happy that he chose her. She appears placid whereas we know Kunal has a tendency of being stubborn and impulsive. She will surely provide Kunal's life the stability it requires." she sighed. "Kunal has been through a lot, which has made him pessimistic and cantankerous. Shreya will bring him back to his original self. She seems to possess all those qualities. I think Kunal is in good hands."

Ridhima hugged her mother. "Ok, Mumma, if you're happy, I'm happy."

Shreya looked around occasionally to look for her family. She was happy as they seemed to be enjoying themselves. She looked around and noticed Vineet standing alone, having dinner.

Suddenly she noticed a girl walk up to him. Shreya saw them talking in a friendly manner, then the girl put her hands on Vineet's arm. Vineet pulled back hastily, and took a step back, looking around and checking to see if anybody had noticed. Shreya found that a little suspicious.

The evening seemed interminable, but then it was finally over and the guests started leaving. This is when the Kohli family also decided to leave. Madhav hugged Kunal, and whispered to him, "Please take care of her."

Kunal patted Madhav's back, "I will, don't worry."

Aastha hugged Shreya, her eyes welling up at the thought of saying goodbye to her best and oldest friend. "The yoga CD is in the red bag, ok?" She sobbed as she hugged Shreya. Shreya nodded, equally emotional remembering that she had promised Aastha that she would start doing yoga as soon as her eyes got better. Everyone then hugged her and blessed her.

She was looking at her mother while they all were walking away. Her mother turned and looked at Shreya. She could feel her daughter's sorrow.

Another Seven Vows Of Marriage

The Kharbanda family returned home tired, but extremely satisfied with the celebration.

They stayed up for a while, gossiping; Rohan and Ridhima were scheduled to leave the next morning.

Kunal eventually escorted Shreya to their room upstairs. "Why don't you have a seat, dearest, you must be tired," Kunal told Shreya. She couldn't bear the sarcastic tone and turned her face the other way.

"Well, as you wish." Kunal sat on the sofa, one foot resting on the other knee, taking complete charge of the discussion to follow. He signalled to Shreya to walk over to him. She walked slowly with a heavy heart and feet to stand mutely in front of him. From an inside pocket of his coat, Kunal pulled out a white envelope and handed it over to her.

"That's your wedding gift."

Shreya looked at the envelope. It had the "Kharbanda Textiles" logo stamped on it. Opening it, she saw an appointment letter made out to her. She smiled at the irony of the situation—her father's premonition of her income in lakhs matching her age had come true!

Kunal now pulled out a scroll it was a well-decorated red parchment tied with golden thread.

He handed it over to her, "This is something you have to live by, every single day of your life."

Shreya was perplexed.

"Well, dear, just forget everything that old priest said yesterday." His voice got sharper. "These are the real seven vows of marriage." He paused. "Make sure they are followed, or else the consequences could be really detrimental to you." Kunal folded his arms.

"So, are we going to have some dramatic and tragic scene here, where you curse me for destroying your life, or can we come straight to the point?"

Shreya stood quiet and stunned.

"So, can I have privilege of hearing them aloud from your mouth?"

Shreya's hands were shaking as she unfolded the scroll. Her eyes blazed with anger and tears as she read the words silently.

"I am waiting, my dear wife," Kunal said unsympathetically. "Can I have the first Vow please?"

Shreya was struggling to remain calm, but she was shivering with fear and shame. She managed to somehow anchor her tears on the periphery of her eyes. She stammered the first vow. *"A ... A...Avoid showing your face."*

"See," Kunal said, "I am actually being considerate here. It's for your benefit. The less you show me your face, the less your miseries will be. The more I see you, the more I will feel like making you pay for what you did," he said sternly. "I don't even want to see your disturbing face."

The Second Vow

"No's are not allowed."

"Precisely! I don't ever want to hear a NO from your mouth. If I ask you to do something, it should be done. I don't want any negotiation or even discussion over my orders. They stand unchangeable and should be executed at once."

The Third Vow

"Mind your own business."

"I am none of your business. I have a separate life, and I don't want you putting your nose in any of my business or personal affairs, or even touching any of the stuff around my room. Remain deaf, blind and even dumb."

The Fourth Vow

"Behave yourself always."

"Very important for you to understand, considering the scene you created last night. Love, you are now Mrs Kharbanda and you are expected to behave in a certain manner at home, in office and in society. I will not tolerate any out-of-place act of yours." He joined his hands together. "Do I need to elaborate more?"

The Fifth Vow

"The past will not be buried."

Kunal looked at her grimly. "It can never be buried, can it? We just met once and we each had a score to settle. You settled it in your way, even admitting you were not being fundamentally correct, but I claim mine to be evil." Kunal frowned. "You'll really regret messing with me."

The Sixth Vow

"For the above five vows to be abolished, you must beg for forgiveness."

"And the last one." Kunal moved closer to Shreya, "What's

the seventh and final vow of our marriage?"

Shreya quivered, her heart beating fast and her face completely red and sweating. Finally the long withheld tears slid down to her cheeks.

"Let me help you read it." Kunal snatched the scroll from her hand and moved closer to her.

"And for you to have my forgiveness, you have to spend a night with me," Kunal read out. He moved his lips closer to Shreya's.

She stepped back, shuddering.

Kunal held her wrist. "What happened?" He narrowed his eyes. "Well, that's what you accused me of isn't it? Though it didn't actually happen then." He pulled her towards him holding her firmly close to him with his arm around her waist. "Let's do that now. And I promise you are free to go."

Shreya struggled to free herself, but Kunal's grip was far stronger.

"Please let go of me."

"Trust me, darling. This is your only way out unless you want to wait until death sets us apart," Kunal said. "Where would you sleep otherwise?"

"I will sleep on the floor," Shreya gave a quick answer.

"But I'll miss the pleasure of being married," Kunal mocked.

"You are more than free to have that pleasure with any other girl." She tried helplessly to free her wrist from his grasp.

"No way, dear. The last time I made love, it was with my love; and I swore the next time I make love, it will be with YOU." Kunal released Shreya abruptly.

"And I am not going to force you. I will make sure that you suffer so immensely under the first five vows, that the last two become inevitable," Kunal proclaimed.

"Next, I want to see you begging for it." Kunal pointed a finger at Shreya. "And that day is not too far."

He now moved past Shreya and pulled the big red cloth from the wall.

It was a wall full of pictures. Pictures of Kunal and Saloni: on dates, at court getting married, on vacations and few other close moments. There were about 15 of them. Shreya looked at them, aghast.

"This is what my life doesn't have anymore. And the reason is YOU!" Kunal said in a heavy voice. "I've been licking my wounds for 17 months now. And they won't heal until I destroy you."

He threw the red cloth into the corner. He then pulled Shreya's hand towards him, and thrust the scroll into her hand. He walked out of the room.

Jab They Met

Shreya continued to stare at the photographs for some more time, now weeping silently. She dragged herself to the bathroom and splashed water on her face, still crying quietly. She looked up at her reflection in the mirror above the sink. Her flushed, swollen face disgusted her. She grabbed the face towel and threw it onto the mirror.

She backed away to the door and collapsed on the floor. As she continued to cry, pages of her memory flipped back. They flipped faster with every advancing second; they finally halted six years back in time.

Shreya had joined coaching classes for the joint MBA exams while in her final year of graduation; she would attend the classes on the weekends. And one day, she became aware of another student.

Gurdip Varma had finished his engineering the year before and was working with an MNC. He fell in love with Shreya at first sight and would watch her secretly during classes. Shreya caught him staring at her several times and would smile to herself. She also thought he was cute but, being shy, she never made the first move.

One day he finally managed to ask her out. Shreya was

overjoyed, and after that first date they started sitting together in class. Occasionally they went out for movies and coffee—those were the early days of love. When Gurdip tried to take the relationship to the next level, physically, Shreya was hesitant; she wanted to wait until they completed their studies. He smiled at her and accepted her decision. Shreya's life was changing, in so many good ways, like a dream being realised.

However much she dreamt of a future with Gurdip, it didn't deflect Shreya's focus from her career even a single degree. She worked even harder to 'Bell the CAT'. All her hard work was rewarded when she got through to the IIM-Lucknow. Gurdip didn't get through to any top college, but since his parents were well off, he applied to a university in Australia for his MBA.

They now had a long discussion over how they would manage a "long-distance" relationship. "It's just two years," Gurdip reassured Shreya one day. "How about we get married after I complete my MBA?"

"You mean it?" Shreya was thrilled.

"Of course," Gurdip grinned. "I've loved you since the day I saw you in class, silly. I'll fix it."

And Gurdip was true to his word—he arranged a meeting between their parents. It was a simple family affair where Gurdip and Shreya exchanged rings.

A month later, Gurdip left for Australia. Shreya left for Lucknow to realize her dreams, her heart overflowing with love for Gurdip and the symbol of his commitment on her finger. She was certainly the happiest girl of the city.

In Lucknow, classes and assignments kept Shreya busy. She didn't live on campus but shared a flat in an apartment building near the college with a friend.

The blow fell one lazy morning of one fine summer day. Shreya was alone in the house as her room-mate hadn't returned from her boyfriend's place since the last evening. Shreya was still half asleep when the bell rang. She assumed it was the milkman.

"What, *bhaiya*, why so early today?" she said yawning.

A voice on the other side of the door rang out, "I am not your *bhaiya*!"

She flung open the door. It was Gurdip. She was thrilled to bits and dragged him into the flat, forgetting in her elation to shut the front door.

They chattered on happily. After about 15 minutes, Gurdip said, "*Arre*, how about a cup of tea? I've been travelling so long, my throat is parched!"

Shreya jumped up laughing. "So sorry," she said. "Come with me to the kitchen while I make the tea."

Few minutes later Shreya and Gurdip returned to the living room with the tea, still talking loudly and sharing jokes.

Suddenly a strange young man walked out of Shreya's bedroom. He was six feet tall and handsome—Shreya had never seen him before. "What's the matter, darling? You are noisier in the morning than at night."

Shreya and Gurdip turned dead quiet. Shreya paled with fright.

Gurdip looked at Shreya. "Who's he?" Shreya was speechless. "Answer me, Shreya. Who's he?" Gurdip asked aggressively.

"I don't know? I swear, I don't know!" Shreya was stammering.

Gurdip kept asking that one question and Shreya kept saying she didn't know, unceasingly.

"Hang on, hang on. Please don't shout. You have already irritated me enough," the other man said.

Gurdip looked furiously at Shreya, whereas she was completely blank. This further fuelled his anger, and he was now shouting at her.

"What the hell is this, Shreya? I curb my desires since I am in this relationship with you. And here, look at you, a man in your room. Maybe it's just me you didn't want to be with." Gurdip stormed out of the house.

Shreya ran after him but he was in no mood to even listen. And then Gurdip did something she never thought he would. He grabbed her left hand and pulled off the engagement ring.

"I hope that answers all your questions!" Shreya was completely shattered. She stared numbly as he walked out of her life.

There was no one in the apartment when she returned home.

How did this happen? Who was that guy and why did he do that? The only answer she could think of was that someone saw the door open and played a prank on her. She had honestly never seen the guy before. She never even saw him again around the campus.

Dejected, Shreya caught the next train back to Delhi to sort this all out. But by the time she reached home, Gurdip's parents had already returned the ring she had put on his finger, a year ago.

Shreya tried to speak to Gurdip, but he refused to talk. And once when he did, he just blamed her for being dishonest and characterless.

She lost all her self-confidence. She would cry all night and stay in her room all day, pretending to be studying. She stopped meeting her friends—they all knew about Gurdip, and she couldn't face the pain of speaking about it. Shreya deleted her Orkut account. She had no answer to their question: "What went wrong?"

Aastha was the only genuine friend who was more worried about Shreya than the broken engagement.

Shreya took time to get back on her feet. She promised her parents that she would not let them down and would emerge a winner in tough situations always. Shreya now had only one ambition in her life: her career. Now she made every possible effort to get to the top. She became a high-flyer and a go-getter. And if some corner of her heart was filled with loneliness, she refused to acknowledge it.

In the midst of all this turmoil in her life, her parents shifted to East Delhi from North Delhi, to a bigger house.

Among the many goals of her life, one goal she left to destiny. And in all her prayers, she just asked for that one thing, since it was only thing out of her control.

"God Almighty, just give me one chance to settle the score with that guy."

She waited for the day she would get her revenge against the man who had snatched away love from her life.

Shreya's Revenge

Shreya tried hard to stop crying and eventually succeeded in controlling her tears a little. When she walked out of the bathroom, the first thing she saw was a thick mattress on the floor lying on the right of the bed, between the bed and the balcony door. Kunal was lying on the bed, on the other side. She walked to the walk-in closet and changed into her nightie.

Her heart was still crying out loud; her deep wounds had been reopened today.

She came back into the room and lay down on the mattress. Now her memory pages travelled forward in time from the tragedy five years ago, and stopped two years back, in Bangalore. Shreya was conducting an audit for a company there and had been accommodated at a five-star hotel.

At the end of her second day there, she was collecting her mail from the reception when she saw a young couple walk towards the reception, holding hands and whispering to each other and giggling. Shreya looked at them disinterestedly—the girl had exceptionally long legs that could have belonged to a model. Then she looked at the man—he was very handsome and tall. Suddenly Shreya stiffened when she saw his face—this was the same stranger who had entered her room in Lucknow and was the cause for her break-up with Gurdip and the misery she'd gone through in the last three years. She was a woman on a mission the next moment.

She quickly looked the other way as the couple approached reception—they were going out and wanted their room number 624, to be cleaned.

"There's a message for Madam," the receptionist said, handing over a note. The girl opened the message.

"Oh, darling, I have to meet Mr Gujral, the movie producer, in 30 minutes!"

The man sighed and said, "Ok, I'll wait for you in the room and order something to eat. Come back soon." The girl went out of the hotel and hailed a taxi and after seeing her off he went back to their room.

Shreya now had a plan—she bribed the cleaner to let her into their room when she wanted. After some negotiations, the cleaner agreed as the price offered was high.

Shreya wasn't thinking straight and had gone a little mad—she'd prayed and prayed for this moment and she wasn't going to let go of the opportunity. She went to the pharmacy next door and was back ten minutes later, lurking in the corridor of room 624. She soon noticed a bearer from Room Service going towards that room with a hamburger and a bottle of beer.

She stopped the waiter. "Is this for room 624?"

"Yes, ma'am"

"Give it to me, please."

"Is this your room, Ma'am?"

"Oh yes. My husband ordered this."

"Oh sure, you can have it in that case. Have a great evening."

Shreya waited for the bearer to leave the corridor and then

opened the beer and put a sleeping draught into it and shook the bottle. She then gestured to the cleaner to take it inside. After about ten minutes, Shreya gained access to room 624 with the cleaner's master-key. She saw the man sprawled on the bed, snoring loudly. She now set the stage for his downfall. She looked through the couple's luggage and found a packet of condoms. She shook one out and threw it into the commode, but didn't pull the flush. She then drained the rest of the beer into the washbasin, even cleaning the glass and basin to ensure no trace of the drug was left behind.

She pulled the sheets off the bed, and planted her bra in the bathroom. She then ran the shower for a while and threw towels on the floor. It was as if someone had had real wild sex in the room.

Shreya left the room gazing at the guy. She had a feeling of a mission being accomplished.

On his marriage bed, Kunal was recalling equally dark memories of how his life had been ruined at Shreya's hands.

Saloni and he had gone to Bangalore and he'd stayed back in the room one evening as she had gone out to meet this movie producer. He must try to persuade her to change her lifestyle, he'd thought, but maybe slowly. They had been married barely two months, and he still enjoyed being the envy of men wherever he went with Saloni hanging on his arm. And she was young. In a few years he was sure she would come around to his way of thinking. He called room service and ordered a beer and a hamburger. He was thirsty and he drank most of the beer in one gulp.

The next thing he remembered was Saloni shaking him to wake up.

Kunal had got up rubbing his eyes hard, and struggling to open them.

His voice was weak. "What's the matter, Saloni? Why are you

shouting?"

Saloni frowned. "Open your eyes. You've been caught almost red-handed."

Kunal looked around the room, and found it little disturbed. "Big deal, Saloni."

"Are you trying to tell me that your sleeping with some other girl isn't a big deal?"

"Saloni. What's got into you?" His head was aching and he was extremely drowsy. "And anyway, can we talk tomorrow morning? I am dead tired."

Saloni waited until the next morning to talk to Kunal, but she had already made up her mind. When Kunal woke up, he saw Saloni sitting in a chair, with her suitcase next to her.

"Hey, good morning. Where are you going?"

"Wherever I wish to."

Kunal moved quickly.

"Is something wrong?"

Saloni's eyes opened wider, and she held Kunal's arm firmly and pulled him into the washroom. "Can you please explain?"

Kunal was completely blank to see the state of the bathroom. He, for obvious reasons, had no explanation. "Who did this?"

"I did," Saloni said sarcastically.

"Come on. I have no clue about this. All I remember is that I was reading something and drinking beer. And then I fell asleep." Kunal was still looking around in shock.

"Oh, really." Saloni pulled out a bra hanging there. "So, where did this come from?"

"Must be yours."

"Don't you try to be smart!"

"You need to trust me, Saloni. We are a married couple now.

We never had this issue, even when we were dating." Kunal was irritated at her allegations.

Saloni said harshly. "I know you were not happy with my assignment of the beach photo shoot, but how could you vent out your frustration in this manner?"

Kunal was now furious too. "Hang on! Yes, I am upset with you getting into stupid assignments like that when I see no need for you to. You can have a good life as my wife and occasionally take a decent assignment. I see no reason for you to be so frenetic about your modelling career. At least respect the fact that you are married now."

"You are married, too." Saloni raised her voice.

"Wait a minute. I did nothing last night, and why would I? And it has nothing to do with your semi-nude stuff." Kunal realised that he was being harsh, and he softened his tone. "See, Saloni, you know I love you very much. Hence this is out of question."

Saloni said, "I know you are very good with words. But trust me, I may not be as wise as you, but I can make out when someone is cheating on me."

She walked out of the bathroom, and pulled her suitcase. Kunal jumped in front of her to stop her.

"Let me go, Kunal," Saloni yelled. "And anyway I was repenting my decision to marry you. You've just given me one last reason to walk out."

Kunal felt as if someone had punched him in the solar plexus. "It's been just two months, Saloni," he gasped.

"Good it's just been so brief. You'll never accept my aspirations and then we would eventually be separated. Why not sooner than later? I didn't grow up to be your wife; I groomed and dreamt of myself as a super-model. And that still remains my priority." She paused. "Let my lawyer speak to you when we reach Mumbai. I've already had a word with him last night. I just want one last thing from you—your cooperation." She pushed Kunal's hand away and stormed out of the room. Kunal stood shattered.

Saloni was very quick in getting all formalities done. In less than two months, the divorce was settled, except for waiting out the legal separation time. Saloni didn't demand alimony from Kunal to avoid any delay in the process. All she wanted was her freedom to pursue her dreams.

Kunal was heart-broken. For the next three months, he lived in a limbo, wondering how suddenly his life had disintegrated.

It was near the end of the third month that Kunal realised someone must have played a dirty trick on him in Bangalore. He flew to Bangalore and stayed in the same hotel. He insisted on staying in the same room, and he now remembered a cleaner had brought him the beer, something not ordinarily done, especially in a five-star hotel.

He located the cleaner and offered money for the truth, but the cleaner declined and pleaded innocence—he had been paid amply for his cooperation and he didn't want to get into further trouble. Kunal then got in touch with a close friend who had contacts in the hotel and was allowed to see the guest list of that day.

He found just one familiar name: Shreya Kohli. Someone, he knew, who had a reason to hit back at Kunal. He was amazed that anyone would go to such lengths for payback! He promised to teach Shreya a lesson when he met her again. But since Shreya had not kept in touch with her old friends and had shifted residence, he couldn't track her down. The address she gave while checking into the hotel was of the company she audited and they refused to give out any detail on their auditors.

He searched for Shreya like a wounded tiger. He swore he would go to any extent to destroy her. He had preserved the pack of condoms that she had opened that miserable night. He swore to use the next one from the pack on her.

Life Moves On

Ridhima and Rohan left for London the next day. Anuradha took Shreya on a tour of the house, introducing her to the staff and making her familiar with their responsibilities. Later that night, the three of them sat for dinner at a table which could easily accommodate 10 people—Anuradha at the head of the table and Kunal and Shreya on either side of her.

Kunal looked down mostly, avoiding any eye contact with Shreya. So did Shreya. Anuradha noticed this behaviour, but thought they were still getting comfortable with each other.

Kunal broke the silence. "Mom, I am resuming office from tomorrow."

Anuradha stopped eating. "No way. Take Shreya out."

Shreya continued to look down.

"Those things can wait. Because of your rush for the wedding, I've been ignoring work for quite a few days now."

Anuradha stared at Kunal for a few seconds and then turned to Shreya. "Dear, you need to keep a check on your husband. It is not really supposed to be my job now."

Shreya looked up at Anuradha and smiled weakly.

"Shreya is not joining office soon, though." Anuradha added.

"Sure. She can join from next week."

The next morning, Shreya chose to be in the balcony when Kunal was getting ready for office. He had restricted access to their room only to one cleaner. He didn't want anyone to tell his mother about Saloni's pictures and Shreya's mattress.

Shreya came down after Kunal had left for office. She spent the entire day with her new mother-in-law, hearing her chat about her NGO. Anuradha's NGO was associated with works for women and children and she occasionally also taught at a small school run by the NGO. She was one of the core committee members of the organization. Shreya was moved by her simplicity and good-heartedness. Shreya was now sure that Anuradha had no role to play in Kunal's satanic plan.

Shreya also spent some time doing yoga as she had promised Aastha. Later in the evening, when Kunal came back from office, she picked up a novel and rushed to the balcony again, while he spent his time on laptop or watching TV. Dinner was quiet that evening too, with both of them occasionally talking only to Anuradha.

While leaving for office the next day, Kunal dropped a folder while putting it into his bag. Shreya picked it up and cleared her throat to get his attention. He turned, and walked towards her and rudely snatched the folder from her hand. She was shaken.

Goddess Durga, please show me some way. I don't intend to bother you to fight my battle; just help me figure out what's my battle?

Shall I speak to Maddy? But he'll be too disturbed, and God only knows what Kunal will do then? I am sure he's waiting for me to appeal to my family and must have planned his next step to humiliate me .

What does Kunal want out of life?

Does he even realize that not only mine but his life is screwed too? I will ride it out for some time. Maybe I have to go through this hell to atone for what I did. Goddess, show me a way.

They hadn't exchanged a word since the night of the reception.

The Match Begins

A burdensome week passed by somehow with Shreya staying out of Kunal's way as much as possible, abiding by his first vow, and spending most of her time getting to know her mother-in-law. Anuradha spoke a lot about her husband, whom she missed a lot, and her children growing up. Shreya could not reconcile the picture of a younger loving Kunal with the devil he had become.

And finally came the day when Shreya joined office.

Kunal drove Shreya to office that first day—wordlessly.

Kharbanda Textiles had leased out three floors of a multi-storeyed office building and employed about 400 associates for various sections.

Vineet was already in office when they arrived and Kunal gave him the job of showing Shreya around. He'd been very excited that Shreya was coming to work with them and kept referring to her as *Bhabhi*, till Kunal pointed out they should not show overt familiarity in office but should treat each other in a professional manner. Since then he'd been calling her by her name.

Vineet introduced Shreya to some of the important employees and also took her on a tour of the office. The first two floors had a similar design cubicles separated by a small wooden wall and furnished with a desk, a cabinet and desktop computer. The management sat on the top floor. There were four big cabins at the corners, and there were fewer staff members in cubicles, than rest of the floors. Each office had its own laptop. Vineet joked that everyone in office was always looking for promotion to the top floor.

He then escorted Shreya to her cabin. It was a spacious room with a glass-topped wooden desk and a small seating area for minor meetings, with a two-seater sofa and two armchairs around a centre table. There were also some cabinets and a white board in another corner.

Vineet's room was next to Shreya's and was of the same size and structure. There was a big conference room next to Vineet's, beyond which was Kunal's room, designed similarly but larger than theirs. All their rooms had glass partitions partially covered with blinds, which gave them a view of the rest of the floor and each other's offices too.

Vineet and Shreya walked into Kunal's room finishing the tour.

"So, Mrs Shreya Kunal Kharbanda, I hope you liked the office?" Kunal asked.

"Yes, it's a good one indeed," Shreya replied.

"My pleasure!"

"So, what do I need to start with?" Shreya questioned.

"Recruitments," Kunal said quickly. "Everyone just keeps coming to me with the need for more human resources in their areas. I am not even sure how many of those requests are really genuine, or whether there are other options to hiring full-time employees."

"I need to dive deep into the daily operations and validate their requests, and come up with the most economical solution possible," Shreya suggested.

"That will be a good point to start with." Kunal smiled, "And if you need anything," he paused for five seconds, "Vineet must be buzzed right away."

Vineet was puzzled with Kunal's statement. And his not being nice to Shreya was also apparent. Vineet also noticed Shreya's unhappiness over the discussion they had in Kunal's cabin. *Did they have a fight in the morning?*

Shreya however smiled and moved to her cabin, where there were two people standing to help her set up her laptop and give her access to office mail. They also asked what name was to be put on the name plate outside the cabin; she chose "Shreya K".

Shreya spent the next four days meeting people from various departments. She took out time to even shadow their tasks, understanding their requirements and challenges. The entire office staff was impressed with her advice.

Vineet, who was with Shreya during all these meetings, was immensely impressed with her management skills. She was quick to understand the process and could provide at least a "first aid" solution to a few issues. Vineet starting looking at her as his mentor.

It was Friday afternoon when Shreya was to discuss her findings and suggestions. All three of them gathered in the conference room. She opened the discussion with an impressive presentation. It explained the entire functioning of the office, and she assigned a priority to all human resource requests.

She suggested more recruitment for IT, procurements and office administration; while for accounting and billing departments, she proposed new improved softwares. She also suggested issuing a warning letter for low-performing associates. She elaborated on improving the performance evaluation process of the company.

Kunal sat at the meeting, paying full attention but with no expression on his face.

Vineet's eyes were wide open in admiration at her professionalism; Shreya was gaining his respect with every slide. He gave Shreya a standing ovation when she finished her report.

"Please, Vineet. You are embarrassing me," she said softly.

"Trust me, I never really knew this company. I am clapping because finally I know it, thanks to you." Vineet was clearly amazed.

Shreya then looked at Kunal, who was still staring at the presentation and hadn't made any remark. Vineet also looked at Kunal for his reaction.

"Do you have any suggestions?" Shreya asked.

Kunal shook his head sideways signalling a 'No'.

"Shall I go ahead and execute these plans?" Shreya asked.

Kunal rose from his chair, looked at Shreya and said, "By all means."

He left the conference room.

Later that night, Shreya was sitting in the balcony reading her novel. Kunal walked up to her.

"I have ordered a new car for you," he said. "I think you should commute to office on your own. Anyway, I am not here to drive for you." Kunal said.

Shreya shrugged. "I have my old car in Delhi. I will get it transferred here. I don't need a new car."

"I am not asking you. I am telling you. And since you are new to the city, a driver has been arranged too. When you gain familiarity with Mumbai roads, you can let him go."

"Please. I really don't need a new car. I am fine with your idea of a driver," Shreya tried to convince him.

"I'd appreciate if we can keep this discussion simple."

Shreya remembered Vow number 2. 'No's are not allowed.' She quietly nodded.

The weekend was quiet. Kunal spent most of his time in his sports club, at the gym, swimming and playing squash with his friends. Shreya again spent time with Anuradha, and accompanied her to her NGO. Anuradha was thrilled to introduce Shreya to her friends and committee members. Shreya really enjoyed being there and for the first time in Mumbai, she genuinely smiled.

On Monday, Shreya left for office in her new car before Kunal came down for breakfast. There was a meeting scheduled for late morning with him.

"I have something important to talk about," Kunal opened the meeting. Vineet and Shreya sat up in attention.

"Vineet, I think with the help of the supporting staff, you can execute the proposals suggested on Friday."

Vineet replied, "Yes, I can. But I would like Shreya to supervise. She's an MBA in operations, and that will really help."

"Just supervision," Kunal emphasized.

Kunal then turned to Shreya. "Vendor Evaluation." He paused. "The financial plan of the company is revised every six months. It's due for revision next month. I would like you to perform an evaluation of all our suppliers and vendors, and check on their performance and commitment to our company. This must be quick, as it will be a crucial input to the financial plan."

Shreya nodded in agreement.

Vineet then escorted Shreya to their finance department's supervisor, Mohit Despande, a senior associate, seated in one of the smaller cubicles on the top floor. Shreya requested reports of all vendors, and also the last two financial plans. Mohit e-mailed them to her and also handed over hard copies of the requested documents.

Shreya put a 'Do Not Disturb' sign on her door and spent the rest of the day studying the financial plan.

Her eyes grew wide in amazement with the brilliance of the content of the plan. She even pulled out her calculator to verify a few of the calculations. She studied it at least four times, before she requested Mohit to come over.

"This financial plan is a masterpiece," an astonished Shreya said. "I have never seen such calculated cost-cuttings, and them accumulating to such huge profit margins." She paused. "From what I gather superficially, profits must have soared at least by 15%."

"No, they rose by 22%," Mohit replied. "I can send out a detailed report on how this plan actually mapped to monetary figures."

"Mohit, you must be a genius."

Mohit's smile weakened. "No, it's not my work. I just execute and monitor the plan. I didn't author it."

"Then whose work is this?"

"Of course, Kunal's," Mohit replied. "It's a credit to his intelligence that we have such an effective financial plan, and we are earning better profits with each passing year."

Shreya could barely contain her excitement and her admiration at Kunal's expertise.

Later that night, Shreya sat late into the night on her mattress, poring over the reports on her laptop. Kunal noticed but said nothing.

On Thursday evening, Shreya requested a meeting on the work she had been assigned.

She categorized the vendors as per department. She came up with a grading system to rank performance in terms of timeliness of delivery, quality and the response to the company's queries. Based on the reports provided, she assigned each vendor a rank on the above criteria.

She highlighted vendors whose services were satisfactory, and suggested their contracts must be extended. And she pointed out those whose performance was 'below acceptance'.

She also insisted that the company should conduct their own independent evaluation on the quality of raw material and not depend on quality reports submitted by vendors.

Vineet had the same expression of being enlightened, but Kunal was plainly staring at the presentation like the last time.

"Does the plan appear executable?" Shreya asked Kunal.

Kunal rose from his chair, and replied. "By all means."

As he was approaching the door, Shreya interrupted. "Extending vendor contracts is a legal thing. I can't do that."

Kunal turned to answer. "We have someone who can help." He turned to Vineet, "Can you please request her to drop into our office tomorrow?" Vineet nodded.

Vineet registered Kunal's indifferent attitude again. He looked at Shreya, but she had mastered the art of hiding her expressions in just three weeks of her marriage.

The next day, Vineet walked to Shreya's room accompanied by a chic girl in her mid-twenties. She had a pretty face, hair cut to just a little lower than her neckline, and she was wearing a very smart business suit which added to her confident look. She looked familiar. Shreya was wracking her brains trying hard to recollect where she'd seen her before.

"Meet Jyothsna Arora," Vineet said. "She's our legal advisor. Her father worked with us for a long time; for the last few months she's been handling our contracts."

Shreya and Jyothsna shook hands. Jyothsna held Shreya's hand a little longer. "I love your *chuda*. New brides look so stunning always." She pointed at Shreya's wrists which were decorated with her wedding bangles.

They spent a few minutes discussing various contracts. In the middle of one such discussion, Shreya exclaimed, "Oh!"

Jyothsna looked up, "What happened?"

"Nothing. Please carry on!"

Shreya recollected when she'd seen Jyothsna earlier. She was the girl who had held Vineet's arm at the reception party. She noticed her taking furtive glances at Vineet, and Vineet avoiding direct eye contact. Clearly a case of one-sided admiration.

When The Going Gets Tough, The Tough Get Going

Kunal now realised that no matter how much work he threw at Shreya, she was capable of handling it efficiently. He needed to come up with something that was outside her forte to execute.

"Pathetic!" Kunal appeared irritated at dinner one day. "It's been an era since I had good home-made food. The Government should consider increasing the prices of spices especially chillies so that cooks go miserly about using them so excessively."

Anuradha patted Kunal's hand. "It's not that bad. And when I say let me cook, you put your foot down so hard."

"Of course. You have done it all your life and then you don't keep good health. I want you to relax." Kunal kissed his mother's hand.

Shreya smiled at the sweet moment between mother and son.

Kunal caught Shreya's eye. "Can I have the privilege of dinner cooked by my darling wife each night?" He smiled. (Sarcastically, of course)

Shreya was taken aback. All she could make was a cup of tea and an omelette—surely that wouldn't suffice for dinner.

Shreya turned to Anuradha. "Mumma, I don't know how to cook." Anuradha stroked her back. "If you can please lend me some of your time and patience; I'll surely pick up fast." Shreya smiled.

"Of course, dear. Let's get started tomorrow morning then." Anuradha gently put her hand on Shreya's cheek. "I don't agree with Kunal. But then he's your husband, and I understand you want his happiness."

Kunal smiled. This is gonna be fun!

Shreya cooked *halwa* the next day under Anuradha's supervision. Kunal took a very little portion. Anuradha later informed her that Kunal's stomach was very sensitive to sweets.

Anuradha had been noticing Shreya's uneasiness of late. She thought of talking to her to help her understand her husband better, when he wasn't home.

"Shreya, are you liking it in office?" Anuradha asked.

"Yes, Mumma. It's very challenging right now. I am enjoying myself."

"How's Kunal with his staff?"

"Very nice; offering best of camaraderie."

"Just like his father." Anuradha smiled. "Kunal was very close to his father. At the age of 26, Kunal's shoulders were burdened with countless responsibilities overnight. It's his biggest grief in life that his father left him when he needed him the most. He's still struggling to cope with it.

"He had been dating Saloni for only three months when Sudhirji passed away. She naturally became the only thing to cheer about in his life." She turned to Shreya. "I think he needed a lot of emotional support from her, but she was too immature to provide it, and what followed was either Kunal's destiny or her strategy." Her eyes went moist. "...But love not being reciprocated is his second grief in life."

Shreya sat quietly; Anuradha had confused her feelings for Kunal.

"I am sure, with a mature and loving wife like you, his life will change miraculously. And his grief will die a natural death." She smiled through her moist eyes. "Pardon him if he said anything inappropriate. His emotions are not very balanced right now."

Late Saturday night, when Shreya was asleep, Kunal got a reminder by text message from his friend about a dance party the next evening. He mercilessly woke her up in the middle of the night.

"Shreya," he called but didn't receive a response. He then shouted her name. In deep sleep, Shreya moved her hand to reach for her phone. She put the phone to her ear, "Hi, Kunal. No, I am not asleep."

Kunal lay quietly. Shreya suddenly realised the voice was not coming out of the phone. It was Kunal in the flesh. She sat up in embarrassment. But Kunal acted as if he hadn't seen a thing. He curtly informed her about the party and said she also needed to attend. "It's a dance party," he said and instructed her to be dressed appropriately.

For the night of the party, Shreya wore an ordinary pink western dress. She was not very good with make-up and accessories yet. Kunal expressed his displeasure at her appearance. The party was actually at a disco, with minimal lighting and loud music. Kunal introduced her to some people and left her with them. Shreya tried speaking to his friends' wives or girlfriends, but then it was her first meeting with them and hence interaction was limited for obvious reasons.

In a while, everyone started dancing and Shreya sat on a couch in a corner, watching everyone having fun. Kunal also was really enjoying the party, dancing close with some of the girls. Shreya sat alone throughout the party.

Vineet arrived at the party a little late. He hit the dance floor directly, and a few minutes later his eyes fell on Shreya sitting in the corner. He looked around for Kunal, who was having a great time dancing with other friends.

Vineet walked up to Shreya to greet her. They had barely spoken a while when Kunal came over to them.

"Hey, bro. You are too late. You missed Ananya's snake dance. The floor was on fire!" Kunal appeared excited.

Vineet was confused. And before he could say anything, Kunal had pulled him onto the dance floor.

When dinner was served, Kunal didn't even ask Shreya to eat, whereas all other couples seemed to be sharing a plate. She didn't eat, explaining to the host that she wasn't feeling too well.

They drove back home, not having shared even a single word all night.

Kunal had a good sleep that night; he was happy to have hurt Shreya. She had no sleep that night—she was crying into her pillow, when she remembered the words: 'When the going gets tough, the tough get going.'

Then she remembered another saying: 'When someone is determined to trouble you, make sure that the troublemaker learns what trouble really means.'

Shreya wiped her tears, and promised her angels she would emerge stronger, and as a winner once again from a tough phase.

Though super tempted to fight fire with fire, her conscience managed to convince her to pick water instead.

Why am I so frightened? If he can speak of my act to the world, even I can expose his fraudulence. He should be equally worried. I am stupidly allowing him to play mind-games with me. He can't insult me without my permission; and he doesn't have my permission. He needs to know now what being a Woman is all about!

The next morning, Kunal shot out an e-mail enquiring the status of the vendor agreements. Vineet was directed to act on it immediately. Then he asked Shreya to come over to his cabin.

Shreya walked in with confidence to know her next task.

"Quality testing," Kunal said. "You suggested that we should have our own testing for vendors." He paused. "I would like a complete analysis and cost estimates."

Shreya nodded, and rose from her chair to leave the room.

"I hope it's not too much work, Mrs Shreya Kunal Kharbanda?"

Shreya turned. "No, it's not. I enjoy working."

Kunal smiled. "I hope you are enjoying cooking too."

"I am."

"So nice of you, Mrs Shreya Kunal Kharbanda."

Shreya put her hand on Kunal's table and leaned a little forward. "Why do you have to say that each time?"

"That's your name. So that you remember."

"Remember what?"

"That you are married to me." He smiled thinly.

"My dear husband, I do remember it at all times, I don't need you to remind me." Kunal looked wary—this Shreya, exuding self-confidence, was not the same shrinking violet he had taken to the party the night before. She gazed at Kunal, "You may want to come up with some way to remind yourself that you are married to me."

She walked out of the room, leaving Kunal flabbergasted.

What's Cooking?

Next morning, Jyothsna dropped into office to get the contracts reviewed before issuing them. They gathered in Kunal's cabin.

Kunal suggested a few changes to the terms and conditions and to the acceptance criteria.

"I will send out contracts for your perusal in a few days." Jyothsna told Kunal.

"Can it be done faster? I need to know the vendors' responses too."

"Actually Dad is out of town too, so some of his work has also fallen on me," Jyothsna replied honestly.

Kunal smiled. "Please get ours done on priority, and a dinner treat is assured."

"Oh no, I don't want a dinner treat from you."

"No, I am not treating you to dinner." Kunal smiled broadly. "Once our contracts are finalised, Vineet will take you out for dinner."

Shreya pressed her lips tight to curb her laughter. Kunal had also registered Jyothsna's interest in Vineet. Vineet didn't respond.

"That maybe against his will," Jyothsna said.

Kunal looked at Vineet, signalling that he should answer.

"It will be an absolute delight to take you out for dinner, Jyothsna," Vineet blurted out, blushing.

Jyothsna's eyes twinkled. "In that case, I'll send out all the contracts within the next two days, Vineet."

She stood up and gave Vineet a naughty look, "I love Italian." Vineet's face turned blood red.

As soon as Jyothsna left the room, Shreya laughed out so hard that her eyes filled with tears. "I am sorry, Vineet, but you looked so cute."

Vineet shook his head and glared at Kunal, who answered him with a mischievous smile. Vineet walked out, and Shreya followed, still giggling. Kunal watched his wife walk out. *She looks so pretty laughing like a child.*

The rest of the week passed as usual. On Thursday, Shreya gave out details on quality testing. As always, her research was impressive, but she had the same expressionless reaction from Kunal: "By all means."

That night, Anuradha expressed her desire to go to the temple with both of them. She humorously added that when her mother-in-law had taken her to the temple for the first time after her wedding, she had forced her to make 200 *ladoos*. Kunal's ears perked up.

"So you mean to say it's a tradition that the new bride should make *ladoos* when she goes to the temple the first time after the wedding?" he asked.

Anuradha shook her head. "No, it's just that she made me do that."

"Well maybe because her mother-in-law also made her do that. It could be our family tradition."

"Maybe." Anuradha looked at Kunal. "Don't worry, I am not going to make Shreya do that. Relax."

"She would love to do that if it's a legacy thing." Kunal smiled at Shreya. "Am I right?"

Shreya looked at him and then nodded. *No No's.*

The next day Shreya was dressed in casuals. "You are not ready for office yet?" Kunal asked.

"I can't make it to office today. I need to make the *ladoos*, it's a full day's job," Shreya replied.

All her nervousness with Kunal had now vanished. She now replied Kunal back in the same tone as his.

"What crap…? I can't give my top executive a day off for making *ladoos*. You should have considered discussing this." Kunal folded his arms.

"You were very well present there, when we discussed *ladoos*."

"I am not asking you to discuss *ladoos*. I am talking about your leave plan." He paused, then said, "Please report to office in the next one hour."

Shreya was irked. "What about the *ladoos*?"

"That's not my problem."

"Ok! Let's discuss this now," Shreya said. "Can I work from home today? This way your office won't suffer and at the same time my husband will be satisfied."

Kunal found that really sweet, but didn't give away his thoughts in his expression.

"That sounds like a good plan. Jyothsna will be sending over the contracts through e-mail. Make sure that you review them thoroughly before you send them out to me." Shreya agreed.

"Alright then. Have a good time making *ladoos*." Kunal left the room.

Shreya worked in her room till Anuradha called her downstairs. She had arranged for a *halwai* to come home to supervise the ladoo-making. Shreya went downstairs with her laptop.

The *halwai* placed a big *kadhai* over a high flame in a makeshift stove in the back garden. He then poured a huge quantity of besan into the *kadhai* and followed it with *desi ghee*. Shreya's phone rang right then. It was Kunal.

"Hello."

"Wait a minute," Shreya said and then looked at the *halwai*. "So much *desi ghee*? Don't you know it's not good for the heart?"

Kunal repeated, "Hello."

"Wait a minute. Don't you get it?" Shreya was miffed at the *halwai*. "*Bhaiya*, how could you do that? It's unhealthy."

The *halwai* was offended. "What, madam. You people are so rich; even then you are measuring *desi ghee*."

Shreya was furious, "What! Being rich doesn't mean we will swim in *desi ghee* rather than water."

Kunal found the conversation funny but suppressed his laughter.

Anuradha emerged from inside the house, and sorted it out between the *halwai* and Shreya. Shreya then spoke into her phone.

"Yes, Kunal. Tell me."

"If you are done with the *halwai*, can you please check my e-mails? I need you to confirm the recruitment list."

"Vineet should be able to give you that information."

"He did; however I would like you to confirm it."

"Ok. I'll revert in a few minutes." Shreya disconnected.

"Come over here, dear. You need to mix it really hard."

Anuradha was pointing at the *kadhai*.

Shreya grabbed a chair and stationed her laptop on it, and she herself stood in front of the *kadhai*, stirring the *besan-ghee* mixture vigorously. Five minutes later, her phone rang. It was Kunal again, reminding her to revert to his e-mail. Shreya was getting irritated now.

"Mumma, do you know how to operate a computer?" Shreya asked.

"Of course I do. How else did I find you?" The women shared a warm smile.

Shreya asked Anuradha to open Kunal's e-mail. Anuradha read out the entire e-mail to Shreya.

"Mumma, can you just hold this ladle for exactly 30 seconds?"

Shreya quickly replied to the e-mail and took charge of the *ladoos* again.

Exactly seven minutes later Shreya's phone rang again. "Yes, Kunal."

"Did Jyothsna send out any contract?" Kunal asked.

"I haven't checked."

"Please do. I want to see them before the end of the day."

Shreya was really nagged. "Yes, Boss!"

Anuradha chuckled; she was enjoying this banter between her son and daughter-in-law. Shreya again requested her to check her e-mails. To her horror, there were five emails from Jyothsna Arora.

Shreya continued to mix harder. "How long will it take, *bhaiya*?" she asked the *halwai*.

"It has just started," the man said. "You have to mix it for another two hours at least."

Shreya took another 30-second break, and opened the first e-mail for Anuradha to read out. That took about 15-20 minutes, with Shreya listening intently as she stirred the mixture. Shreya now took a five-minute break, and gave to Jyothsna a few corrections. She then opened the second e-mail and took control of the mixing again. This was repeated five times, and Shreya managed to answer all her e-mails with Anuradha's help.

In the meantime, the mix was cooked to the *halwai*'s satisfaction, but it needed to be cooled for three hours.

Anuradha and Shreya now found time to relax. After lunch, Anuradha gave Shreya one of her *banarasi* silk sarees and expressed the desire for it to be worn when they went to the temple the next day.

Just as the *halwai* was showing her how to make perfectly round *ladoos*, her phone rang again. It was of course, Kunal.

"Did you hear from Jyothsna?"

"I did revert to her with corrections. I am awaiting her final versions."

"You may have to call her to send them soon."

"You can ask Vineet to do that."

"She has literally scared Vineet away. He's not even watching Italy's Soccer matches now."

Shreya laughed, recalling Vineet's face the other day.

She then called up Jyothsna with one hand, while making *ladoos* with the other. Twenty minutes later, Jyothsna e-mailed all the documents.

Shreya sat with her legs crossed, with her laptop on a table at eye level, scanning through the documents while her hands were making round *ladoos*. She started slow, but then both activities accelerated simultaneously.

Anuradha couldn't hold her laughter. "Oh, my MBA *bahu*!" she giggled.

But Shreya admitted she couldn't have done her day's work without Anuradha's help especially without her computer skills.

By the evening, all the *ladoos* were ready and all the documents had been reviewed. Shreya sighed with relief.

Anuradha and Shreya then packed the *ladoos* in small boxes for proper distribution. Shreya's eyes fell on the wall clock; it was 7pm.

"Oh, God! The day went so fast." Shreya looked at Anuradha. "It's seven already, and I haven't started preparing dinner."

"It's fine. I'll ask Gopal. You must be very tired." Anuradha patted her back.

"No, then Kunal will complain of spices and make faces on the dinner table. It doesn't take long; I'll get started right away." Shreya hurried to the kitchen. Anuradha's eyes became moist. Her fondness for Shreya grew manifold.

They left for the temple at around 8:30 in the morning. Shreya was dressed in Anuradha's saree while Kunal was also dressed in the Indian attire of kurta-pajama. The famous *ladoos* were loaded in the car. Anuradha performed a few *pujas* with the two of them and then gave some sweets to the priest.

"My daughter-in-law prepared these herself," Anuradha said proudly. Shreya touched the priest's feet for blessings. Kunal joined hands in a formal Namaste.

Anuradha then offered a *ladoo* to Kunal, "You must try them. They have lots of love for you."

Shreya cast her eyes down. Kunal took a very little portion, "Not bad!" he said.

Anuradha then walked around the temple to distribute them. Kunal and Shreya were standing in the middle of the temple.

"Is this my mother's saree?"

"Yes. She wanted me to wear it to the temple today."

"I see. You take such good care of everyone's desires. I feel so blessed being married to you."

"You are standing in a temple, Kunal. You should consider being honest at least here."

"No, I mean it."

"Just relax in this holy place, you don't have to be sarcastic all the time."

Kunal's phone rang and he moved to a corner to attend it. Anuradha now called Shreya to accompany her to distribute sweets to the beggars sitting on the stairs leading to the temple. There were about 20 stairs, and they started distributing from the topmost. Someone had broken a glass, and Shreya told her mother-in-law to be careful where she stepped. Kunal now emerged from the temple and was hurrying downstairs, unaware of any danger. Shreya quickly held on to his arm as he passed by her to save him from walking over the glass. He turned back to Shreya in amazement; their glances held for a few seconds before Shreya released his arm hastily.

"There's broken glass on that step. Please be careful." Shreya said softly.

Kunal was stupefied. His mind raced in confusion. *I've been treating this girl so harshly and she still feels some concern for me as a human being!*

His feelings became ambivalent for a while; but the former feeling of rancour emerged stronger.

Horror Date

Anuradha was very satisfied. "Everything went off so well."

"I need to go to the club." Kunal said.

"What is this club thing every weekend? And why do you always go alone?" Anuradha asked.

"What will she do while I play squash or swim?"

"You can teach her too."

Shreya interrupted, "Let it be, Mumma. We'll go to the NGO in the evening."

"No way. Kunal is taking you out for a movie today." Anuradha insisted.

"Movie!" Kunal and Shreya yelled together.

"Is something wrong, guys? Sometimes I think you two behave very weirdly."

"Come on, Mom. We are both just too busy putting things in place at office." Kunal consoled her. "It will be my absolute pleasure to take her out for a movie tonight." Kunal smiled at Shreya. "Followed by dinner." His smile broadened. He knew how much it tortured her to be alone with him.

Shreya dressed up in a smart top and jeans for the evening. She tried her best to do a better job with the make-up. She looked pretty. And somewhere in a corner of her heart, she was excited about the evening.

Kunal drove her to a cinema-hall nearby and purchased the tickets from the window.

Shreya was aghast to see the name of the movie.

"Horror film?" Shreya said.

"Yes. I like horror genre. It will be fun." Kunal smiled.

"You should have told me." Shreya was really upset.

"Are you afraid?"

"It's not about being afraid. I find them nasty."

"Is that so?" Kunal paused. "Then I definitely picked the right movie." Kunal was thrilled. "If you find a scene really scary; feel free to look at me or hold me. I'll cheer you up."

Shreya replied bravely, "You know, watching a nasty horror scene is far better than watching your face."

They exchanged a bull and matador look again.

Shreya hardly saw the film—there were so many nasty scenes in it that her eyes were shut throughout. Kunal was smiling as they left the hall.

"The evening is not over yet, my dear wife. I have a lavish dinner plan for you." He said.

"It's alright. I am not hungry."

"No way. You must remember this date always. I need to ensure that I do everything possible for that to happen."

Shreya realised Kunal was hellbent to make an ugly scene, so silence would be the best plan to pursue. Minutes later, they arrived at a bustling street. Shreya saw the sea in the distance. She looked around, smiling in amazement.

"Is this Chowpatty?"

"Yes, it is. Hope you like my idea of a romantic dinner at Chowpatty."

Shreya was thrilled and delighted to be here. "This is really amazing. I always wanted to come here."

Kunal's smile weakened. He saw Shreya scamper out of the car. "*Pau bhaji* please. I have heard lot of great things about *pau bhaji* at Chowpatty."

Kunal's plan had failed! They ate silently. Shreya thoroughly enjoyed her dish. "If it's not too late for you, can we walk a little closer to the sea?" Shreya asked. Kunal nodded.

Shreya took off her shoes while walking on the sand; she was smiling like a child at the beach for the first time. She opened her arms wide and took in deep breaths of air, skittering away laughing whenever the surf touched her toes.

Kunal watched her quietly. He was surprised to see he was actually enjoying watching her have fun. He suddenly felt guilty for being rude and unfair to her. He'd seen her good qualities and calmness and was realizing that Shreya was a very nice girl.

All women aren't alike.

Accident At The Factory

The next month passed more or less in the same fashion. The only change was in Kunal's attitude to Shreya. He was less harsh and he did not pass too many biting remarks now, but they had frequent verbal battles—mostly witty arguments in office. Shreya still found Kunal's words sarcastic; she avoided talking to him and made sure all his rules were followed. She never made any attempt to get close to him; she maintained the distance he had created. But because Shreya was a beautiful soul, it was her nature to be nice and warm to everyone else.

The only person whose life was really changing for the better was Vineet. He was gaining confidence with every passing day, observing Shreya's style in operational discussions and watching how she mapped her thoughts.

Shreya sharpened her culinary skills as things settled into some sort of a routine. She had now started preparing dinner without Anuradha's supervision, though Anuradha would stand next to her to chat and spend time with her new darling.

One day, mid-week, while Shreya and Vineet were gathered in the conference room with Kunal, his phone rang. Kunal listened to the conversation and then put down the phone with a worried face. "Talwar uncle called," he said. "Some worker fell from the second floor of the factory onto the machine and died on the spot." Kunal was really upset. "All workers have stopped working and they insist on my visit."

"You must leave right away," Vineet insisted.

"That's exactly what I am thinking." Kunal looked up at Shreya and moved out of the room.

Shreya turned to Vineet, "Can you please take care of operations for the day? Call me if you have any problems."

Vineet smiled. "Don't worry. Please go."

Shreya hurried to her cabin, picked her purse and then ran to Kunal's office. "Can I please come with you?" Kunal nodded.

When they reached the factory, over 150 workers mobbed their car. Mr Talwar and a few other senior supervisors demanded calmness from the workers. Kunal requested the presence of the Union leader, Prakash, in the office.

The Union leader was in a belligerent mood. He was especially angry with the allegations of the floor supervisor that the dead worker Manohar had been drunk on his shift.

Kunal questioned the supervisor who was adamant about his allegation. Prakash got further agitated, and warned the management of dire consequences.

Kunal pacified Prakash by assuring him that if the post-mortem report suggested the supervisor was defaming the dead worker, he would fire him and take legal action against him. At the same time he firmly requested Prakash to be cooperative and not to worsen the situation further. "All our workers are always well taken care of, and their safety has always been our prime concern," he told him.

Shreya was watching from a distance and felt proud at the way

Kunal was approaching the issue so calmly and maturely.

Just then a worker walked up to Prakash and whispered something in his ear. The Union leader's whole demeanour changed—his face went pale and his gestures also mellowed down.

"Kharbanda *sahab!*" he said hesitatingly. "I've just got news that Manohar was indeed drunk. In fact, he had been drinking all night and came straight to the factory from his friend's place." He paused. "He didn't even go home. His wife was also looking for him all night."

Kunal's eyes grew wide in shock. "He was married? Yet he has acted so irresponsibly."

Prakash paused and then added. "He has a seven-year-old son, too."

Kunal slapped his forehead in frustration. He turned to Mr Talwar, "Uncle, I would like to visit his family."

"No need, Kunal. Things are under control now," Mr Talwar replied and walked with Prakash to the door of the room.

Shreya now walked up to Kunal in the meantime. "You must go," she said softly.

Kunal looked at her and nodded. He then turned to his uncle. "Can you please call Prakash? We need to visit Manohar's home." He looked at Shreya. "Please come along."

At Manohar's home, everyone was mourning, and some women were holding Manohar's wife, who was completely shattered by the loss of her husband. Shreya walked up to her, and expressed her condolences. Kunal saw the little boy sitting in a corner and his heart went out to him.

Shreya said to Manohar's wife, "I can't compensate your loss. But can I at least help you take better care of your son."

Manohar's wife calmed down a little. "How can you help,

ma'am? He was the bread winner of the family."

Shreya gripped the widow's shoulders. "There's no rule book that says only men can be the bread winners. You must make sure your son is well-educated. You have a big task to accomplish."

Manohar's wife started sobbing again. "What can I do?"

"You can work in our factory," Shreya said firmly. "You are more than welcome to start as soon as you want. I'll personally make sure that you are taken care of." Shreya then opened her purse and gave all her cash to the woman. "You need to perform a dual role for your child. Life makes a few decisions for us without our consent. Your life doesn't allow you to lose courage. Be strong."

The widow folded her hands in gratitude and Shreya joined Kunal. He was moved by Shreya's actions, but every time he looked at the little boy, his eyes filled up.

"He'll be alright Kunal," Shreya said.

Kunal turned to her, speaking with a heavy voice, "Does he have any other option?" Kunal wore his sunglasses to mask the emotions pouring out of his eyes.

The ride back to Mumbai was in complete silence. Kunal was clearly very disturbed with the tragedy. Shreya now realised that his wounds were very deep, and his frustrations were actually a culmination of all the unfortunate incidents of his life.

Later in the night, Kunal was sitting in the balcony for a change. "Are you okay?" Shreya asked gently.

Kunal nodded. She sat next to him.

"It was not your fault." she said.

"Still, a father's loss is irreparable." Kunal's voice still heavy.

"Yes, it's a big loss, but life needs to move on."

"It's easier said than done."

"But it's an eventual truth." Shreya paused. "And then why

can't you look at it this way, that you lost a father but got blessed with an angel." Shreya's voice filled with emotion. "An angel who's also watching over you and showering his blessings on you. An angel whom you need to make proud."

Kunal looked up at Shreya in surprise, remarking once again the depth of Shreya's understanding and maturity. She turned to walk into the room. She had won some form of respect from Kunal that day. It might be a bad day for the factory, but it was indeed a good day for their relationship.

Kunal looked at her walking away, and his heart took its first step towards her.

Quality Testing?

The next Monday, Kunal called an urgent meeting. He elaborated on a marketing plan and a list of potential customers. He pointed out an export house that was a top priority. He mentioned that a lunch meeting had been scheduled for the day after tomorrow. He instructed Vineet to get the details listed.

"Shreya, I would like you to join in at the lunch too," Kunal said after Vineet left.

"You know I am a complete disaster at marketing," Shreya replied.

"Still, I insist you join us." Shreya agreed. She had to.

All three of them met the potential clients at a pre-decided venue. Shreya's eyes were opened to Kunal's command of marketing strategy. He left no stone unturned to crack the deal. She was mesmerized by his eloquence and meticulous flow of ideas. She remembered how his words had moved her in the courtship period.

She wished that ugly night had never happened. He was actually the kind of man she thought she could have easily loved. Her self-control on her feelings weakened for a while; but she reminded herself that she was the face that disturbed him the most.

I need to maintain a distance from Kunal. I can't allow him to play any games with my heart. Maybe this is all part of his plan to jolt my life further.

Shreya was now determined not to weaken where Kunal was concerned.

All this, while Shreya and Vineet became very good friends. They would talk very warmly, crack jokes and take a long coffee break each afternoon. They would also play bets during meetings on who would pay for the next coffee. Whereas with Kunal, Shreya was still extremely reserved. Even during meetings, she would give brief and pertinent answers to Kunal's questions. At home too, she spoke only to Anuradha. Kunal's mother noticed the silence between the two, but kept her peace.

Shreya's obvious ignores were disturbing Kunal now. His second grief in life was amplifying. He was hoping for her attention; someone to talk to; someone to spread some smiles in his life too. Ever since the factory mishap, he'd been just thinking of her all the time. He now uselessly picked fights to get her talking to him. Shreya would mostly surrender to keep it simple. It was dinner time and Shreya was talking to Anuradha about some needy lady at the NGO.

"Can you please pass that dish?" Kunal said abruptly looking at Shreya.

Shreya picked up the dish and passed it while talking.

"That one, please," Kunal interrupted again. She did so.

"Not this one, the other one." Kunal said. Both ladies turned to look at him.

"There are only two dishes; I can't give you a third one." Shreya said in a not-so-pleasant tone.

"What's in the third bowl then?"

"Curd."

"That's what I wanted." Anuradha looked at Kunal's plate. He already had a bowl full of curd.

Kunal detected Anuradha's observation. "I meant the salad."

"That's right in front of you," Shreya said pointing at the salad.

Anuradha continued gazing at Kunal for some more time and then smiled.

The two women didn't know it, but Kunal's irritation that evening was the culmination of a whole day of watching Shreya and Vineet laughing over office matters—wherever he looked, they seemed to be giggling like teenagers!

After dinner, he walked out onto the balcony where Shreya was sitting on a chair with her feet up, reading a book. He grabbed another chair. She sat up straight and lowered her legs.

"Can you please take them off?" He said pointing at her *Scavin eyewear*. She still needed reading glasses despite her lasik surgery. She put her glasses on the table. "Most of my office time is consumed with finance these days. I was wondering if we can use this time to discuss operations," Kunal said with some hesitation.

Shreya was baffled. "Anything in particular you want to talk about?"

His uneasiness grew. "Nothing. Just generally."

"I did send out the weekly status report yesterday. That is all I have to say."

"I did look at the report. But..."

"But?"

"Maybe you want to mention anything that report doesn't encompass." He joined his hands in front of his mouth to hide his nervousness. She gently shook her head to signal a 'no'.

"Any escalation?"

She shook her head again. She was bewildered; her face bore a big question mark.

Kunal was now getting frustrated. *Am I so difficult to read? Can't you make out what this is all about? You need to talk to me as well. If you also behave as I do, what will be the difference between me and you?*

"Anything else?" She asked softly pretending to be completely blank.

He gestured a 'no'. She opened her book and wore her glasses again.

A few days later Shreya received the quality testing report of the major vendors. She noticed that the quality of an important vendor was much below the acceptance level.

Shreya walked to Kunal's room to bring this to his notice. Kunal was slightly vexed since they were one of the oldest; in fact they had been very close to his father. Kunal arranged for a meeting with the owner, Rajeev Bhalla, for the next day. He insisted on Shreya joining him.

"You are like my son, Kunal," Mr Bhalla said at the meeting. "Sudhir was such a good friend of mine. It's so unfortunate that you walk into my office with such an allegation."

"Sir, it's not an allegation. We have a quality report from an independent agency. We have no reason to make up a story," Kunal replied.

"It's all rubbish. Our quality is flawless."

"If quality needs to be improved, it's beneficial for all of us."

"I hate it when young kids argue so much," Rajeev showed his irritation.

Kunal tried his best to evade an argument. "All I know is, it's never harmful to learn, especially if it brings profit," he said.

Rajeev was a stubborn middle-aged man whose ego wouldn't allow him to accept a fault, and that too from someone much younger to him. "Leave it, Kunal. Tell me, how is *bhabhiji* doing?"

"Mumma's good. Thanks."

"And, how's your new wife?"

Kunal realised Rajeev's game. He kept quiet. "What happened, Kunal? You are not answering," Rajeev gave a cunning smile "Filing a divorce again? You should consider quality testing for yourself next time you plan on getting married."

Kunal rose from his chair. "I think we should leave now. I just thought we could resolve this amicably because of our old relationship."

"Exactly, my boy. We've been together a long time. And you must understand who needs whom more desperately." Rajeev Bhalla stared at Kunal.

Shreya and Kunal drove back to the office quietly. Kunal did turn to Shreya at times, but she chose to avoid any eye contact.

On reaching office, they discussed various options to safely eliminate Bhalla as their vendor. It took a lot of time to plan these details; when they finally called it a day, the clock had already struck 9:30 pm. Anuradha had already gone to bed, and Kunal and Shreya sat down to dinner after freshening up.

"I hope you are not thinking about Rajeev Bhalla's remarks? He has a filthy mouth," Kunal said.

"No, I am ok. And anyway you can't really control people's mouths."

"Yes, I agree. But I just want to make sure you are not disturbed by him."

Shreya smiled sarcastically. "It will be my first divorce, so it will not be that disturbing to hear. Maybe you will be more disturbed."

"Don't react to the statements of a sick person."

"We need to prepare ourselves to hear this kind of talk more often," Shreya said. "It's the eventual and inevitable truth of our marriage. We got married to be divorced one day." She paused. "For our vendetta to stand settled."

And before Kunal could say anything, Shreya walked away. Kunal sat stoically, though he could really feel her pain.

Jyothsna was requested to terminate the contract with Rajeev Bhalla's company the next day. Kunal explained the entire issue, and with the respect due to old association, said he didn't want to charge any penalty or file any law suit. Shreya was amazed.

He has such high quality business values. I wish I'd had a chance to meet his father, too. If the shadow is so amazing, the real figure must have been even more inspiring.

"When can we have the papers ready?" Kunal asked.

"It should be quick," Jyothsna replied.

"Great. I don't have to bribe you this time," Kunal smiled.

Jyothsna frowned. "Anyway, your people don't respect your words. So, even if you'd offer a bribe today, I would have outrightly rejected it." Jyothsna walked out.

Shreya stared at Vineet. He looked sheepish.

"Vineet, can we talk? In my cabin. Five minutes." Shreya said briskly. "Please."

Shreya walked out of the boardroom. Vineet followed.

"Is this the right way to treat a lady?" She asked Vineet with her arms crossed. "She's pretty, intelligent, smart and most importantly she really likes you. You really behave very awkwardly. I did notice that on the day of the reception, too." She paused again. "Do you already have someone in your life?"

Vineet shook his head.

"God dammit! Then say something."

"I have no answer." Vineet looked confused. "I know I should have taken her out for dinner. But I couldn't."

"Exactly why?"

"I know she likes me. I also find her very attractive and nice. But I just don't think it would work out."

"How can you jump to that conclusion? The truth is that you haven't even made an attempt yet." Shreya tried to explain. "You are equally smart, capable, good-looking and nice. You should not underestimate yourself." Shreya smiled. "Trust me," she put her hand on Vineet's shoulder. "It's worth an attempt." She winked, "Italian food may taste really good!"

They laughed.

"I will ask her out over the weekend."

"You promise."

"I give you my word, dear."

"Great." Shreya exclaimed. "So, can I have the honour of a hug now?"

Vineet gently hugged Shreya. Kunal again saw the entire incident from his room.

Over the weekend, Kunal stayed home trying to spend time with Shreya. She, however, avoided him: she was either in the kitchen or with Anuradha doing the NGO work.

On Sunday evening, Kunal returned from his club, dead tired

and walked into his room without switching on the lights. He sank down into the sofa facing the dressing table, put his feet on the table and shut his eyes. His head was low enough for him to go unnoticed.

The sound of the latch opening broke his sleep. Shreya emerged from the bathroom, having just had a bath. She walked straight to the dressing table, wiping her wet hair, humming a song.

She was wearing a knee length golden strappy nightie; due to the low light in the room it was as good as wearing nothing; the soft material clung to her curves evidence that the yoga she was doing had toned her body. It was tempting for Kunal; he was seeing her like this for the first time. And no way can you take your eyes off an Indian girl with wet hair, especially if you have an inclination—his body was sending him thrilling messages he hadn't received in a long time.

Shreya sat in front of the dressing table. She picked up a bottle of skin lotion and started applying it on her body; hands and neck first. She then rested a leg on the table and poured lotion onto her leg and started massaging it into the skin in long smooth strokes. Kunal started squirming on the sofa and was forced to pick a cushion nearby to place on his lap. When Shreya moved her leg down, her foot hit Kunal's favourite *Scavin Aviator* sunglasses. She hastily picked them up and he saw her quickly putting them back on the dressing table. He noticed her nervousness with his belongings.

As she was massaging her other leg, the phone rang. It was Aastha.

"Hey. Let me put this on speaker." She pressed a button on the phone and continued massaging her leg.

"Ok. Has Maddy returned from Singapore?" Shreya asked.

"Not yet," Aastha's voice was soft but clear. "The weekend is so boring, I wish you were here. How's Kunal?"

"He's good. You tell me, how's work?" *Dammit, at least talk about me if not to me.*

"Forget work, let's talk naughty. So, what's the score?" Aastha asked laughing.

Score!! Even girls talk like that!!

"I wish we could have our secret dance party while Maddy is away."

"I hate it when you say such things. I am not your backup husband," Shreya teased.

"Hey, let's dance," Shreya exclaimed.

"Great idea, I'll just play our song on the laptop and keep the phone close. It should be audible."

Aastha said. "And I bet I'll do a better job than you."

"No way. I've mastered the song. I can win a national award for my performance," Shreya chirped.

Kunal was eagerly waiting for the song to play and to witness the show. He had never seen Shreya so happy and uninhibited. But the song she played made him squirm even more.

"Bheege hooth tere, pyasa dil mera…. Kabhi mere saath….oh oh hoooo"

Shreya's performance was seductive; she held the comb as if it was a microphone and she frolicked and grooved freely, the material of her dress clinging in places he was now dying to explore. Kunal's cushion erected: he didn't even blink, wishing his first thought about her golden nightie being skin was actually true.

While dancing, the comb flew out of her hands near the sofa. She bowed down to pick it up, giving a very generous view of her cleavage. And then she noticed him.

Shreya screamed.

"What happened?" Aastha said.

"Nothing. I'll call you later." She disconnected her mobile.

Kunal sat upright, red-faced, pressing the cushion down.

"How dare you not speak up?" said an incensed Shreya. Kunal was staring at her heaving breasts.

"Take your eyes off, do I need to tell you that?"

He turned his head away. She walked to the closet angrily stamping her feet and Kunal rushed to the washroom with the cushion, dry-mouthed.

Delhi and London

The next few days were so busy in office it was as if the impromptu floor show had never happened. Shreya was gaining popularity in office, and if a few people still preferred going straight to Kunal to discuss their departmental issues, he directed all such matters to her, emphasizing her status as operational head.

Shreya took a keen interest in attending all the financial meetings, although her invitation was marked as optional. Even Vineet preferred missing those meetings.

But Shreya wanted to learn how Kunal's brain worked. She was overwhelmed by his business acumen and ingenious calculations. Her accidental 'Wow' made Kunal feel extremely flattered.

One thing they both knew; they were intellectually compatible—both seeking joy in working hard; seeking adventure in problem solving; and feeling good on delivering outstanding results.

What was drawing Kunal to her most was her promptness and spontaneity. Personally, though, he noticed she reciprocated his mood; when he was humble, he was treated humbly; if he delivered attitude, he suffered attitude. He realised that she was living a marriage of 12 vows—respecting the fact that she and Kunal co-existed under the same roof and that her only job was to help him take the right decisions in office. It was breaking his heart.

It was in the middle of July when Shreya sent out an e-mail to Kunal with the subject, "Leave Application". The body of the e-mail had a leave request from 5-14 August.

Kunal replied back, asking for a valid reason. He received an instant reply, "To visit family in Delhi, to celebrate *Rakshabandhan*."

Kunal replied back, "Tentatively Rejected." He waited. Exactly 45 seconds later, he heard a knock on his door. He smiled; he was very sure of who it was.

"Yes, Shreya. Please come in."

She stormed in angrily and stood on the other side of his desk with both her hands on the table.

"How could you do that? How can you be so merciless, always? At least you can be humane enough to a colleague, if nothing else. How could…"

Kunal interrupted her tirade. "Relax, relax. Take it easy. I was just kidding."

Kunal stood up and walked around the desk to her. "Sit down please. I was just teasing." He offered her water. Shreya sat on the chair drinking water and Kunal sat on the table facing her.

"And thanks for reminding me, I need to book my ticket for London to see Ridhima."

Shreya calmed down. Kunal picked up the calendar on his table. "Aren't your dates a little unplanned? May I make a suggestion? You must be back by *Janmashtami* in Mumbai—it's a treat to watch. So, 2 Aug – 7 Aug would make more sense." He looked at her. "Does that suit you?" Kunal asked. Shreya nodded joyfully.

"So when I call my travel agent for the London tickets, I'll make your reservations too."

"I'll do it myself. It's a simple online booking." Shreya replied.

"I know it's simple, but allow me."

Shreya left the room feeling happy about her plans.

About 20 minutes later, Kunal received a call from his mother. Shreya had informed her about the travel plans. Anuradha now told Kunal to stopover in Delhi and escort Shreya back to Mumbai. Kunal also hadn't paid the Kohli family a visit since the wedding and he agreed with the plan. He would go to Delhi from London.

Shreya arrived in Delhi to a warm welcome and a joyous reunion. Shreya had bought gifts for her entire family- she was extremely delighted to be home. Her mother had cooked *Kadi-Chawal* especially for her. It was good to be back home, in her own bed after a long time. She slept like a baby that night.

The next day, Shreya spent all day telling her family about her life in Mumbai, her work, and Anuradha and Vineet; she also fabricated a few anecdotes about Kunal.

At the dinner table, conversation flowed.

"So lots of travelling these days Maddy?" Shreya said.

"Did my growing belly suggest that?" Madhav raised a brow.

"Yes partially, but mostly your activity on *Happytrips*." Shreya teased.

"Oh well!" Madhav chuckled, "That is what it's all about, if you're happy about a trip, put it on Happytrips."

"Share your experience and do good for others." Madhav added smiling.

"Does Kunal like your food?" Aastha broke into the conversation.

"He's never complained. So, I guess he should be ok with it." Shreya replied matter-of-factly.

Her reply caught Sandhya's ears. Sandhya saw deep beyond the façade. She knew that something was not right but it wouldn't be easy to pull it out from Shreya.

Later in the night, Shreya was looking forward to another comfortable night sleeping in her bed. The phone rang.

"Hello, Kunal."

"Hi, there. Hope you are having a good time."

"You bet."

"Good to hear that."

"Good night then." Shreya wanted to keep it short.

"So soon?"

"Yes, please. I am too sleepy, and I don't want to hear any sarcastic remarks."

"That was rude."

"I am sorry," she said. "Does that help?"

"What's wrong?"

"Nothing." A pause. "Good night."

"Take care."

The next day, Sandhya tried to get some more information about her daughter's married life. Shreya had insisted Madhav and Aastha go to work, so she had the whole day with her. Shreya narrated lots of incidences, but whenever Sandhya wanted to talk more about Kunal, Shreya would either keep it very short, or just deflect the topic smartly.

That night the Kohli residence's landline phone rang. It was Kunal; he greeted everyone and conveyed his regards. It was not the first time he'd done that; when Shreya would call her family from Mumbai he would also say hello. Recently he'd been doing it more warmly ever since his guilt was worsening.

Later Kunal called up Shreya on her mobile.

"I hope you are in a better mood than yesterday," Kunal said.

"I am never in a bad mood at home."

"Mumbai too should feel like home by now."

"Haven't you heard? Home is where heart is," she replied.

"Then make sure that you pack your heart, too, when you leave Delhi this time."

Shreya smiled, and then she remembered how Kunal's calls had made her nights beautiful a few months back. It had all been an act, she now knew. Maybe he was still acting.

"So, I hope you are not missing me?" Kunal asked.

"Kunal. You don't really have to do this."

"Do what?"

"Call me up for formality's sake." She added. "You know it would be more than fine with me if you just tell Mumma that you called, but you actually didn't."

"I don't get you."

"You are calling because Mumma asked you to." Shreya said. "And I know I am right."

"No, she didn't. I called up on my own."

"You want me to believe that?" She paused. "Please relax and pack up your stuff; you too have a flight tomorrow."

They hung up.

Rakshabandhan was celebrated in high spirits at Delhi and London. It was a special day for both the families, a day when a brother makes his sister feel really special. With brothers progressing in life and career, gifts also grew in size and price and Shreya made sure Madhav paid big time this year too like all others; there was no denying the close bond she shared with her brother.

Sunday arrived in no time and with it, Kunal. He was welcomed to the Kohli residence traditionally and whole-heartedly. He looked at his wife. *I missed you, Shreya, but how do I say that? You may literally bite back.*

In the afternoon the entire family sat down for lunch in the same seating arrangement as always. This time however, Kunal sat on the other end of table, opposite Mahesh, next to Shreya and Aastha.

"Good you joined us today, Kunal. Mumma mentioned a few days back that the sixth chair should be occupied now," Madhav said.

"That's not what I meant, Madhav," Sandhya replied, smiling.

Aastha and Shreya looked at each other. "The pressure is mounting," Aastha said and they both giggled. Kunal watched Shreya looking wonderful, laughing her heart out like a child.

Sandhya pretended not to be amused. "It's a crime these days to express such desires. Family planning is such an in-thing."

Shreya gave a hug to her mother. "You need to take it easy. It's just been a year, and you have to give credit that they waited eight years to get married."

"Eight years!" Kunal exclaimed.

Everyone looked at Kunal in surprise. "Don't you know that?" Madhav said. "Shreya loves to talk about it to everyone."

Shreya stopped laughing abruptly.

Sandhya saw this as a good opportunity to know Kunal. "Shreya said you don't talk much."

Kunal looked at Shreya; she looked uncomfortable. Sandhya continued, "Maybe that's why she didn't mention the story."

Shreya breathed easy with Sandhya's mild answer, but she saw Kunal looking at her with an unfathomable look on his face.

They got ready to leave for the airport after lunch. Shreya was upset and feeling miserable about leaving Delhi again, hugging everyone and continuously crying.

Kunal tried to cheer her up. "Shreya, you are really making me feel bad now." He pretended to be offended. Everyone laughed.

Shreya cried all the way to the airport and was sad and quiet on the plane. Kunal cracked silly jokes occasionally in a clumsy attempt to make her feel better. But she didn't feel any better, and he felt helpless knowing she was really miserable.

The Joy Of Giving

The next day, Kunal drove Shreya to office hoping to speak to her. But she cut short all his attempts at conversation; she was clearly in no mood to talk to him since the Delhi visit.

A message arrived from the factory—600 metres from Rajeev Bhalla's raw material had been manufactured by mistake. As the management had decided to discontinue usage of their supply, the cloth was going waste. Shreya moved to Kunal's cabin to talk it over. "Can I have it?"

Kunal was stunned. "Do you plan to drape the house?"

"No, some other use. But can I buy it? Please."

"You don't have to buy it. It's ours until we sell it."

"But there must have been some cost invested while manufacturing."

"What's this crap, Shreya? It belongs to you as much as it belongs to me."

Shreya stood quiet.

"How and when do you want it?" Kunal asked.

"ASAP. Packed in a hundred packets of six metres each."

"Sure, ma'am. And where do they need to be delivered?"

"To our residence."

Kunal smiled at Shreya's answer. "The pleasure is all mine."

The packets arrived two days later and were kept in the storeroom.

Janmashtami arrived and Kunal was right—it was indeed so much fun; the entire city was celebrating. Kunal planned to take Shreya to the *matki-phod* event in a nearby area, but before he could even discuss with her, his mother expressed the same desire.

That is the price you pay for an extra vocal mother. Your idea always appears redundant, as they are always the first one to say it, if not the first one to think of it.

So, for poor Kunal, the event went down in history as yet another *mumma-asked-you-to-do-so event* of their life. Kunal wished he had a mute button for his mother, and a talk button for Shreya.

Later in the day, Shreya requested Anuradha to get ready. She got the packets of cloth loaded into the car.

"Where are we going, Shreya?" Anuradha asked.

"To the NGO. There was about 600 metres of cloth of little inferior quality for international standards, which was rejected. So I thought of cutting it up into six-metre pieces and donating it to your NGO. It can serve as a saree, or if they want to make some other use of it, it's up to them."

"I am so proud of you," Anuradha hugged Shreya.

Kunal was sitting around watching this warm moment.

"Are you busy with something?" Mother asked son.

"Nopes," he replied.

"Then why don't you also join us?"

"Your daughter-in-law didn't ask me." Kunal smiled.

Anuradha smiled as Shreya said, "Please join us."

The women and children at the NGO were delighted to have a special surprise. And Kunal was watching Shreya; her every action was steadily filling a gap in his heart.

He smiled at Shreya, "There's no joy as the joy of giving, right?"

"Right. It's a good feeling."

"You do that quite often," he said.

"Me? No, not really."

"Well, the joy of giving could be just some moments of happiness. Look at my mother; she seems your mother more than mine in just four months." Kunal smiled. "Thank you, Shreya, you've really given her many reasons to smile. You've sparked a new life in her, and I owe this to you."

Shreya turned to him in amazement. This was his first ever appreciation of her. She chose to be silent though and just simply nodded.

Kunal now started the strategy of complimenting Shreya's proposals in office. She chose to be silent and expressionless whenever he did that. He was frustrated at her lack of reaction and ran himself ragged finding ways to soften her. The next opportunity came one evening at dinner in early September, when Anuradha was away to attend some religious gathering. Kunal started eating.

"Delicious!" He said. Shreya turned to him in confusion; after a few seconds she looked down at her own plate and took a spoonful of the food.

"Appears alright to me," she said.

Kunal grew tense. "I said delicious."

"Which implies that something is terribly wrong with the dish today."

"How come appreciation implies that?"

"Well, if you are appreciating anything of mine, that's the only possible inference."

"I am not that bad."

"No, you're not. To others."

Kunal rubbed his index finger over the lines of worry on his forehead. "Listen, my dear...."

"There you go again," she interrupted. "I am anything but dear to you, even the servant Raju knows that and mocks at the situation." Raju was the only servant with access to their room.

What the hell, man! All I said was 'delicious'. But I need to monitor my temper with her; she's had too much of it already.

"What can we do to make our situation better?" he asked.

She was awed by that question. "As of now, can I just have my dinner, peacefully?"

"You must, it's delicious. You've mastered the kitchen too. What next?" he asked meaningfully.

She looked shocked and then shook her head and didn't answer.

Enough for today, I need to keep a check on the dose as well. Her second prejudice is even more lethal.

In the second weekend of September, Kunal received an invitation for another dance party. After the last experience, Shreya refused to join him. He tried to pursue the topic in his own clumsy style—cracking jokes. "See, I am ready to leave. You can have ten minutes to get ready."

Shreya picked up her laptop and sat on the sofa. "I am genuinely not interested," she said. "Thanks for asking, though."

"Dance parties are fun."

"I saw you having lots of fun last time. I am sure you must be looking forward to this one too."

"You too can learn. Dancing is no big deal."

"Please, Kunal, leave. You are just wasting your time."

"Did you notice girls in the party the other day?" He turned to her.

"Yes I did. What about them?"

"Don't you think they were very hot?" Kunal said dramatically.

"I don't find girls hot."

"Mumma has told you so many times to keep a check on your husband. And you are allowing me to go to such a party alone."

"It's more than fine, Mr Husband. Even if you don't come back home tonight, you know I would have no problem with that."

Kunal was a little offended. "What does that mean?"

"Well, hot girls can have hotter intentions. And you seem to be already fantasizing."

"Fantasizing!" Kunal was miffed, but controlled his anger.

"Talking about fantasizing" Kunal moved closer to Shreya, "When was the last time you fantasized?"

"No luck there. I was not as lucky as you were." Shreya pointed to Saloni's pictures. "She must have been real fun."

"Shreya, you are getting nasty now."

"When you start a nasty discussion, you shouldn't complain of being hit back." She frowned and stood up.

"I was just kidding."

"I really don't understand how playing with someone's emotions is "kidding" for you? Each conversation has to be sarcastic, and eventually ugly."

"I just wanted you to come to the party, that's it."

"I know that. You truly and desperately wanted me to join.

You really enjoy putting me into such situations. They are your winning moments."

Kunal stood too. "Shreya, we need to talk."

"Yes, we need to talk. I need a date from you on when my suffering will finally end." She took a shaky breath. "I sincerely feel you've had enough fun, and if need be, I can speak to Saloni. I will be more than happy to bring you both back together, if that makes my life better too. Handing over the 'Mrs Kunal Kharbanda' tag back to her will be my ultimate joy of giving." Shreya's eyes seethed with anger. She walked to the washroom and didn't come out.

Kunal walked downstairs and sat in the garden for a long time. He was distressed as he'd truly just wanted Shreya to accompany him to the party so that he could make up for his callous behaviour at the last party. He knew he needed to prepare himself better to deal with Shreya's frustration, of which he was the perpetrator.

He and Shreya needed a few light moments, the rest would follow naturally. But even as he thought that, he realised he had a bigger task to accomplish—he needed to win her trust.

Fasting Time

Shreya was now mostly taciturn. She sat in all the meetings with her eyes down and refused to attend the marketing meetings. Kunal's increasing attempts to mollify her failed. She asked Anuradha if she could now take off her *chura*—she found the wedding bangles irritating and uncomfortable. Anuradha requested her to hold off until *Karvachauth*, the festival when wives fast and pray for their husband's well-being. Shreya didn't want to upset her, so she agreed to her request.

When Kunal reached home one evening, he found Shreya sitting on the sofa, blowing hard on her newly-applied *mehndi*. Kunal had never seen Shreya doing that before, and he went and sat next to her, hoping to finally break the ice.

"What's this?" Kunal asked.

"It's called *mehndi*."

"I meant to ask, why have you applied it?"

"Many married women do that. It's not a new concept."

"I know, but I've never seen you do it before."

She was struggling hard not to indulge in a sweet conversation with Kunal. She knew that road only led to deeper pain.

"Just to remind you, Mr Kharbanda; I am still your legally

wedded wife."

Kunal grinned triumphantly at the answer—in his heart of hearts. Outwardly, he just smiled benignly.

"You very much are. But the way you said "legally" it appeared you may ask for half the property next." Kunal winked.

"Don't worry. I haven't even asked for half of the bed; half of the property is far distant."

"Bed!!" Kunal passed an elfish smile. "Interesting! I can see someone getting really desperate."

"Yes, truly and madly desperate to be sleeping on a bed again, all alone." Shreya moved back. "And regarding half of property, you can keep it safe for your third wife."

The argument now seemed to be getting out-of-hand. Luckily, at that point, Anuradha came out of her room.

"You are home, Kunal?" Anuradha said.

He stood up and hugged her mother. Shreya also stood up.

"Today was alright. But you need to be on time tomorrow. It's a very, very special day." Anuradha was sounding like a little girl in her excitement.

"Someone's birthday, Mumma?"

She lightly cuffed Kunal on the head. "As if you don't know!" Anuradha walked to Shreya and gently moved her hand over her hair.

"Tomorrow is my daughter-in-law's first *Karvachauth*."

Kunal's face gleamed. Shreya kept her eyes pinned to the marble floor.

Anuradha continued, "Better be home on time. She will be awaiting you to break her fast."

Anuradha's phone rang, and she walked to her room to answer it. Kunal walked to Shreya, whose eyes were still inspecting the cleanliness of the floor.

"You should have told me." Kunal said.

"Mumma did. One and the same thing."

"No, it's not. It's a yours and mine thing. I needed to know this from you."

Shreya gave no answer and turned to leave. Kunal held her arm at the elbow to stop her.

"You need to ask me to be home on time tomorrow. Otherwise, you'll tell me that I did so because Mumma asked me."

"Even today's time is okay."

"I could be even later tomorrow. So you need to smile and ask me to come home early."

"To be hungry for a few extra hours will not be a trouble. You return at your regular time."

"Shreya, you are unnecessarily turning it into an argument."

"It's a matter of perception. I see no reason that I should ask you to make your work suffer."

Kunal gasped. "Fine, then. Tomorrow I'll come home only when you call me."

Shreya set the alarm for 4 am. She took a quick shower and dressed up and joined her mother-in-law downstairs for a *puja*. She returned after some time and slept again. Kunal was unaware of this ritual and a little confused when he woke up and saw Shreya sleeping in a heavy salwar-kameez and jewellery. She looked like one of the bahus in the daily soaps, who sleeps with full make-up and expensive sarees.

Shreya pretended to be still sleeping to avoid talking to him while he was getting ready for office. She walked down only after he had left home.

Anuradha gifted her daughter-in-law a traditional gold

necklace with matching earrings. Shreya was reluctant to accept it, but Anuradha had her way. She loved to shower gifts on Shreya; she was the apple of her eye.

In the early evening Anuradha took Shreya to the big community hall nearby. There were over a hundred ladies in attendance, all dressed in their best sarees and jewellery. *Karvachauth* is celebrated with full enthusiasm and ritual by all the married ladies.

Shreya wasn't very happy; when the other ladies talked about their husbands, she chose to be silent. Her heart was bleeding in anguish for being in such a complicated relationship.

The news of the moon's arrival at around 8:45 pm spread like a jungle fire. Anuradha wished to call up Kunal, but Shreya told her he was busy with US clients. At about 9:30 pm, Kunal called up Shreya.

"Just a gentle reminder. You need to ask me to come home."

Her emotions were running wild; her struggle to keep herself calm was failing. "Nobody is waiting. Take your time." She hung up the phone.

Shreya requested Anuradha to go to sleep, as her health might be affected. It was 10:20 pm when Kunal finally arrived home. He saw a servant in the living room when he entered.

"Where's my *Dharam patni?*"

Shreya rose from the sofa and answered. "I know you have nothing to do with *patni*; you should have showed some respect for *dharma* at least."

Kunal's eyeballs nearly fell out seeing Shreya. She wore a red and green saree and looked beautiful. Kohl, bindi, jewellery and sindoor made her look the epitome of pulchritude.

Shreya picked up the *puja thali* and gestured Kunal to follow her to the rear garden. He simply followed; even the view of her back was a treat to watch. Today she was carrying the deep cut *choli* with greater comfort. Her hair had been twisted into a knot and decorated with a jasmine garland. Kunal was mesmerised by the physical beauty of his wife.

Shreya now stood where the moon was clearly visible. She knew Kunal was staring at her, but she ignored his gaze. She handed him a small goblet, filled with milk diluted with water and then looked at the moon and then at his face through a sieve, as per the custom. Kunal didn't move.

"I am waiting, Kunal," she said.

"For what?"

She was a little amazed. "You don't know?"

"No."

"You haven't done this before?"

"No dear, this is my first *Karvachauth* as well." He smiled gently, still captivated by her charisma.

"You need to offer me that mix."

"You can have it. All yours."

Shreya was perplexed. "Haven't you seen *DDLJ*?"

"I have. Several times. "

"Don't you remember that iconic dialogue of Kajol?"

"No, though I do remember Shahrukh's. *Bade bade desho mein aisi choti choti baatein hoti rahti hain, Senorita.*"

Shreya gritted her teeth. "I am talking about the *Karvachauth* scene, and Kajol's dialogue; and no Senorita."

"What's the big deal, you can help me remember." He sighed. "Why does everything have to be so long-drawn out?"

"Ok. Alright." Shreya closed her eyes for few seconds, exhaled a deep breath, and when just about to say something, she closed her lips again. This continued three times; before she finally uttered: "Well, Simran said to Raj..." Shreya said hesitatingly. Kunal didn't miss this opportunity; and stepped closer to her. "She said..." Kunal nodding encouragingly. "She said..." Kunal moved even closer.

"She said, for today's fast to be successful; the first drop of water and first bite of my food shall be from your hands."

Kunal's face lit up. Shreya's face flushed too, but she looked at the grass at her feet. Kunal's heart swelled—even in the make believe *Karvachauth*, she had really made him feel hugely special. He now wanted her to be his wife forever; he wanted a happy family life, with Shreya. Today marked his complete acceptance of Shreya as Mrs Kharbanda.

His decision of showing up late that day served the dual purpose he had targeted. First, he could finally see a ray of hope in their marriage; second, he could humbly keep his mother and chiefly her excitement away from their private moments.

Kunal brought the glass near Shreya's lips. She broke her fast, blessing the moment. Kunal then picked a piece of *mithai* from the plate, and put it in her mouth. He gently touched her quivering lips while doing so, which Shreya perceived as an unintentional mistake.

They sat down for dinner. Kunal kept staring hungrily at her, resting his eyes a little extra on her curves. *Revenge was indeed a two-edged sword.* He regretted coming home late and missing a longer view of her beauty. He kept asking her to pass dishes so that he could touch her hand. He cursed himself for creating this marital mess and missing a golden opportunity to "make it happen" that night.

Mumma Finds Out

Next night, Anuradha came out of her room for water and noticed Shreya's gold earring fallen near the sofa. She considered it important to hand it over to her right away. She looked at the stairs. *Once in a while it should be fine. Even temples have these many stairs.*

She saw Raju coming downstairs and the door was still ajar, so they must be up, she thought. Anuradha climbed the stairs cautiously and finally reached the door of their room. Looking in, she saw Shreya half-asleep on a mattress on the floor and Kunal in bed, working on his laptop. She gasped in shock. "Shreya!" she said, horrified.

Kunal fumbled to see his mother at the door of his room. Shreya jumped up, hoping it was just a bad dream. But Anuradha was there, leaning weakly against the door, nearly crying in shock. "Why are you sleeping on the floor, Shreya?"

"Well Mumma. It's just that…." Kunal tried to answer.

"I am asking Shreya." Anuradha stared at Kunal furiously.

"Nothing really significant." Shreya struggled to find an answer. Her eyes fell on Kunal's laptop.

"We just had this little fight. Kunal wanted to keep working,

I wanted to sleep. So, when he didn't listen, I pulled out the mattress. It's as simple as that." Shreya was shivering, hoping she accepted the answer.

"Exactly. That's exactly what happened." Kunal added to support her reasoning.

"Hang on, you two," Anuradha shouted. "I am not an idiot." She took a deep breath and then her eyes fell on the pictures of Saloni.

Shreya was terrified; she had no explanation. Anuradha walked closer to the pictures to confirm what she was seeing. Kunal slowly moved towards his mother, calling out "Mumma...," but she raised her hand, stopping him in his tracks.

Anuradha fainted and fell on the floor.

Kunal and Shreya ran to pick her up. Shreya was freaking out and Kunal was standing in shock, looking at his mother lying helplessly.

"Quickly, Kunal." Shreya had to shake him out of his stupor. "I'll pull out the car. Bring her down. We need to rush to the hospital."

In the hospital, Anuradha was taken to the emergency ward and examined. Shreya was crying, and she noticed Kunal was speechless and still in shock. She gently put her hand on his shoulder. "She'll be alright. Have faith." Kunal held her hands between his and stood quietly.

After about 30 minutes of examination, the doctor came out of the ward.

"She's out of danger now," he said. "Was it sudden anxiety or some kind of shock? You need to be careful while dealing with a heart patient. Her blood pressure shot up rapidly. She has responded well to medication and is sleeping now. She can be discharged tomorrow morning. Don't worry."

Shreya looked at Kunal. "She's alright." He still held her hand tightly. And then he put his head on Shreya's shoulder and started sobbing. She stood still, astounded. She hesitatingly rested her hand on his head to soothe him. Kunal raised his head and looked into her eyes. "I almost killed my mother today," he wept. Shreya had no answer.

They spent the entire night sitting on the hospital bench. Kunal didn't release Shreya's hand even for a fraction of a second that night. She found the situation really difficult to handle—even if she wished to support him, it would have made her emotionally even weaker. As it is, it was really difficult for her with Kunal always being around. But perhaps for today, he really wanted someone to hold him. Her kind heart couldn't let her pull back her hands.

But the next morning, when they visited the patient, Anuradha pulled back her hand from her son's grasp and turned her face to the other side. He tried speaking to her at which she got restless.

"Give her some time," Shreya whispered to Kunal, holding his arm. At home that afternoon, things were no different. Shreya sat beside Anuradha gently massaging her head. Kunal was standing at a distance, but Anuradha was in no mood to speak to him.

"I need to sleep. You guys can go and take some rest too." Anuradha spoke stumbling.

"Mumma. Can you just give me one minute of yours?" Kunal begged.

"Shreya, can you please ask him to leave."

Shreya was flummoxed as to how to deal with the situation. She gently gestured Kunal to leave and she followed him out.

After some time Shreya walked up to Kunal, who was sitting listlessly on his rocking chair.

"Kunal. You need to give her some time. She's in shock. You need to understand that she had an impression that we have a happy marriage."

He slowly opened his eyes, and stood up. "I don't even know how to face her. What explanation can I offer?"

"You don't have to worry about that. She's wise enough to make out."

"To make out what?"

"That you still truly love Saloni. And that her place in your life and heart is irreplaceable."

He was struck dumb by Shreya's line of thought. She continued, "Well, you know, there are always two sides of a coin. Hate is nothing but love going sour, or unrealised. It's your love for her that made you ruin my life."

Kunal was staggered. He had no idea that Saloni's pictures on the wall were still giving Shreya such a false impression. Initially, he did put up those pictures to torture Shreya, but later he had hoped someday Shreya would become jealous and throw those pictures out herself.

"Similarly, your mother's anger is another side of her concern for you." Shreya added. "You need to speak to her at a suitable time, and plan your life accordingly." She paused. "The only thing I ever feared happened last night. Our relationship status is now out in the open." She looked up at Kunal. "I think it's time for me to take an exit from your life and house."

Kunal realised that his life was in a real mess. His giving her time to get over the initial trauma had actually resulted in an even bigger problem. He regretted not destroying those pictures earlier.

"Can you please keep quiet for some time? I don't think it takes a genius to analyse my present mental state." Kunal replied with irritation.

"I just wanted you to feel better by offering the best solution."

"You really want me to feel better?" Kunal asked.

She nodded.

"Can I ask for a favour in that case?"

"Sure."

"Can I have a cup of tea?" He said out-of-the-blue. "Strong and just one spoon of sugar."

Shreya was a little stunned. She, however, started heading towards the door.

"And do you really want to make it even better for me?"

Shreya turned to look at him.

"Then please make it two. We had an awful night yesterday; we both need to feel better, and a good cup of tea will really help." Shreya did as he desired.

Kunal was however mostly quiet over the tea, deep in thoughts tossing his newly discovered coin. *Even the archaeologist who first discovered Harappan culture coins wouldn't have been this puzzled.*

Initially she made attempts to make our marriage work and now when I have started making moves, she's retreating. Today I have the first piece of my puzzle. She thinks I am still stuck to the past. Vow number 5—Hell! That's the only thing she registered.

When Vineet came to visit her that evening, Anuradha told him to shut the door and then started crying. She narrated the entire incident to Vineet and was surprised that he didn't appear shocked. He also knew what was going on! "Why did you never tell me this?" Anuradha was a little angry.

"You know, *mausi*, my loyalty lies with Kunal more than anyone else on this planet."

She narrated Shreya's wedding night reaction. Anuradha's voice choked. "Shreya is such a wonderful girl. What's Kunal's problem?"

"She's an angel. But he's not been nice to her until very recently," he said thoughtfully, "Day one she reacted so strongly seeing Kunal! But why? She had met Kunal twice before the wedding."

"You were there when they met in the coffee shop, right?"

"Not exactly. I left after Kunal's prank was over for him to call her up and reveal the suspense. He told me later that he did speak to her, though very briefly."

"Not only Shreya's reaction, even Kunal's reaction when he saw Shreya's pic for the first time is very fresh on my mind." Anuradha's memory leaped a few months back in time.

"Please Mumma. Don't start again." Kunal had said with mild irritation; seated in Anuradha's room while she tried to show him a picture of a suitable girl on her laptop.

"You said that I can choose."

"I did. But every second day we can't be talking about this."

"You never even give a look to any girl I propose. I think you just said so to change the topic."

"You are too stubborn. Let's do it then."

"Let it be. It's already gone sour. Do you even know how much it hurts to see your own child in pain?"

"I am not in pain. I am solving the purpose of my existence by taking dad's dream to new heights."

"I know. But trust me, even Sudhir would have wished that you'd smiled more often, and wholly." Her eyes were moist.

He hugged her. "Ok, Mumma. I am sorry. Let's see your favourite website, *BharatMatrimony.com;* your homepage; the first thing you see each morning."

The first profile was nixed in less than 10 seconds.

Next, she pulled out the profile of "Shreya Kohli". Kunal's face turned demonic. He swiftly moved towards the laptop and checked her education details. He stared at her profile for a long time.

"You want to consider her?" Anuradha said with hope in her voice.

He was still gazing at the picture in the laptop. She waited until he broke the silence himself. "Mumma, I want this girl. And at once." He turned briskly before she could react. "You are too much into *pandits*. I am sure they will have a big say on the wedding date."

"No, no," Anuradha said hastily before he changed his mind. "April 13 is *Baisakhi*. That's a suitable date. Are you sure?" She was confused at this sudden haste after months of refusal to even think about marriage.

"No later than April 13 if you really want me to tie the knot. Otherwise this topic stands closed in our house forever."

Anuradha was befuddled. His words were not matching his expressions; and the topic being ignored for months now, had finally found a resolution in seconds. And he wanted to be married in a few weeks.

"Are you sure?" She asked again.

"Very sure." He said. "An MBA Operations is exactly what the company also needs." He smiled ironically. "And such beautiful eyes too."

Anuradha now looked at Vineet tearfully. "Did I accidentally cause her to be his punching bag?"

Vineet hugged her. "I'm afraid the answer is yes." He paused. "But Kunal is mellowing now and he's always trying to get her attention."

"You think so?"

"It's not what I think; it was an obvious thing to happen."

"Tell me more."

"I am a guy myself; so it's not so difficult to read another guy. Take a girl like Shreya—even if she lives in the neighborhood, a guy would be impatient for her. Shreya lives in his house, sleeps in his room; how long can he resist her?"

She smiled. Vineet's smile weakened. "I am more worried about Shreya's point of view. She really had a hard time."

Her smile broadened. "It's been millions of years yet men fail to understand a woman." She sighed. "It's very simple for one woman to read another." Her moist eyes also smiled. "Now I clearly understand what she has been doing all this time. Truly a mature girl. Kunal deserved to be handled that way."

"What next?" Vineet asked.

"Let's cause agitation at both ends, simultaneously. They both haven't been tested together, that is all we need to ensure now—that they become one unit in facing the world."

"Great then." Vineet clapped. "Let's stir both of them up; I am sure we'll have a good show to witness." He smiled impishly.

"Vineet, I was about to call you." Shreya said when she saw him coming out of Anuradha's room.

"I came over to see *mausi*. I hope she gets better soon."

"It's a cascaded effect of events; we need to fix the root cause."

"I don't quite understand that." Vineet pretended to be completely unaware.

"I need your help." Shreya requested. "We need to get Kunal

and Saloni back together."

"What?" Vineet freaked out. "Are you in your senses? It's an absolute useless thought to even consider!" he asserted. "And for heaven's sake, don't mention this to Kunal."

He left their house, and headed straight to Jyothsna's office. He took her into full confidence on the entire situation. They both worked on her laptop until late night, finalizing some documents.

Very late in the night, Vineet visited Anuradha's room almost secretively. He handed over the desired documents to her.

The next morning, Kunal made one more attempt to speak to his mother. She asked him to close the door and keep the discussion highly confidential.

"You are part of my body and my soul. No matter how disappointed I am with your actions, I have to stand by you always. You remain the most important person of my life," Anuradha said with an upset face.

"Thank you, Mumma."

"But, in all these months, I have developed a very special bond with Shreya too."

Just when Kunal was about to say something in his support, Anuradha interrupted. "I know things have changed. Marriage is not considered a pious bond anymore." She paused. "I don't move well with the times. I think I was being too orthodox to look for a girl for you. I am sorry for pushing you to get married."

And that's another piece of my puzzle! Shreya's also angry with me for being disrespectful to the pious bond of marriage.

"Keeping the entire situation in mind, I have only one solution to offer. And it's not a request but an order," Anuradha said with authority.

"I'll do whatever makes you happy, Mumma." Kunal begged.

"Good." She pulled out the papers from her side drawer. "These are your divorce papers. I want you to free Shreya. She deserves to be happy too, if not with you maybe with somebody else. I want that good soul to experience a life she deserves. To see her smile, genuine smile." She looked straight into his eyes.

Kunal was devastated, as if someone had slipped the ground from underneath his feet. Not even in his wildest dreams had he expected his mother to take this stand.

Kunal stood there shocked for about a minute and then turned around and strode out of the room, leaving the documents behind. Anuradha gave a weak smile. She hoped the arrow had hit the target.

Kunal went to office that day to avoid the chaos at home; Shreya chose to stay home to take care of Anuradha.

When Vineet walked into Kunal's cabin, he found him standing at the window looking outside.

"Hi. Are you okay?" He asked. Kunal just nodded.

"Something you want to talk about?" Vineet stood a couple of feet away from him, leaning on the window, so as to see his face.

"I really appreciate that, Vineet. But it's a mess I created myself. I don't even remember why I did so. But it's now traumatizing me."

"If I really matter to you, you would allow me to help you out." Vineet sounded concerned.

Kunal looked at him, and realised his sincere desire to help.

"Mumma wants me to divorce Shreya." Kunal closed his eyes in pain.

Vineet paused for a few seconds. "So, what's the issue? You've been married for about six months, and while you may have become amicable colleagues, no way are you a couple."

"I always thought you really liked Shreya." Kunal was vexed.

"I do. She's my mentor in a way. I have tremendous respect for her, and I will always have it. But the question here is not whether I like Shreya. The question here is: Do YOU like Shreya? And the answer is NO." Vineet replied clearly. "And I don't blame you either."

"Vineet, your words are confusing."

Vineet chuckled sarcastically. "No matter how much girls keep saying all men are the same, we know we aren't. We have different preferences, we like different kinds of girls. She isn't your type and that's it."

"What crap?" Kunal was offended. "What kind of girl do you think is my type?"

"Well, Kunal, you are more an admirer of beauty than brains. Though I think Shreya's pretty, you've always dated—women with seductive faces and sexy figures. You even married one, didn't you?"

Kunal turned to him angrily. "Are you calling me vain and shallow? You need to give me a break here. You can't really put that tag on me."

"I don't see it being such a problem. Beauty is an admirable thing. But personally, I don't consider it as the only criteria for a spouse or even girlfriend. I am not in college anymore; I would like her to have a few additional qualities as well. I need to spend many days too, and not just a night with her."

Kunal's eyes opened wide with pride for Vineet. "You've grown up, bro." He paused. "But I am disappointed you think this of me."

"I've spent five months sitting next to Shreya, watching her being disappointed daily. You have no idea what a high character and intelligence your wife possesses; as you never care to give her a look. That's because you don't have the eye to admire such qualities. So please set her free."

Kunal stood quietly.

"And maybe if we put the same question to Shreya about you, the answer will be the same."

Kunal was now really irritated with everyone telling him the same thing. "And how do you know that? Did you ask Shreya?"

"Not exactly. But when I went over to see *mausi* yesterday, Shreya said something that supports my statement."

Kunal narrowed his eyes. "What did she say?"

"You really want to know?"

"Yes, I really, really want to know." Kunal was impatient.

"She asked me to help her put you and Saloni back together."

Kunal banged his hand on the window really hard.

"Careful. I refused. So it's sorted out."

"You know she's not right. But she won't believe me, but I've seen her listening to you." Kunal paused. "I beg you Vineet. Please take that out of her mind. She needs to know the truth." Vineet instantly agreed.

However, Shreya had decided to set the ball rolling. In another part of the city, she had managed to get hold of Saloni's manager. When Saloni heard someone from "Kharbanda Textiles" wanted to meet her, she agreed immediately.

Shreya went over to her shooting location, and they met in the make-up van. Saloni was seated at her dressing table, rollers in her hair and make-up on in thick layers for the shoot. Her skimpy dress showed her long legs to perfection.

"This is really surprising, to see that Kharbanda Textiles still wants to speak to me." Saloni raised her eyebrows.

Shreya introduced herself. "We still have a deep connection with you. I am here to make a confession." And then she narrated the Bangalore hotel room incident to Saloni.

Saloni heard the whole story and then shrugged and raised her eyebrows. "I was anyway looking for a reason to call it quits with Kunal. Thank you for giving me one."

"What are you talking about? Kunal really loves you."

"I don't get this crap. His love is the way he defined it. I dated him hoping he would help me in my career but he in turn eclipsed my career. Then he was mad to get married; he wanted it and so I had to. Again, I hoped that his contacts would help me." Saloni was furious. "Within two months of marriage, he almost destroyed my career. He even dropped me as brand ambassador of his own company, saying that I was family now. He's one middle-class jerk. I wasted too much time with him."

"He truly is still yours," Shreya asserted.

"That is more bullshit. He has moved on in life too, Textiles has a new mistress now."

"Well, she sits right in front of you and her marriage is meaningless." Shreya said with a heavy heart. She told Saloni about the photographs.

"Gosh !! He's pissed you off, too." Saloni smiled sarcastically. "His mother also does a great job in pissing off people."

"Mind your language, Saloni. Not a word against her." Shreya made her stand clear.

"Wow! I am impressed." Saloni clapped dramatically. "Anyway, Shreya, my life has moved on. Kunal is a closed chapter, and not in my worst nightmare do I plan to reopen it. Thanks for dropping by."

Shreya walked out, nearly bumping into a middle-aged woman who was walking into the van. As the door closed, she heard Saloni say, "Mom".

But Shreya didn't register their conversation. She walked away, disappointed at Saloni's rejection. But the burden on her heart had lightened; she was not the reason Kunal and Saloni had split. She felt a deep empathy with Kunal; she felt sorry for his feelings being misunderstood. He had wanted to protect Saloni, and she had perceived it as male chauvinism.

When Shreya reached home she saw Vineet's car in the driveway; she was looking forward to speaking to him. She walked into Anuradha's room, where she found him chatting with his aunt. Anuradha, still resting in bed, extended her hand to Shreya. Shreya came and sat next to her.

Anuradha rested her hand on her face expressing affection.

"I need to ask you something, something very important that I need to know." Anuradha paused. "And if even for a single day you truly loved me, please be honest."

Shreya could sense the gravity of the matter. She sat quietly, looking into Anuradha's eyes.

"Do...you...like...Kunal?"

Emotion rolled down as tears from Shreya's eyes. She gently pulled back her hands from Anuradha's. "Mumma, for me, to even ask this question of myself, I don't have Kunal's permission." Shreya answered chokingly and she ran out of the room.

"Talk to her, Vineet," Anuradha urged and he nodded. Vineet quickly left the room and gently caught Shreya's hand as she was about to climb up the stairs to her room. He pulled her down to sit on the steps and held her hand between his and waited for her to calm down before he started speaking.

"I always thought you are a very honest person," he said.

"Now you too have doubts."

"Well, I just developed that doubt a minute back. I don't believe you when you say that you have no feeling for Kunal." Vineet smiled. "You've handled his temperament, you've stood by him in tough times and you are always so concerned about him. I can't buy that you have no soft corner for him."

Shreya took a deep breath. "We co-exist under one roof and we are colleagues too. I owe it to Kunal to be supportive."

"Shreya, you are not being honest again. I share my deepest feelings with you. I don't deserve this in return."

"I honestly did tell you all yesterday. You refused to help me."

"That's all rubbish. I've known Kunal since childhood. He was disturbed for few months during his divorce but no way does she even exist in his mind anymore. I can swear my life on that."

"He himself told me that. You don't have to endanger your life here."

"You know Kunal, he has this habit of blasting off. I am sure it must have been one of those moments," Vineet said assertively. "*Mausi* told me about the pictures. I visited Kunal's room almost every weekend before your marriage and I always found that wall vacant. Trust me, it could mean anything but what you are thinking. And I beg you to trust me on this."

'Kunal truly is hot-tempered. Maybe he put those pictures up just to make me feel jealous. I've actually never seen him looking at them,' she thought.

Vineet changed his tone to make the conversation pleasant.

"I only see one amicable solution to this entire mess." He smiled broadly. "My two favourite people, staying together, happily married forever."

Shreya smiled weakly. "It's not going to work."

"How do you know when you have not even made an attempt." Vineet winked as he repeated Shreya's own words to her.

"Things are different here. You and Jyothsna really liked each other; it was just a matter of making the first move."

"Things are the same. You need to give up your adamancy."

"I am not being adamant."

"You are. I see you puncturing Kunal's attempts very often. He asks you to join marketing meetings, you decline. You don't go to parties with him and he just keeps sitting there, lonely. You are always ignoring him in office." Vineet paused. "I know he didn't behave well in the initial days of marriage, but I also observe your absolute refusal in giving him another chance." He looked into her eyes, "I think he really likes you now. He feels very close to you. Don't you agree?"

Shreya looked at Vineet in amazement. She'd had an impression that Vineet was a happy-go-lucky type of person; to her surprise, he was deep and observant. "It's difficult to read Kunal. He always appears angry to me," Shreya answered.

"I do notice him being much more at peace with himself lately," Vineet said. "Bear with him for some more time. The memories of the bad times are wearing-off. He's a darling. I am sure he'll make a great husband." He said hoping that he'd cheered her up to some extent.

Vineet gently rested his hand on her shoulder. "And the most important question." He paused. "How do you manage to resist Kunal?"

She shrugged Vineet's hand from her shoulder and pretended offence, but she couldn't help grinning at his mischievous question. Vineet laughed lightly. "And you know what. You are indeed the most compatible match he could ever have; in terms of beauty, brains and attitude. You are actually the female version of Kunal minus his temperament. Thankfully." Vineet said rolling his eyes. Shreya laughed out loud.

"And you know there's this one pathetic old saying that the way to a man's heart is through his stomach. It's extinct now. Good food is readily available everywhere," Vineet said. "A way to today's man's heart is through his eyes and ears. Look good; talk good and you can have him on his knees."

Shreya's eye opened in astonishment. She had never witnessed this side of him. Vineet in turn had been practising for hours for this discussion; most of these lines were actually written by Jyothsna.

"And you anyway always look gorgeous, but Kunal is little stylish. Let's go shopping and change your wardrobe a little." Vineet stood up and stretched. "Your battle is already half won. We only need to ensure that he's on his knees soon. What the hell does he think of himself?"

And he said snarling: "ATTACK!"

Attack—The Siege Begins!

Vineet drove Shreya to one of their designer clients. Jyothsna accompanied them and helped Shreya pick some of the smartest western business suits.

Shreya looked the price tag of the dress; her eyes opened wide. Vineet noticed that.

"You don't have to worry about that," he joked. "They're worth every single penny, Mrs. Shreya Kunal Kharbanda."

Shreya reached home at about 5 pm. She hurried to her regular parlour nearby, and requested basic classes for make-up. The owner agreed to let one of her most experienced helpers teach Shreya basic make-up and party hair-do for a friendly amount of money. Shreya started the classes, sitting there for about one-and-a-half hours.

Anuradha was thrilled to see the change in Shreya's stand and wished her best of luck to teach a tough lesson to her own son. She also got into the mood of the campaign and suggested that she would pretend to be sick for the next week as well, so that Shreya could be home post-lunch and find time for her make-up classes.

Anuradha partially disagreed with Vineet, and insisted that the stomach should also continue to be attacked. They laughed out aloud, and Anuradha recovered magically.

Kunal returned home later about 9 pm in an extremely bad mood. He had cancelled all his meetings for the day, and had been mostly sitting in his cabin in solitude.

Shreya was arranging her closet when she heard glass breaking in the room. She hurried out and found Kunal throwing the pictures from the wall, all over the room.

She was a little frightened watching Kunal being insanely furious.

A piece of glass pierced Kunal's thumb. Shreya hurried towards him, pulled him by the wrist, and made him sit on the bed. She sat on her knees right in front of him.

"What's up with you? It's bleeding." She gently pulled the glass out. She was angry at Kunal's behaviour.

"Do you realize that you have this big issue of anger management?" She frowned. "You actually end up hurting yourself more than anybody else."

Kunal looked into her eyes, calming himself down. The cleaner arrived.

"Please clean this up. And send the broken frames for repair," Shreya said.

Kunal, whose back was to the door, mouthed at her to "Shut up!" and then he turned around and said to the cleaner, "Take the broken frames, as well as the ones on the wall to the backyard and burn them." He said firmly. "I want to see the ashes from the balcony in two minutes, and if the clock ticks the third minute, you are fired."

Shreya sat quiet, and waited for the cleaner to leave to speak. "Burning them will not help," Kunal snarled at her. "Shut up. I don't want your *gyan*." Shreya looked down.

A few seconds later, Kunal spoke. "Do I really need to tell you that I need first aid here?" Shreya pulled out the first aid box from the side table, and started dressing his thumb.

"Why are you always so silent when with me? Does it really cost to talk to me? Or is it just me who's not even worth talking to?" said a disconsolate Kunal.

"You asked me to shut up," Shreya replied.

"And you always do what I ask you to. Right?"

"Ideally, I should not be even showing my face to you."

"But you actually do that very often."

"I am sorry, I'll take care of that from tomorrow."

"Don't be sorry for obliging me. Just like the difference between right and wrong, there has to be a difference between you and me."

"Right or wrong is matter of perception. There's no absolute right or wrong." She finished the dressing. He still held her hand, amazed at her calmness.

"What kind of a person are you?"

"I am an idiot."

"That's your perception. But I and my people don't think so."

"They all do. I am an idiot, hence I am here today. Had I had brains, life may have treated me differently." She choked. "But no hard feelings. I don't want to give life a victorious feeling of defeating me."

"You can never be defeated. Your enemies learn this the hard way. They make futile attacks to bring you down, and they stoop so low that they fail to see even their own reflection." They looked eye to eye. Kunal's state of mind was well communicated through his moist eyes.

"Do you even know what you want out of life, Kunal? Such an ugly scene today was not needed." Shreya realised he must have had a bad day. "Would you like some tea?" She smiled. "Or dinner first?" Kunal melted with Shreya's smile, and chose dinner.

Later that night, while everyone was sleeping, Kunal walked to the rear garden. The ashes of the frames were still hot. He stared at them for a while; suddenly rain started falling. He stood quietly in the rain; the drops camouflaged his tears. Shreya's pain flowed through his eyes that day and the rain washed away his leftover bitterness, cleansing his soul.

He looked up at his room and his heart finally made a long-awaited confession.

I shouldn't have done that. It wasn't about only me and her; our families were involved too. It's so sinful of me to have abused the sacredness of marriage. If she's right and Papa is actually watching me as an angel, he would be so disgusted. And why? I blame her for the loss of my love; however, the truth is I never even had it. Maybe that's the reason God doesn't consider me worthy of it.

A beautiful soul; a blissful face. My wife is my biggest treasure. I can't afford to lose her. She isn't going anywhere, she belongs to me. More than Mumma, it seems Papa chose her for me.

I'll prove myself worthy of her.

That Saturday was a working day for the three directors of the board. Kunal had postponed an important meeting with a potential customer to today. Vineet showed up at the Kharbanda residence with the final presentation and sales figures.

"I wish I could join this meeting today, but I have this movie plan with Jyothsna." Vineet said.

"That will be okay, Vineet, you can carry on with your plan," Kunal replied.

"That's great. Jyothsna was anyway not happy with me going away to Pune the last two weekends." Vineet said.

"You know what? She actually means you should give her more attention and divide your time evenly." Shreya said.

"I am not sure if she means that."

"I am sure," Shreya said. "It's easier to make out what a girl really means; men are just so unpredictable in their thinking."

Kunal gazed at her realizing that 'men being unpredictable' was actually aimed at him. Vineet too registered the barb.

"You know what? They are actually not that unpredictable if you keep your prejudices aside," Kunal replied instantly.

Vineet considered it just the right time to leave their room and let them sort it out.

"I have no prejudices," Shreya said.

"You do. And they are so unshakeable." Kunal said. "Firstly, whatever I say, is sarcastic. No matter how sweet it is or how positive, if it's coming out of my mouth, it lands on your ears as sarcastic." He paused. "Secondly, I am always scheming. Whatever I do pertaining you, for you it has a secret agenda. You really need to let your prejudices go."

Shreya stood quiet. 'He's right,' she thought.

"Can you please get ready now?" Kunal said.

"See, here you go again," Shreya said, "You know I have no contributions to make in those meetings. I am just sitting there, listening and smiling artificially. But you keep bringing up this topic again and again."

"Is it really that difficult to understand why?" Kunal said.

"Difficult for you to understand…?"

"You really want to know why I ask for your presence."

"Yes, please. One good reason will really help." Shreya said.

"And I can be assured, you'll trust me."

"Be assured."

"In that case, Mrs Shreya Kunal Kharbanda, your mere presence makes me feel stronger." Kunal looked straight into her eyes. Shreya went quiet.

It was the first time he was acknowledging her as a supportive wife. She smiled to herself.

Shreya wore one of her new business suits for the meeting the next day. When she walked into the room, she saw Kunal noticing, but he remained silent.

The meeting was extraordinarily longer than usual. After lunch, two rounds of coffee also followed. It was about 7 pm when the deal was finally closed. They sat in the car, Kunal smiling and Shreya yawning. Kunal decided to take her to Chowpatty to cheer her up.

To his utter surprise, Shreya wasn't chopping his conversations. She was talking, listening and replying. Her voice may not have been as extraordinary as Kunal's but her words were. Her cordiality healed his soul and he was happily smiling after such a long time. But he still couldn't see the end of the horizon.

Later in the night Shreya was sitting on her mattress cross-legged, busy on her laptop. Kunal was lying on the bed. He turned to Shreya, resting his head on his hand.

"Shreya."

"Hmm?"

"I always wanted to ask you something. It has been bothering me for about two years."

"Tell me." Her eyes were still fixed on her laptop.

"How did you gain access to our hotel room in Bangalore?"

Shreya raised her head, keeping the laptop aside. "Before I

tell you, I need to know the answer to a similar question." She paused. "What was that all about in Lucknow?"

"I paid a visit to my engineering college friend. It was my first and only visit to Lucknow. I was going down the stairs and you guys were so loud; the door was open. I used to be a real prankster back then." Kunal paused. "Are you still mad at me?"

"No." Shreya meant it. "Not at least after my own Bangalore act."

"Yes, tell me, how did you get inside the room?"

Shreya smiled naughtily. "I bribed the cleaner."

"And drugged the beer."

"And finally, I searched your luggage for the condoms," she said with pride.

"You are quite a schemer. I am so impressed." Kunal said shaking his head.

"One more thing, how did you know my name? I never knew yours." Shreya asked.

Kunal scratched his nose. "I felt a little guilty about my prank later that day. I asked my friend for your details. I even dropped by in the evening to apologize but the house was locked. I had to leave the city the same night. I knew your name, college and batch and vaguely remembered your face."

Shreya nodded. "I remembered your face very clearly. I even drew a sketch of yours, and made sure to look at it at least once a day. I could have recognized you even with a moustache and beard."

"You almost did. In fact, I am so proud of Vineet for cracking a joke at the right time, to take your eyes off me."

Shreya was puzzled. "Off you? What do you mean?"

"You remember that yellow-turbaned Sardarji in the coffee

shop?"

"Yes. He was quite irritating."

"Well, I've been irritating you ever since then."

Shreya was thunderstruck as she realised the Sardarji had been Kunal in disguise. She finally broke her silence. "You win. You're the bigger schemer." Kunal laughed.

"One last thing," he said. "How did you get a reputed hotel to change their protocol to let a cleaner serve the beer?"

Shreya sighed. "The waiter delivered the stuff. I was standing right there, and took it from him to give to the cleaner when he left. Simple."

"And why did he give it to you?" Kunal questioned.

"Well, I told him that it was my room and my husband ordered it."

Shreya realised what she'd said after the words left her mouth. Life had indeed come a full circle.

Kunal smiled gently and said. "God must have been watching."

That Sunday, Anuradha and Kunal spoke normally to each other. There was still some formality, mainly on Anuradha's side, but Shreya knew her mother-in-law was putting on an act. She smiled secretly.

Kunal got a reminder for the Diwali cards party at a friend's place. He had initially refused because of Anuradha's health, but the friend was insistent. Kunal asked Shreya, and after some persuasion she agreed to accompany him. Shreya wanted Kunal to accept this marriage not under pressure but to willingly make way for her in his life. And she was now also ready to meet him half-way.

At lunch time, Anuradha expressed the desire to conduct

a religious ceremony at home. After considering a few options, Shreya suggested *Mata ki Chowki*, to which she joyfully agreed. Anuradha was very excited. Her son and daughter-in-law appeared to have worked out some sort of reconciliation and she wanted to thank God in her own way. They planned out the details—the singing party to be called, the menu, sweets and chairs etc. Anuradha roughly calculated the number of guests, saying there would be an 'additional 100 guests'. Kunal said his guest list would have around 70 people. The date decided was Monday; it was *Bhai Dooj* and a good time to spend with the family. It was also an optional day-off in the company.

Kunal sat listening to the two women discuss the plans—he had no contribution to make and no one asked him anything. He now understood how Shreya felt at the marketing meetings.

Just then the phone rang—it was Ridhima. And when Anuradha heard her news, her plan to pretend to be ill for the next week flew out of the window. She turned to Shreya in excitement.

"You'll be a *Mami* soon."

"What happened? You ladies look very happy." Kunal asked.

"It's an ultimate happiness for a woman to experience motherhood." Anuradha was emotional.

"And I think the ultimate happiness for mothers is to throw puzzles at her kids," Kunal said sarcastically.

"You are such a moment spoiler." Anuradha grinned. "I meant Ridhima is going to be blessed with a baby soon."

He hugged his mother and expressed his joy. Anuradha hurried to the temple at home to thank her God.

Kunal looked at Shreya. "Are you of the same opinion?" he asked her.

"About what?"

"About this ultimate happiness of a woman..."

She was looking uneasy at the question and it was exactly what Kunal wanted. She stressed her mind a lot to find an appropriate answer but in vain. "I don't know." Bad answer indeed.

"What will be your ultimate happiness?" Kunal paused. "Don't tell me it is going back to Delhi."

"Is there anything wrong with that?" Bad answer again.

"What's so exciting about Delhi that Mumbai doesn't offer? Were you associated with some skydiving or biking club?" Kunal was in full flow.

"No, it's just peace."

"You just planned a religious event a few minutes back to attain some peace."

"You know what? I just realised what my ultimate happiness would be."

"Tell me dear. I am dying to hear it."

"It would be to win an argument with you." Good answer delivered at last. "It's just next to impossible to do so."

"And my confusion is," Kunal winked. "Why do you even attempt?"

Shreya blushed and turned to leave.

"And a wise man said; if you can't beat them, join them." Kunal had the final word.

That evening, for the card party, Shreya wore the outfit she had worn to the coffee shop in Delhi.

This time she was correctly dressed for the occasion. Shreya recognized many of the people she had met at the dance party, so she felt more comfortable. Mingling with the women now, she realised that the last time she had spoken about her work too much. Most of them didn't even know what business their husbands were associated with and preferred to gossip about designer clothes, shopping malls and cosmetic brands.

The men had already started playing cards. They were all seated on the floor on a thick mattress with colourful pillows scattered around to make the ambience more vibrant. Cash was flowing heavily with every bet. Eventually, nobody really loses or wins big time at such parties; it's just a reason for friends to get together and have a good time. You don't return financially poorer or richer than what you arrived with.

Kunal was dressed in a long kurta and jeans and lounging comfortably against a cushion. Vineet was seated a little distance away, but he could tell that Kunal clearly looked at peace after long. After some chit-chatting, the ladies' group dispersed either for food or drink while a few of them sat down to play cards as well. Three women joined their husbands in the main card playing area. Shreya also walked towards the men's group. Kunal brightened up when he saw her coming towards them, but was disappointed when she sat next to Vineet instead.

Vineet and Shreya talked softly, almost whispering.

"Do you know the game?" Vineet asked.

"I'm a Delhi girl, Vineet, we all play cards before Diwali."

The two sat together, whispering and giggling at his cards, and Kunal got more upset as they were ignoring him completely.

Cards were distributed once more. And most of the people surrendered. Vineet had a strong hand—King-Queen-Jack in the same colour—he couldn't lose! Good enough to bet even your last penny in the game. The betting was hard and furious, but eventually, there were only two left in the arena—Kunal and

Vineet. Kunal looked very confident, staring hard at Vineet.

Vineet whispered to Shreya, "What do you think he's thinking?"

"You know I find men unpredictable." They laughed out aloud.

Kunal doubled the bet.

"But he seems confident," Shreya said.

"There are just two possibilities here. One, he has a triple," Vineet whispered. "And the second, he's bluffing."

Vineet tripled the bet.

Vineet was really enjoying Kunal's expression—he was beginning to look desperate to win.

People started flocking to the cards area—this promised to be a good round! A few ladies were even cheering now.

Kunal and Vineet were eye-to-eye for this one. Kunal now put the last bit of his bucks on the bet.

Vineet, realizing that the game had gone far enough called for 'Show'.

Kunal held his first card between his fingers and flipped it. "8"

Vineet and Shreya looked at each other. What if he really had three 8s? Did he actually have a triple? For the first time, Vineet was worried.

He also showed his first card. 'Jack.'

There was silence all around. There was big money in the centre. Everyone held their breath, waiting for Kunal to expose his second card.

Shreya looked up at Kunal; she thought he looked angry. Kunal held his second card between his fingers and slowly turned it over. '9'.

Shreya exclaimed, "Yes!" Raising her hand up in the air, as an umpire signalling out, she high-fived Vineet.

Vineet now showed his Queen and King. He had won! Everyone was surprised that Kunal had bet so high on relatively weak cards; he was known to be a good player otherwise.

Vineet and Shreya were as elated as the Pakistan team claiming Tendulkar's wicket in the first ball of the match.

Kunal sat still, expressionless for a long time. Vineet bent forward to collect his winning money, looked up at Kunal and winked. Kunal smiled bleakly and turned away. Some of their friends joked: "Not your fault, Kunal. Lady luck was on Vineet's side." *Yeah, in the form of my wife*, Kunal thought jealously.

The next morning, Kunal was quiet on the drive to office. They were going in together—Kunal wanted time alone with her and had made the excuse that they had an important meeting to attend. Shreya smiled. She knew the day's agenda, and nothing had been put on her calendar, so she understood Kunal was again bluffing.

She now decided to begin the conversation—after all, even she had to make an effort! She also felt a bit guilty about her sudden thrill after he lost at cards the night before. "Kunal, as a child, were you mischievous or sorted out?"

"I don't remember." Kunal was still sulking from last night.

"Which school did you go to?"

"I'll send you my resume when we reach office."

"Did you and Ridhima fight often?"

"She bugged me often."

"No way, she's such a sweetheart. I am sure it must be you. Anyway, brothers have nothing better to do."

"Sure. All sisters think alike."

"All sisters experience alike."

"They are the precious darlings of the house, so even if they make a mistake; it's always overlooked," Kunal said.

"Of course, they deserve that treatment."

"True but Mumma used to be on my side mostly. I think it works the same in every house."

"Yes it does, and it's wonderful. Mothers always ignore a son's mistakes."

"True. She has always been patient with me. Back to your first question; I was mischievous, a prankster and a pain in the neck."

"So, you agree that she had offered you maturity, patience and care always." Shreya said.

"By all means."

"Good, then it's simple. Please be patient with her. She's not well and our situation hasn't helped. As far as I know her, she doesn't hold a grudge for long. She'll be fine with time."

Kunal closed his eyes gently; his heart moving even closer to her.

"Open your eyes, Kunal! Truck ahead!" Shreya screamed.

Kunal was startled. He applied the brakes in time.

"You okay?" Kunal turned sharply to Shreya.

"Yes." She was breathing fast. "You?"

"Yes." He put the car in gear and drove on carefully.

"Sure?" Shreya asked. Then she smiled.

Kunal's smile broadened. "How am I expected to react?"

"No reactions at all. Just input and output through your ears. Don't bother your mind's CPU."

"That's not what I am talking about."

"What else are you talking about?" Now Shreya was puzzled.

Kunal turned his wrist to check the time. "It's not even been

10 hours."

"Oh, that!" Shreya laughed. "Your cards were not bad actually. But wasn't it a little stupid to bet so high?"

"I say shut up!" Kunal said, laughing ruefully.

Shreya was now giggling uncontrollably. Kunal's heart warmed—he loved to see her laughing, so carefree, forgetting their grim situation for the moment. So beautiful and happy!

That evening Shreya tried a recipe for lasagna that she'd seen on the Internet.

While it was cooking, she almost scolded Anuradha, saying she should stop overacting where her health was concerned as Kunal was worried about her.

"I just want to understand what's on Kunal's mind," Anuradha said.

'Don't worry," Shreya said. "He's already confused and too much worry may defeat the purpose."

Anuradha promised to take care in future. They hugged.

Kunal reached home at 7 pm, earlier than usual. The two ladies were in the rear garden, watering plants. Shreya served him tea. Anuradha and Kunal spoke normally, and he was relieved to see his mother nearly looking her old self again. Later at dinner, Kunal asked which restaurant they had ordered the lasagna from. Both women laughed at this huge compliment.

Mid-Anniversary

Shreya was ready 15 minutes ahead of Kunal. She wanted to drive her own car to office so that her return was flexible, not only to check on Anuradha but also to complete her make-up course. The day before she'd had to take a cab. Today she was wearing a knee-length tight black skirt and a formal shirt in yellow—yet another new addition to her wardrobe. But she left before Kunal could see her. He had to drive in to work alone.

His phone rang as he sat in his car. "Hi, it's me, Aastha," the voice at the other end said. "Madhav is driving. We are on speaker, though."

"Nice to hear from you. How are you doing?"

"Very well, thanks. We were trying to reach Shreya but she isn't answering."

"She must be driving. I'll inform her once I get to office."

"You guys are working today?" Aastha sounded disappointed.

"Yes, it's Tuesday here. What's the day there in Delhi?" Kunal joked.

"Same for us, but today should be special for you guys."

"Aastha, can you please clear the suspense? I know it's not her birthday today."

"It's your mid-anniversary. You guys have completed six months of being married. Shreya celebrated ours big time, how come she has no plan for hers?" Aastha sounded plaintive.

Kunal was quiet for a few seconds. "You know what, Aastha, she must be very sure about me not remembering this. And the worst is she's right." They all laughed. "Now, can I ask for a favour please?" Kunal asked.

"Don't be so formal," Aastha replied.

"When you speak to Shreya today, please don't tell her I know. Let me plan something special for her." Kunal paused. "You know, I have this constant complaint from her that I do things only because Mumma asks me to; I don't want this one to become 'because Aastha asked you to'."

Aastha and Madhav had a huge laugh over this, and they agreed. Later, Aastha finally got through to Shreya and gave her their travel plans for the *Mata-ki-Chowki*, to which they'd also been invited.

"Akash Uncle's son, Prateek, is getting engaged a week after *chowki*," Aastha said. "So Madhav and I will attend the *chowki* on Monday and leave for Pune for the rest of the week. We'll return to Mumbai on Saturday morning to attend his engagement and fly back to Delhi on Sunday night, how's that?" Shreya was thrilled to be seeing her best friend again.

"And Mumma and Dad?" Shreya asked.

"The parents plan to be in Mumbai for three weeks; one week to visit Shirdi and another additional week to help Akash Uncle finalise the wedding details," Aastha told Shreya. Shreya was thrilled to hear the plan.

On reaching office, Kunal requested Shreya to come to his cabin. He was speechless for a few seconds—she looked stunning in her new outfit.

"Office staff really appears lazy these days," Kunal said.

"I know. Nobody really wants to work. Everyone is in a festival mood. But it should be alright, they deserve this break," Shreya replied.

"You are right. I think we all deserve a break. By the way, we need to go to the factory on Friday, a day before Diwali." Kunal informed her.

"Anything in particular?"

"Yes, Diwali *Puja*. Feast lunch organized for workers and other staff. We do that every year."

Shreya nodded smiling.

"Talking about a break, I think you can also take a break for today. We actually are just sitting idle." Kunal said.

"Yeah, good idea."

Shreya had picked up a report from Kunal's desk and was now looking at it. It had some graphs, which always interested her. *I am a Commerce student, yet this Engineering guy is much better than me on these financial figures and stats.*

"Shreya...."

"Hmm...?"

Kunal cleared his throat. "Movie.... tonight?" he asked with hesitation. His eyes clearly bore the guilt of the last time.

Shreya helped him out sooner than he expected. She nodded okay.

"Thank you," Kunal smiled in relief. He was pleasantly surprised at this easy victory; no you-remember-what-you-did-last-time look.

"Followed by dinner." Kunal blinked his eyes.

Shreya kept the report back on the table. "What time?"

"We can plan to leave by 6 pm. Is that okay?"
"Fine with me."
"Any preference for the movie?" he asked.
"No. Whatever you choose." Shreya smiled gently.
"About dinner?"
"Ch..."
"No," Kunal interrupted. "No Chowpatty, please."
"You should have let me finish," Shreya smiled sweetly. Kunal nodded. "Chinese. Will that be okay with you?"
"Chinese is perfect." Kunal smiled. "Thank you."

Shreya left his cabin, and headed home within the hour. She attended her classes, and practised what she had learnt to make her evening special.

It took Shreya a lot of courage to put herself together and to learn to trust Kunal again. She could see his attitude changing and his words transforming verbal attacks into verbal healing. He now sounded like the Kunal of their courtship period. She was enjoying his attention. Her world was changing once again.

That evening Shreya wore a royal blue sleeveless top, a pair of white capris and white wedged heels. A smart clutch bag and round earrings matched her attire perfectly. She tied her hair in a loose pony tail, allowing it to bounce around her head. She looked strikingly beautiful; a western beauty with the pure heart of the east. As she finished, she looked in the mirror and growled "Attack!"

The 'attack' was well registered. It raised the eyebrows and enchanted the heart of the targeted victim. Kunal opened the door of the car for Shreya—it was the first time he'd ever done that.

"I think we need to laugh," Kunal said. "Comedy, okay?" Shreya nodded.

It was exactly the change the couple needed. Some time away from the world, off work and off complications. The movie was not the best of its kind, but it was the best time they'd had together. Kunal had reserved a table at a high-end Chinese restaurant of the city. "Looks like a good place, ambience is great," Shreya said appreciatively.

"Yes. I really like this one. The food is great too. What would you like to order?"

"Anything nice, but veg please." Shreya replied.

"Why so? "

"Today's Tuesday." She looked up at him. "You don't follow the 'no non-veg on Tuesday' rule?"

Kunal smiled broadly. "I am mostly neutral about it. But since you've mentioned it, let's stick to veg for the day."

Kunal glanced over the menu. "Do you want wine? Let's limit Tuesday only to food. Drinks can be exempted."

Shreya's eyebrows rose. "I've never tried it."

Kunal looked at her skeptically.

"Trust me," Shreya smiled.

"You don't have to mention it," Kunal said. "Consider trying it for today."

"No. I've heard of people getting drunk, puking, creating scenes…"

Kunal intervened. "Hang on! It's wine and just a glass will not cause any of these."

"What if I do get high?" Shreya was concerned.

"You'll be driven straight home; safe into the bed. Can I order now?" Kunal asked and Shreya nodded smiling.

Drinks and appetizers arrived soon.

"Cheers." Kunal touched Shreya's glass with his. She was

hesitant, but finally she took her first sip. "Tasteless." Kunal laughed at her verdict.

"So, how were you as a child?" Kunal asked.

"I've been nice mostly. I had many friends and was reasonably but manageably naughty. My mother tells me I've always been the logical one."

"You don't seem to have many friends now?"

"Right." She hesitated, running her finger along the top of the wine glass. "I'm not in touch with any of my school or college friends; all I have is Aastha and Madhav. And now Vineet."

"Oh yes. That reminds me, I need to know the story you enjoy telling everyone." Kunal said. Shreya narrated how Madhav won her childhood friend Aastha pretending to help her with studies.

Kunal smiled. "You must have been the first one to notice?"

"No," Shreya said laughing. "It was my mom. She was the first one to notice that in the midst of all these teaching classes, some other subject was developing."

"Really?" Kunal was surprised.

"My mother has this inbuilt intuition system that works in a mysterious way. She just has this vibes technology kind of a thing. It's really surprising to see how it works. But it does. Then she has these detective tendencies; as children, Madhav and I used to tease her by calling her Sandhya Holmes," Shreya said.

"How did her system try to help you?"

"She was against our marriage." *Shit! Now I've screwed up the evening.*

But Kunal didn't react. "She didn't like me?"

"No, it was even before she met your mother. She just had this intuition that something was not right, and that I would have a tough road ahead," Shreya said.

Kunal grimaced. "Well, she was right. I really gave you a hard time."

"My mother says it's the hard times that mirror your character. It's always during bad times that you get to evaluate how well learning translates into righteous conduct." She paused. "And honestly speaking, in hindsight, I don't think I've done a good job. I really lost my cool at times."

Kunal was startled. "No, you've been amazing. It's me who's been out of my mind. I really feel ashamed." He paused. "See Shreya, I know I've been a jerk. You didn't deserve it."

"Kunal, there's one more thing I've wanted to say for a long time now, particularly after Mumma's ill-health. I have this strong feeling that you feel guilty about everything, always."

"Yes, I do feel guilty," Kunal burst out. "And for heaven's sake, everything is not about Mumma. I've been trying to speak to you much before that. But you offered no cooperation. I understand your frustration, and I take all blame. But we really need to talk."

Thanks for confirming but I had already put this piece on the puzzle board. But hey! Wait a minute. Are you thinking I am doing all this, so that she can be a grand-mother soon?

Shreya was also thinking along these lines and she immediately felt guilty about thinking the worst. "You have mentioned that many times, tell me what do we need to talk about?"

"I'll keep it very simple," Kunal said humbly. "Can we start by being friends?" He smiled. "And trust me, I won't disappoint you this time. Can we just bury this awkwardness between us?"

Shreya concurred smilingly. She was happy to take her relationship with Kunal to a new level.

Kunal, for his part, felt he had surmounted a great obstacle. But he knew there was still a long way to go. He needed to pull

Shreya out of her shell and he was glad he could, finally. But he had no intention of being only Shreya's friend. He wanted her for life—as his wife, his companion. And he better hurry up, he thought. He had already wasted a lot of time.

Happy Diwali Indeed

Diwali was an extremely busy period for the Kharbandas. On Friday, Shreya and Kunal went to the factory. Unlike their last drive to Pune, this one was far more pleasant. Kunal drove, pointing out all the landmarks on the way.

They were very warmly welcomed at the factory. Union leader Prakash, trying to make up for his behaviour the last time, was overly effusive to them both. The workers had even collected some money to buy a gift for Shreya.

This time Kunal voluntarily took Shreya on a tour of the factory, showing her the manufacturing plant and other departments. When they finished the *puja*, they stepped out to meet the workers. A female worker walked up to them, offering tea.

"Hello, Ma'am," she said to Shreya. "Do you remember me?" It was Manju, the widow of Manohar, who had died in the accident.

"Of course I do," Shreya said warmly. "How's your child doing?"

"Very well, ma'am. He goes to a good school, and he stood first in his class in the last exam."

"That's great. Ask him to keep up the good work," Shreya smiled.

Happy Diwali Indeed 187

"Ma'am, I wanted to return your money. You gave me too much. I should be thankful enough for the job."

"You don't have to mention it. Which section do you work in?"

"I work in the canteen. I made some of the food for today's *puja* also. In fact, this tea is also prepared by me," Manju said happily.

"Good tea," Shreya said to boost her confidence.

Manju turned to Kunal, "Sir, I hope you too liked the tea?"

Kunal smiled. "It's good. But you know, my wife does a much better job with tea."

Shreya smiled, amused at Kunal's banter. Manju laughed. "Ma'am, you get time to make tea?"

"Not only that. Your ma'am cooks too. You can even learn that from her," Kunal replied proudly.

'God bless this couple,' Manju prayed. "You both look so great together. May love always blossom in your lives," Manju said emotionally and left.

"Now that's what I call a blessing straight from the heart." Kunal was touched by her honest blessing. Shreya lightly nodded.

Diwali followed the day after. Shreya was dressed in a pretty salwar kameez when Kunal woke up. He walked up to her and wished her Happy Diwali; She wished him back with a glowing smile. They both walked up to Anuradha next, to convey Diwali greetings and get her blessings.

They were scheduled for a Diwali *puja* in the office later in the morning. All associates were invited, but not mandated to do so.

"You are going as you are?" Kunal asked.

"Yes. Is this dress not alright?" Shreya asked looking down

at her outfit.

"Hmmm... Let me think." He paused. "You know what; it is only alright, not great."

"Oh! ok. I'll change in that case." Shreya turned to move to closet area.

"Listen." Kunal called. "Consider wearing a saree."

Shreya turned back with amazement. "Saree?"

"Yes. Is it too much trouble?"

"Not really. But ...."

"But what?"

"Nothing. Just give me about 30 minutes here. It's a time consuming activity," Shreya replied with a shy smile.

"Take your time. We have some time before *puja* begins."

Shreya wore a peacock blue silk saree. She looked beautiful as always. The couple arrived at the office before anyone else. Vineet was at the Pune office. Shreya quickly decorated the idols at the entrance of the third floor. She was checking the decorations when Kunal came and stood behind her.

"Does it look good?" Shreya turned around and asked Kunal.

"Looks great," Kunal said, looking at her. Then he grinned and looked at the decorations. "Isn't it little strange, that we worship God so many times during this festival season. There will be one in the evening at home, and then the day after is the *chowki*. Too much *puja*!".

"It should be fine. We pray for prosperity."

"We pray too much, that's our problem."

Shreya looked at him with a little confusion. "Are you an atheist?"

"No, I don't think so. I am not that extreme."

"Are you an agnostic?"

"Hmm. That's a good one. Let me think." He paused for a few seconds. "No, I think God does exist. It's just that he doesn't like me but he's omnipresent. I am not sure if the dictionary has any word for me."

"You shouldn't feel like that. I think God does take care of you."

"You think so?" He paused. "Please elaborate."

"For instance, you are very intelligent and talented, but there are many others like you who don't have a platform or means to achieve what you have done at the young age of 29. You should be thankful to the Almighty always, to be blessed with that." He nodded at that compassionate reply.

"By the way, thank you."

"For what?"

"You just complimented me for the first time." Kunal got flirty.

"What did I say?"

"You said 'intelligent and talented'." He paused. "On second thoughts, they are not actually a compliment. You should come up with better words."

"We have many other important things to do right now."

"No, we are not doing anything else unless I say so." Kunal held Shreya's wrist and twisted it to tuck it behind her waist and pulled her close. Shreya struggled to get loose, but she felt immobile.

"Ok. So, tell me quick before someone else shows up. I don't intend to entertain others," Kunal said.

"I am not able to think of anything," Shreya was still trying to free herself.

"I'll help you." He paused. "How about 'good-looking'?"

Shreya blushed, and planned to deal with it playfully this time.

She turned to him, raising her eyebrows. "Not really."

Kunal's eyes widened. "You sure?" Shreya bit her lips to keep from laughing.

"Average or above average?" Kunal asked.

"Below average." Shreya's laughter broke out.

Kunal tightened his grip. Shreya ouch-ed.

"Ok. Next one." Kunal said. "Attractive?"

"Nah!" Shreya replied instantly.

"You sure again?" Kunal was enjoying the moment. "Maybe you wanna give me one look before your final answer."

Shreya turned to him and glanced at him from head to toe. "Very sure. No chance."

Kunal pretended offence. "You are really hard to get in that case." Shreya's laughter got louder.

"You can't deny this one," Kunal said. "Charmer?"

Shreya turned her face in the other direction to hide her reaction. "Forget it." She replied playfully.

"Sure? You aren't charmed?"

"Cent percent. No effect at all."

"You know what, I give you exactly 30 seconds to come up with a compliment for me; else I am gonna smooch you right here." Kunal's pretense of offence continued.

"You can't do anything like that in the office premises. We have a strong policy against sexual harassment," Shreya replied breathlessly, trying hard to get herself freed.

"I don't care about your policy. It's my company; and to make it sound more dramatic, it's my dad's company. I can't be fired." Kunal said dramatically. "And your 20 seconds are up. 10-9-8-7…"

"Hang on. This is unfair. It's torture."

"4-3-2…"

"Talkative." Shreya breathed easy having mentioned one attribute of his.

"You are too talkative and authoritative. Take two." Shreya flashed her playful smile.

Kunal smiled back in the same spirit. "That is all you could think of?"

"Yes, given 30 seconds and a threat like that." She giggled. He released her.

"Sexy?" Kunal said.

"You asked for one. I gave you two. Game over." Shreya said massaging her wrist.

"No, that's for you," Kunal said. "You look very sexy in this saree. You look gorgeous." He smiled at her with sincerity in his voice.

Shreya's playful smile faltered with emotion. "Thank you."

Later in evening, yet another Diwali *puja* was conducted, this time at the Kharbanda residence. The house had been lit up for the last three days and the Diwali *diyas* added to the glow. Anuradha again pulled out an expensive gift for Shreya. Thereafter followed gift distributions to servants, and some crackers were burst with the neighbours. It was a joyful evening for everyone. The Kohli family called up to convey their wishes. Kunal too spoke with everyone and greeted them with "Happy Diwali".

For Kunal, it was an auspicious start to a new year.

A Divine Evening

On the day of the *Chowki*, the whole household was put to work—a *pandal* was set up in the rear garden where the *puja* would be held, and idols and decorations were polished and set out. The front of the house was also getting decorated. Calling up the caterers and confirming the boxes of sweets to be distributed to all guests was Shreya's task.

She picked an orange *anarkali* suit for the occasion. It had a long flared skirt edged with navy blue. Although her "attack" on Kunal's senses was getting heavier with each day, today she didn't really have to try—the orange colour of the dress was reflecting on her face, the glow adding to her already clear complexion. Her hair was curled at the ends and swung gracefully as she walked down the stairs. Kunal's heart missed a beat. She looked graceful and enticing.

Kunal had chosen to wear a cream-coloured Lucknowi kurta-pajama. Shreya's self-control weakened when she saw him.

The Talwar family was the first to arrive. Shreya gently hugged Vineet. He gave her a huge compliment on her looks.

The Kohli family arrived ten minutes later. Shreya was elated to see them all and introduced Vineet as her 'Mumbai Madhav'.

Madhav joked about not having recognized Shreya, stating his sister had never looked so beautiful.

They all sat around the drawing room and Shreya brought out the *Bhai Dooj thali* and applied a *tilak* to her brother. Then she rubbed her hands, and opened her palms up to Madhav.

"Ok, let's see what you've got me this year," she asked excitedly.

"You know what, I couldn't go shopping for a present for you. So, I have cash this year," Madhav replied with a naughty smile.

Shreya snapped her fingers, and pointed to the door. "Get out." Everyone guffawed.

"Aastha, can you please pull it out of the purse quick? Next she'll ask the security to throw me out," Madhav joked.

Aastha pulled out a shining new iPhone from her handbag.

"Wow! Now that's really mind blowing," Shreya exclaimed. She hugged Madhav and Aastha together, an arm around their shoulders.

"But you know, the phone has a contract." Aastha said.

"What kind of contract?" Shreya asked.

"The contract says that you need to call Delhi at least thrice a week. This phone is to ensure that you remember us," she said. Shreya embraced her emotionally.

The *puja* started in the rear garden and guests started arriving soon after. Shreya and Anuradha welcomed the guests. Kunal was standing at another corner discussing something with Vineet in a low voice; but his attention seemed to be elsewhere. Vineet noticed his eyes continuously following Shreya.

"You are staring at her. Others might be watching," Vineet whispered in Kunal's ear.

Kunal turned to Vineet. "I don't think anyone should have an objection to that, including you."

"But it looks odd, someone staring at his own wife. What exactly are you thinking?"

"You know what, for the first time in my life, I fail to read a girl." Kunal sighed.

"You know what, for the first time in your life, you are with the right girl." Vineet replied with a smile. And then gently patted Kunal's back in affection.

Suddenly Kunal noticed Shreya looking worried; she appeared to be counting the guests. He also noticed that the flow of guests seemed to be steadily growing, more than they had catered for. He moved towards the house looking for her and met her at the doorway. She was looking frantic.

"I was about to come to you." Shreya said. "The guests are much more than we expected. The number is already 150. And none of your friends have turned up as yet. Mumma also says she's expecting a few more guests. I fear the number could rise by another hundred in the next hour." She was worried.

"How come that happened? Numbers were a simple calculation."

"I remember Mumma saying 100, and you 70; hence total of 170, the maximum should have been 190 or 200. I ordered everything accordingly." Shreya's worry was worsening with every second. "I've called up the caterer. Since we've informed him in time, he said it's manageable. I want you to call the tent house for additional carpets, fans and chairs. And I think we need to allow access to the ground floor of the house during dinner. We can't accommodate 250 people in the garden. Also, we need to order additional 40 boxes of sweets and that's my biggest concern. Because of the festival today, I am not sure if he can supply the additional boxes at such short notice." She was nearly in tears now.

"Relax. Relax. We'll work it out." Kunal said. The Kohli family noticed Shreya looking uneasy and walked over to pacify her. Kunal meanwhile called up the tent house. The *mithaiwallah* declined the request; he said he was out of stock. "Relax Shreya." Kunal said. "It's no big deal. Don't be so worried."

"I planned it out. If it fails, then I am to blame," she said, contritely.

"No one is blaming you. It's just a simple miscalculation."

"It's a big mess."

Kunal finally got through to one of the sweet vendors and confirmed the order.

Suddenly two delivery boys arrived with a big parcel—it was huge and rectangular and was being held by both very carefully. Kunal frowned. "This was to arrive five days ago."

"Sorry, Mr Kharbanda. Our workers were on Diwali vacation," the vendor replied politely.

Kunal turned to Shreya, who was still upset. "Ma'am, can I please have the key to our room?" Kunal requested. Everyone smiled. Shreya opened her purse and passed the keys.

Kunal escorted the delivery boys inside the house. Anuradha moved from the *pandal* with Vineet, looking for them.

"Where's everybody?" Anuradha asked.

"Nothing Mumma, just a little problem. But it's all resolved now."

"Let's go then." Anuradha said. Kunal also came out of the house.

"Mumma. How come we have 250 guests against 170 counted? You said 100." Kunal said with a little anger.

"I never said 100. I said an additional 100. 50 are immediate family; they are not guests, they are like hosts." Anuradha replied, fuelling Kunal's irritation.

"Mumma, you need to speak clearly. We almost landed in a mess."

"What's the big deal? Why do you create a fuss over everything, Kunal?"

"I am creating a fuss?" he fumed.

Anuradha was now offended. "For heaven's sake, Kunal. We are doing something in the name of God. Nobody invites anybody to the deity's feet, everyone only comes if they are destined to," she said philosophically.

Kunal looked like he was about to burst and Shreya swiftly moved between the two of them; signalling Kunal to cool down. She also moved her eyes, to make him aware that people were watching him. He calmed down and stood quietly.

"Good, Shreya. Some control finally," Anuradha said smiling.

Vineet was the first one to laugh, everyone also smiled along. Kunal blushed at everyone's reaction.

Then everything started happening like clockwork—a truck with additional tents, rugs and chairs arrived. Anuradha requested everyone to move to the *pandal* and enjoy the devotional songs. Kunal lightly pulled Shreya's *dupatta*, to hold her back while everyone walked away. "Cheer up," he said. "You are the most important person today; you can't be in a bad mood. Please smile." Shreya smiled.

"Little broader. If you don't smile like my wife at the count of five, you know what will follow."

She blushed as she smiled widely. "There you are." Kunal smiled back warmly.

About an hour later, the sweets arrived. And tripping hastily in her high heels and obviously uncomfortable in her saree, came

Jyothsna.

"Jyothsna," Shreya exclaimed. "So late? This is not done."

"I know. These sarees are so clumsy. I am not even able to walk, leave alone drive."

"You could have avoided wearing a saree in that case," Shreya said.

"He told me his parents are also attending, so I thought a saree would make a good impression." Jyothsna said, blushing.

"Oh, I see." Kunal grinned. "The saree was mandatory in that case."

Shreya too smiled broadly. "Jyothsna, you need to relax your grip on your saree. I am sure his parents don't want to see your knees," She said jokingly.

Vineet meantime emerged and blushed on seeing Jyothsna in a saree.

"How do I look?" she asked him abruptly. Vineet turned red, and gave no answer. Kunal had a good laugh looking at his expressions.

"You could have taken it easy," Vineet said in a low tone to Jyothsna.

"You told me your parents would also be attending."

"What does that have to do with a saree?"

"What type of question is that?" Jyothsna was disappointed.

"You need to relax. I have a lot of family members around." Vineet was feeling self-conscious.

"Ok, ok." Kunal interrupted them. "You guys can sort it out later. Just come inside Jyothsna, you are most welcome."

"Vineet, please escort her inside," Shreya said.

"Let's all of us go together. If I take her alone with me, my mom will bombard me with questions." Vineet was hesitant.

"Holy crap! Then answer her questions." Jyothsna freaked out. "That you are wasting your time with me since the last five months." She was very loud; thankfully the *bhajan* singer was louder.

"Take it easy," Shreya consoled. "Come inside. And you look gorgeous." Shreya stared at Vineet with disappointment. She took Jyothsna to Aastha, and asked her to take care of her for the evening.

They walked inside. Shreya thought of talking to Vineet but Kunal dragged her to his side and sat down. "You haven't married Vineet that you go and sit next to him each time," he whispered angrily.

"How cheap!"

"Yes, how cheap..." he paused, "of you."

"Actually I thought if I leave you alone for some time, you may have some luck with some hot girls."

Kunal turned to her; she wore a naughty smile. "You are sitting in a place no less than a temple; you should check your words." He was echoing Shreya's words to him at the temple. "And talking about hotness, you beat any girl I've ever seen. You are emitting fire today." He winked.

Shreya was stunned at his frankness. Her eyes opened wide with wonder. She then smiled charmingly, feeling flattered and shy at the same time. His face also glowed with pride and joy. They shared a heartwarming smile; her face radiating his admiration. The expression stayed on their faces for a long time.

Anuradha and Vineet were enchanted to see the moment. Anuradha's eyes filled up—it had been very long since she'd seen her son smiling genuinely.

The priest now requested Anuradha and Shreya to start the

aarti. Anuradha refrained, letting Shreya and Kunal do the job. The priest was holding a big plate that had a bronze lamp with about 21 *diyas* illuminated on it. He now extended this plate to Shreya for her to do the *aarti*. Instantly, the entire weight of the heavy lamp shifted to her hand; Shreya lost her balance but before she could drop the plate, Kunal caught her wrist in time, avoiding any mishap. He held it with his right hand, and stood behind her holding her left arm above the elbow. Once she had regained her balance, he slowly moved his right hand over her fingers so they were both holding the *diya*. He now put his left hand on her waist, inducing shivers in her.

The priest had started chanting *mantras* and asked everyone to stand up for the *aarti*.

Kunal gently whispered in Shreya's ears. "I know you have this trust issue with me, so you won't believe me otherwise. But you know me enough that I won't lie standing here right next to you in front of the goddess." Shreya turned her eyes, to look into his. A perfect eye contact. He said, "Hot girls was a terrible joke, and I have no explanation for those pictures on the wall. But I swear I am not holding on to my past. My life moved on long back, though it's never appeared this ecstatic before. Thanks for helping me find myself again. It had been ages, and it's a divine reunion."

"Are you still mad at me for that hotel incident?"

Oh! Another puzzle piece. I may still remember that incident someday and be mad at her again. This one was an absolute surprise.

"No. I should have never been there in the first place. You opened my eyes to the ugly truth of my relationship; what my own people had been alluding to for long. I should have been thankful. But you know, I am a moron and I do things that eventually hurt me more than anybody else. You know me so well."

"*Om Mangalaya Swaha*" – the holy words marked the end of the *puja*.

People started walking to where dinner was being served under Shreya's supervision.

Kunal was also walking around, ensuring his guests comfort when he saw Vineet approach Shreya, and gently holding her wrist over her bangles, whisper something in her ears. Kunal saw Shreya's, eyes sparkle as she nodded happily. Vineet still looked hesitant, and whispered to her again. She gently pushed him away, and mouthed "Go". Vineet blushed and walked away. Shreya's eyes followed him, Kunal's too.

And they saw Vineet walk up to Jyothsna, who was sitting alone. He held out his hand to her; she turned sharply and passed a shy smile. Vineet then took her to meet his mother. Kunal walked up to Shreya in the meantime.

When he introduced Jyothsna, she bent down to touch Anita's feet; Vineet turned pale and he shut his eyes hard to control his blush. Anita looked startled and confused; she had had no idea of the friendship. However, she greeted Jyothsna very warmly, looking at Vineet for a clearer introduction of Jyothsna; but he was looking in the other direction to avoid any such situation. He signalled to Jyothsna to go after a few minutes and she did so. Anita pulled Vineet's arm asking him the obvious question. He shrugged off his arm, and walked away without answering. Shreya and Kunal had a good laugh, looking at the expression on Vineet's face.

Shreya then gently touched Kunal's arm. "Let's go meet your friends."

Shreya had this feeling that she and Kunal had never displayed togetherness in front of his friend's circle; they had never stood as a couple. She was conscious of rumours about their marriage and thought it was important for them to be seen together.

Kunal was delighted that Shreya had expressed a desire to meet his friends; he felt it would strengthen the bond between them. They walked around spending some time with each one of them, and shared light moments. They then joined Shreya's family. Akash uncle invited them to his farmhouse near Pune for Prateek's engagement. Kunal accepted the invitation whole-heartedly.

One of Kunal's guests, Mr Pujari, was passionately religious and he continued sitting near the *pandal* at the deity's feet even after all the guests had left. He finally got up only when the idol was being taken away and the vendor wanted to pick the last carpet he was sitting on. As he was leaving, Shreya and Kunal went to the driveway to see him off.

He looked at Shreya while speaking to Kunal.

"Mr Kharbanda, it was mean of you not to have mentioned that the beautiful lady sitting in the business meetings is actually your wife." He continued before Kunal could answer. "I really like your thought, to have your Laxmi sit on your left in important meetings, to seek good fortune."

Kunal shook his head at the man's effusiveness. "And brother to the right," Kunal said, pointing at Vineet.

"So, it's like Ram, Sita and Laxman !" Their guest shook his head from side to side. "God works in mysterious ways!" He was still shaking his head wisely as he left.

Everyone was laughing as they went into the house for their dinner. Now it was only family. Kunal now asked Shreya to relax and let the servants serve them. Anuradha sat at one end of the table, with the Talwar couple on one side and the senior Kohli couple on another. Vineet sat at the foot of the table, Aastha and Shreya on either side followed by their husbands. Sandhya sat next to Madhav. Kunal now pulled Vineet's leg on his expression over Jyothsna meeting his mother.

"Kunal you need to stay out of it; you know we have this unsigned treaty of no personal remarks," Vineet said. Kunal nodded laughing.

Aastha, Madhav and Vineet had also become good friends by now. "I am still not able to understand—if you planned to do so, why did you upset her when she walked in?" Aastha asked.

"You don't know Jyothsna. She has this weird habit of throwing things at me in public. I fail to frame a proper answer and end up saying utter rubbish. It took me two hours to coolly think of what I really wanted to do." Vineet sighed.

"That should be alright, Vineet. It's the happy ending that matters. It's all part of being in a relationship," Aastha said smiling.

"So Madhav," Vineet smiled. "Does she also freak out like mine does?"

"Oh yes! It's all part of being a woman," Madhav replied, looking at Aastha. She elbowed him in the ribs.

"I never saw Shreya freaking!" Aastha said, hoping to counter the remark about women freaking out.

"Me, neither," Vineet added.

"Good. That's something only I have witnessed, thankfully," Kunal said.

"You just tarnished my image," Shreya grumbled.

"When was this?" Aastha was surprised to hear of her calm friend freaking out.

"Once," Kunal said. "I deserved it. My jokes get really ridiculous at times." They exchanged a smile.

"What did you say?" Vineet asked.

"Gentle reminder of the treaty," Kunal reminded his cousin

of their pact.

"Kunal, did you compliment Shreya? Stunning is an understatement for her today." Vineet winked.

"I did."

"When?" Shreya turned sharply to Kunal. He rolled his eyes helping her recall. "Oh, that's not called a compliment." Everyone laughed.

"Let's help you come up with a better compliment." Vineet rubbed his hands.

"No PDA, please," Kunal smiled back.

"What's PDA", Aastha asked.

"PDA stands for Public Display of Affection. It's when a guy says something cheesy and sugarcoated; or displays his emotions cinematically to his girl in public. You know you've done a good job, when girls around exclaim 'Awwww' or 'Cho-Chweet'; and guys broaden their chests for having found a 'murga' for the next booze party.

When the girl exhibits PDA, the outcome bears just one change; the 'murga' is grilled even harder."

The Talwar family left after dinner. Madhav called up for a taxi for Pune, and Aastha asked Shreya to show her room. Aastha entered first. Shreya was standing near the door, facing the balcony.

"Wow! What a lovely picture." Aastha pointed at the wall next to the main door. Shreya frowned, wondering what was on the wall. She turned swiftly to that side and gasped when she saw what was hanging there.

It was a picture of Shreya and Kunal at their wedding reception. It was a huge portrait, covering the entire wall. Shreya remembered the photographer asking her to smile; the picture didn't reflect any of her sorrow; it only reflected Kunal's determination to move forward.

"What happened? You look worried." Aastha noticed her expression.

"Just that it wasn't here until yesterday." She paused. "Maybe this is the delivery for which Kunal asked for the keys."

"I see." Aastha said. "Isn't it lovely? You both look so compatible." Shreya smiled warmly, looking at the portrait. She had never seen herself standing next to him before; she felt truly emotional. *We truly look awesome together.*

As everyone was taking leave, Anuradha insisted on Sandhya and Mahesh staying over at their house for a few days while in Mumbai. Mahesh was hesitant but Sandhya spoke abruptly, "How can we offend you by refusing, Anuradhaji? We'll come over again tomorrow with our luggage and will be here until Friday."

Mahesh intervened. "We need to help Akash with marriage arrangements."

"But that's post-engagement. We can be with Shreya and her new family until then. Won't you be offended if Anuradhaji comes to Delhi for three weeks and doesn't stay at our place?" Sandhya replied.

"Absolutely right, *bhaisahab*. Please allow us to offer hospitality."

Shreya was still staring at the portrait when Kunal appeared from the closet area. "Isn't it beautiful?" Kunal asked, walking up to her.

"You didn't have to do this, Kunal."

"I just realised a few days back that putting the right pictures on a wall is so critical."

"Hmmm…"

"We don't really need a filler here. You should have something to say."

"You remember?"

"Of course I do. I called up myself. I didn't outsource my phone calls."

"I know you called. I can't make a mistake in recognizing your voice."

"I am flattered something impresses you about me. At least something is above average."

"I didn't say it's impressive, all I said is, it's recognizable." Shreya started walking towards the closet. Kunal held her forearm, and pulled her back.

"It's important to be honest at times," Kunal said smiling.

"I've always been." She said playfully. "Same voice, same face, same me."

"I know, I know." Kunal nodded dramatically. "But you know if I would have shown you my face, this pic wouldn't have happened." He pointed at the wall. "Isn't it great? You still need to answer my question."

"Kudos to Ridhima. I never thought I can look this pretty."

"You perhaps never were this pretty. It was a life changing event for you."

"What does that mean?" Shreya pretended offence.

"Well, remember what Madhav said this afternoon. My sister never looked this beautiful ever." He looked at her. "He was right."

"He has a pathetic sense of humour."

"Your brother, after all." Kunal laughed.

"Isn't it great?" Kunal said. Shreya turned to the picture again. Her true emotions finally took over. "Yes," she said softly.

Kunal's Ma-in-law

Sandhya was on the warpath.

"What made you choose that freaky Kunal for my delicate Shreya?"

If you have an Indian mother, you very well know how it goes.

"What's got into you now," Mahesh asked. "I thought you had reconciled yourself to the match. You even said so, before the wedding. They are a happily married couple now."

"Oh, really?" She stood right in front of Mahesh. "Look into my eyes and say that."

"It's an arranged marriage," Mahesh mumbled.

"Marriage is eventually a marriage. And more than that, it's Kunal's attitude that really bothers me."

"Mind it Sandhya. You are talking about your daughter's husband."

"Of course, had he not been my daughter's husband; I wouldn't have even paid heed." Sandhya's anger grew.

"He's such a well-established guy."

Mahesh got interrupted. "Both my kids are equally well established. Only thing that is different is the size of their houses and cars; which will also diminish in due time. Shreya didn't marry him for his money." She turned to him. "When Shreya was worried over the large number of guests, did you notice his behaviour?"

"He tried to soothe her; exactly what he was supposed to do."

"Yes, but not how a husband is supposed to do. No gentle hug, no warmth; and he's so bellicose. Also if he's talking to his mother like that in front of so many people, God only knows how he's treating Shreya."

"All mothers-sons do that. Even our house is not an exception."

"My Madhav is far more humble. Don't compare Madhav to Kunal, I warn you." Sandhya fumed.

"Sandhya. You should treat Kunal no less than Madhav. You should accept him, he's part of family."

"Huh! Forget it. I need to get to the bottom of it. There is something terribly wrong."

"No, Sandhya. It won't be the right thing to do. We should refrain from prying into their personal lives."

"I want to know why my daughter doesn't talk about her husband. My child deserves to be happy." She started crying. Mahesh comforted her and promised to cooperate.

Shreya chose one of the upstairs rooms for her parents' stay, so that if they needed anything at night they could reach her.

She left office around 3 pm with the driver to pick up her parents. She still wasn't very familiar with Mumbai roads, and when she mentioned this to her parents, Sandhya inferred that it must be because she hadn't been out much.

At home, Shreya prepared dinner with the help of the cook.

"Great food, Shreya," Mahesh exclaimed, rubbing his stomach. "You cook so well. I am so proud."

"Mumma taught me." Shreya pressed Anuradha's hand gently with affection.

"Ideally, I should have done it," Sandhya said. "But she only came to the kitchen to make her tea. You motivated her to be interested in cooking, which is quite impressive," Sandhya said. Mahesh winced. Sandhya's campaign had begun.

"It's alright. Even Ridhima was the same," Anuradha smiled. "Things change post-marriage. And it's not me but Kunal who motivated her. I was actually reluctant but he doesn't like the cook's preparations."

"I see. You could have changed the cook in that case," Sandhya said jokingly.

"You know what he meant," Anuradha smiled, "The personal touch."

Kunal grew uneasy; he didn't like such discussions. "He's happy now that he gets good food."

"Really? Did he tell you that?" Sandhya said. "When I asked Shreya in Delhi if Kunal liked her food, her answer was that Kunal doesn't complain so she guessed he's okay with it." DIG(1)

Everyone stopped eating.

"Well! Had it been me, not complaining would mean good," Mahesh broke the awkward silence, to bring back the peace. Kunal recalled Shreya's description of Sandhya Holmes.

Post-dinner everyone moved to their rooms. Sandhya came over to Shreya's room and looked around it like a detective. Kunal figured out that Sandhya could show up at odd hours at night or early morning and remarked it wouldn't be a good idea for Shreya to sleep on the mattress.

"Where shall I sleep then?"

Kunal cleared his voice. "On the bed."

"Really?" Shreya got into her playful mood. "You sure?"

"Very much." Kunal's eyebrows rose. *I am sure you won't come that easy.*

"Where would you sleep in that case?" He was proved right too quickly.

He said hesitatingly. "On the other side of the same bed."

Shreya blinked her eyes fast. "High hopes. That's not happening." She paused. "Let me think." She looked around. "Sofa? How about the sofa? You can sleep there for a few days. I was anyway thinking we should take turns on the bed. The mattress really hurts my neck." She gently massaged her neck.

Kunal's jaw dropped. "It's my house. I'll sleep on the bed. I was trying to be nice."

"It's my parents-in-law's house. So, my comfort is equally important," she said with a flourish. Kunal gaped at her. She picked up a bed sheet and pillow and handed them over to him. She got onto the bed and stretched her arms, yawning, "Ah, such luxury. Good night. Sweet dreams."

He stared at her for a few minutes, not believing what had just happened. He moved to the sofa; no way was he going to be able to sleep tonight. He tossed and turned all night, hoping for morning as Shreya always got up early for yoga.

She woke up earlier than usual. And no matter what time you wake up, there's always one place everyone goes to first thing in the morning. When she came out she was amused to see Kunal already lying on the bed, almost lifelessly. She suppressed her laughter, and went closer to check if he was sleeping. He was snoring.

Everyone was finishing breakfast, when Raju came from the kitchen to the table at 10:30 am.

"Ma'am, Kunal sir called up on the kitchen's intercom. He's asking for tea," Raju said.

Anuradha and Shreya looked at each other with confusion.

"Then ask Gopal to make it; it doesn't require approval," Anuradha answered.

"He insisted that Charaya madam should make it," Raju said.

Everyone smiled as Shreya moved to the kitchen to do so. Kunal came down in the meantime and greeted everyone.

"Anyone could make tea, why did you have to bother Shreya particularly?" Anuradha scolded Kunal.

"Because you've recruited a bunch of buffoons who fail to understand what strong and one spoon of sugar mean."

"Shreya's also my discovery, so you shouldn't be saying that." Everyone smiled at that.

Shreya came with the tea, smiling at Kunal mischievously, feeling so proud of herself for his sleepless night. She sat down next to him, still grinning.

"Your eyes look puffy, Kunal," Sandhya investigated. "Didn't you sleep well?"

"Well, actually I overslept. I planned to give office a miss today, so that I could take you guys around, so I disabled my alarm," Kunal managed to come up with a good answer, giving Shreya a side look.

"Well, you really slept long. We just finished our breakfast except for Shreya." Anuradha said.

He turned to Shreya. "Why didn't you have it?"

Sandhya interrupted, "What kind of question is that? Isn't that obvious?" DIG(2)

"Well, we usually leave at different times, so breakfast is mostly separate. Only on weekends we eat together," Shreya said.

"Well, so today is actually a weekday that feels like a weekend. My question was wrong indeed," Kunal said.

Sandhya continued. "Anuradhaji, Shreya really talks about you a lot. Even if we ask her anything regarding Kunal, she ends up answering about you. *Karvachauth* for instance; we asked about Kunal's gift and she ended up telling us about yours." DIG(3)

"There need not be two gifts," Shreya said gently.

Sandhya was relentless. "What time did you come home that day, Kunal? I called Shreya at 9:30 and you weren't home yet." DIG(4)

"He was late, Mumma," Shreya said curtly. She was getting irritated with her mother's interrogation. "He had this call with some US client."

"Oh, I see. He was in the US."

"No, Mumma. Call to the US."

"Are there special phones to call the US? I thought the US could be called from any handset?" Sandhya said.

"Mumma, would you like some tea?" Shreya asked her mother, glaring at her to be quiet. Sandhya held her peace.

Anuradha stayed back when they all went sightseeing, but called Shreya before they left and asked her if Sandhya knew it all. Shreya explained that her mother had very keen observation, but she had never discussed her marriage with her.

With Mahesh to act as a peacekeeper, the day went fine. Sandhya still took occasional minor digs at Kunal, which Shreya fielded very well. She admired Kunal's patience with her mother. Had it been his mother he would have blasted her by now.

It was dinner time again.

"So, how's work, Kunal?" Mahesh asked.

"Very well, Dad. We are doing even better than before. We were very worried about our operations until some time back; Shreya sanitized them big time."

"So, you must be keeping very busy these days?" Sandhya asked.

"Not really," Kunal replied warily. The way Sandhya was going, one never knew if one was giving the right answer or not!

"So you have relatively free time now. Am I correct?"

Kunal nodded.

"So it's not a shortage of time; and by God' grace not a shortage of money that you newlyweds failed to go on a honeymoon." DIG(5)

Shreya was shocked at her mother's onslaught. Kunal froze. Mahesh was perplexed and embarrassed. Anuradha was on the verge of tears.

Shreya looked at her father, begging him to bring her under control. Sandhya ignored their looks; she was not the least guilty.

Anuradha stepped into the breach. "Actually, I was unwell and so they couldn't plan anything. And then the festival season happened."

"I see." Sandhya said. "Then that should have certainly been their priority." She smiled artificially.

Kunal looked up and met his mother-in-law's eyes. She conveyed a very clear message *I don't like you.*

"What the hell do you think you are doing, Mom?" Shreya was fuming.

It was after dinner and everyone had retired to their respective rooms.

Sandhya shrugged. "I just asked him the questions you should be asking."

"Do you realize you are indirectly disturbing the peace of my home?"

"Peace of mind is more important. What the hell does he think of himself?"

"He took a day off to take you around the city; he's been so considerate throughout. Yet you are embarrassing him each time, for no good reason."

"Cut the crap, Shreya. He's being unreal. He's one arrogant guy who has no regard for what you do for him, or feel for him."

"Dad, you need to ask her to relax. Meal time is not the time for useless banter. Kunal must be so disappointed."

"Shreya." Sandhya screamed. Shreya gestured to her to lower her voice as Kunal was in the next room. "You need to think about your disappointment before his. God dammit, it is allowed and required to be selfish at times."

"Stop it, Mumma, I know you don't like Kunal. But please, you need to understand that I am married to him. And I didn't elope; Madhav chose him as the best match possible for me." She choked.

"Don't give me this Madhav angle." Sandhya was livid. "You are intelligent, pretty and independent. You should voice things if you aren't being treated right."

"There you go again. I am perfectly fine."

"I am not blind. You may be fine, but you deserve much more from life. It's not that I don't like him; I hate him," Sandhya said harshly.

"Your opinion doesn't matter to me," Shreya burst out in anger. "He's my husband, and I demand respect for him."

Sandhya started crying—she realised her little girl had grown up into a mature woman. Mahesh rested his hand over Sandhya's shoulder firmly, signalling her to stay quiet.

Shreya left the room. Sandhya turned to Mahesh and sobbed. He hugged her tight, and said humbly, "Dear, you should have avoided messing with Shreya Kharbanda." She smiled through her tears.

Kunal watched her storm into their room. "I am sorry about

my mother's behaviour," Shreya said. "I apologize on her behalf."

"Relax. It's alright. You don't have to make it appear too big."

"And thank you for today. I appreciate you took out time to take them around the city."

"My pleasure." Kunal paused. "But what do I get in return?"

Shreya smiled weakly. "Well, you get to sleep on your bed. And I am sorry for making you sleep on the sofa."

"Shreya. Please don't blow it out of proportion. We can have a good conversation rather than this depressing one."

Shreya looked up at him, "It's really unlike you, not being mad at my mother."

Kunal smiled. "I know I've made a bad impression on her. It will take me an era to make amends." Shreya smiled too.

Next day, Kunal left for office but Shreya worked from home, staying back to keep her parents company. Both breakfast and dinner had been amicable. Sandhya made no conversation with Kunal—not even an eye contact. When he asked something, she answered looking down. Shreya wasn't very happy with her mother's responses, but chose silence as long as her mother wasn't making snide remarks again at Kunal.

On Friday, Shreya dropped her parents to Akash's home before going to office. Kunal walked over to her cabin just when she arrived.

"I hope you had a good time off from office. You need to get into action now."

"I've been aware of everything. I agree I have been physically less available, but my presence could be felt at all times."

Kunal smiled sweetly. "Yes, ma'am. You were always felt around; but I would like you to frequent office regularly now."

"I still don't get your concern." She looked puzzled. "No

work has suffered, I can prove that. I completely justify the salary I take home."

"Salary?" Kunal exclaimed. "Salary is the last thing I am trying to communicate here."

"Kunal, for at least once in your life, can you please state it clearly."

"Mrs Shreya Kunal Kharbanda, I missed having you around."

Final Bastion

Soon it was time to leave for Prateek's engagement. Shreya packed her dress for the evening and her night suit. Kunal selected his clothes and asked Shreya to pack them with hers. They arrived two hours ahead of the function as promised. Kunal was partially ready, while Shreya was still in casuals. She went up to change and Madhav invited Kunal to the terrace for a drink. Akash Uncle had rented a farmhouse with a big garden to accommodate about 70 people. "So, how's life Kunal?"

"Good." He paused. "Super-duper good."

Madhav sighed. "Mumma is always very worried about Shreya. I think it has more to do with the distance than anything else. "

"It's alright," Kunal shrugged. "I too have an Indian mother. Worrying about their kids and hoping for grandkids is their favourite pasttime." Madhav nodded in agreement.

Shreya came out of their room, and Kunal caught his breath. She was wearing a light green saree of net fabric; she had realised her curves were in good shape, thanks to Yoga, and she was now comfortable flaunting them. She wore a *choli* that was deeply cut at the back and tied with a string knotted between her shoulder blades. She had curled the tips of her hair and left it open. She had also mastered the skill of walking in high heels, wearing a sari and Kunal's breath caught in his throat as she walked elegantly towards him. She almost growled 'Attack' again; she was still on her mission.

Kunal's dress was simpler; he just needed to put on his tie and blazer and that too he forgot. Shreya had to run to their assigned room and get it for him even as the bride's family arrived. As a result, they were standing at the periphery of the crowd when the engagement ceremony began. Shreya craned her neck to see over people's heads and she dropped her phone. As she bent to pick it up, the strings holding the choli up at the back unwound. She quickly stood up, holding the strings in one hand, but there was no way she could tie them up. Kunal was having a good time watching her struggles. He finally pulled her towards him by the waist to make her stand her in front of him.

He moved her hair to the side and grabbed the strings, his fingers sending up chills across her naked back. He gently tied the knot, and pulled her against his chest and blew air into her ear.

Shreya's breath fluttered; she turned pale and looked back into his face. "What are you doing? Leave me." She was conscious of the people around them.

"What do you think I am doing?" Kunal whispered flirtatiously.

"Someone could be watching," she whispered back.

"They are all looking in the other direction. It's just me and you watching each other."

Shreya stood still, looking into his eyes. A perfect eye contact again.

"I want to ask you something." Kunal paused. "It's high time now, when are we meeting without it?"

Shreya was confused. "What's 'it'?"

"It is something we manufacture daily near Pune." He said caressing her waist.

Shreya's eyes widened. She stumbled over her words. "How… How can you talk like this to me?"

"Who else should I be talking to regarding this? I am your man."

"This is not the right place for a question like that."

"I don't care. I want my answer."

"We are just friends. Remember?"

"I lied. You are my wife." He brought his face closer to hers, stopping just an inch away.

"Kunal, stop. There are many people around. I am sure you don't want PDA like that."

"You give me a date and time; and I'll behave myself."

"Well, that's not happening. Your last vow says I am free after that. Do you want me to leave?"

"You don't have to mention that disgusting act of mine each time; and you don't follow the rest of the others either."

"I did. You changed your stand."

"I didn't know then that you are so wonderful."

"What did you think then?"

"Nothing. I don't even want to remember what I was thinking. All I care is what I am thinking now; and you are in even graver danger than before." He winked. "So, when are we making that happen?"

"We'll see."

"What!"

"We'll see. I am not impressed yet." Shreya got playful.

"Give me one chance, I'll surely impress you. You want a trailer?"

"No way, you have to earn it. I am not so easy to get."

"I don't care, I want it. I know my rights as a husband."

Shreya was shocked. "How could you even think that?"

"You are leaving me with no option. Your wardrobe arsenal has been lethal recently. And this saree is like an ultimate assault. I am a man after all," Kunal said reddening. Shreya burst out laughing.

People close by turned to look at them. Kunal released her, feeling conscious. Madhav and Aastha's eyes had been watching the couple for some time now and they smiled at each other. *Mumma was unnecessarily worrying.*

The rest of the evening was beautiful too, and Shreya spent most of her time catching up with Aastha. Kunal kept catching her eye, delighted when she blushed and smiled at him. Kunal was falling in love with her expressions and her witty answers. *She is really very hard to get. But she's worth it.*

They all walked to where dinner was being served. Kunal joined Shreya but didn't pick up a plate.

"Where's your plate, Kunal?" Shreya asked.

"In your hands."

"This is my plate."

"No, this is our plate." He paused. "Look around—all couples eat like that."

Shreya's heart smiled at this new milestone they had reached. That night Mr and Mrs Kunal Kharbanda ate from same plate for the first time.

Later at night, Kunal looked at their sleeping arrangements. Their room had a relatively smaller bed than the one at home, and there was no sofa; no way could one couple ask for an extra mattress. Kunal looked up as Shreya walked in with a cup on a tray.

"What's this?" Kunal asked.

"Your green tea." She chose to look down; Kunal was on cloud nine that she'd thought of bringing his nightcap.

"I hope it's not drugged?" He asked playfully.

"Be assured. You are safe."

"That's exactly my misery—being safe is troubling me now." Shreya blushed. She also looked around the room; she was tired and wanted to sleep.

"What are our options?" Kunal asked. "Chair?" He paused. "Hope you don't want me to be in the chair for the night?"

"No, that's out of question. It's my uncle's house in a way; and you are a special guest."

"That's so considerate of you. What else can be done?" Kunal said. "I have an idea. We can share the bed; I promise I will behave myself. But you need to promise the same. My head is getting heavier with this green tea already. "

"Don't be so hopeful. " She looked around again. "But I guess that's the only choice for tonight."

"Just for tonight. You too need not be hopeful." She laughed lightly as he said that.

Kunal finished his tea and switched off the light; he lay down on the bed. Actually, he was hopeful!

Shreya took a deep breath and then lay down on the bed with her feet facing his head. Kunal was disappointed. *She's getting impossible to get.*

"Shreya, your feet are ugly."

"It's okay. As if you like any other thing about me."

"I really like a lot of things about you. Especially below and above the neck."

Shreya was flabbergasted. *He's trying too hard,* she thought.

Kunal was getting desperate but he knew his presence was affecting Shreya and he was determined to capitalise on it.

The next day, when the couple was preparing for office, a mischievous idea struck him. He tried pulling out a button from his shirt sleeve, and when he couldn't do it with his hand he bit at it to pull it out. Then he called out to Shreya.

"Mrs Shreya Kunal Kharbanda, did the Kohlis only teach you how to operate a laptop, or did they teach some of the household work, too?"

She was confused, but she knew a joke was coming. "Don't you get dinner each night?"

"That my mom taught you. No credit to the Kohlis there."

"What is the service you are looking for?"

Kunal showed her his loose button; Shreya went to the closet to get a needle and thread.

"Can you take your shirt off? It will be quicker." She said.

"No way. Don't be hopeful."

Shreya sighed artificially and stood in front of him. He extended his arm.

She started with the repair, keeping his hand in front of her, at stomach level. As she started stitching, Kunal playfully tickled her belly with his fingers. She moved his hand away, but then she couldn't reach the sleeve.

She turned to his right and raised his hand up. He moved his arm closer, almost touching her bosom. She slapped his arm down. He then rubbed his arm against her belly. She looked up to scold him, but Kunal kept his expression innocent. He now moved closer to her and turned her gently so that her back was aligned with his chest and she could stitch the button with his arm around her waist.

Now he gently rested his chin on her shoulder and breathed in the fragrance of her wet hair. Shreya closed her eyes and slowed her breathing to savour the moment.

When she finished, she put the button in the hole. That is when she discovered wet lip marks around hole. She looked at him and grinned. Kunal was startled. *Having a smart wife can be disadvantageous at times.*

Shreya smiled; she was enjoying this phase. But this new Kunal was affecting her. She was absent-minded in office the rest of the week; she would forget the agenda of the meeting; go to the wrong floor; go to the printer but forget to collect the printouts. Once she even walked into Kunal's room to get an important document signed and blushed when she realised she had forgotten to bring the document along. She was clearly daydreaming.

They were invited to a dance party on Saturday night and this time Shreya prepared for it two days in advance. She had decided to take the 'Attack' to the highest level now. *The hell with eyes, ears and stomach; she had hit the right spot to get her man on his knees.*

She dressed up in a red strapless knee-length cocktail dress. The high heels she wore made her legs look longer. Today she had straightened her hair and left it loose. Kunal got ready earlier and went to his mother's room to say goodbye. Shreya had already said her goodbyes; she was shy and hesitant to meet her mother-in-law in the revealing dress. She walked down and waited for him to come out of Anuradha's room. She felt triumphant when his jaw dropped.

Kunal walked into the party with Shreya's hand held tightly to his side. They met everyone, and then the male and female sections split up. Shreya had become good friends with some of the women by now, and she was comfortable being with them. They loved her dress, and gave her lots of compliments.

Vineet joined the party late and immediately looked for Kunal. Kunal was walking towards Shreya, when Vineet patted his back.

"Hey, bro. Let's have a drink," Vineet said.

Kunal showed him his glass. "I have mine, you get your own." He continued to walk towards his wife. Vineet almost jumped in front of him. "That's rude, at least give me company at the bar."

"Talking about company, I think you should start getting Jyothsna to the parties."

"That reminds me, is Shreya here today?" Vineet turned and spotted her. "There she is. I want to dance with her."

"Mind your own business," Kunal growled pulling his arm back.

"What do you mean? She's my friend."

"She's my wife. And I can take care of her this evening." He snapped his fingers. "Get out of the way."

Vineet moved out of Kunal's way, smiling broadly. The music had changed to a soft and slow song as Kunal reached Shreya. Kunal felt it was a signal from God.

"Come, let's dance," Kunal said, holding out his hand towards her. Shreya was thrilled and gently put her hand in his. They walked onto the dance floor.

He rested both her hands on his shoulders and held her around the waist, gently pulling her towards him. Shreya was the happiest girl at the party. Her battle was won.

Kunal tucked strands of her hair on her face, behind her ears.

"Do you know how you look tonight?" Kunal asked.

"I think 'nice'. Hope I didn't disappoint you?"

"You never disappoint me; it's my job to disappoint you always."

Before Shreya could answer, he spoke again. "Sshhh. It's not mandatory to answer every question. You can just let me speak at times." He paused. "So, did someone tell you that you have beautiful eyes?"

Shreya's eyes filled with tears of joy; it was the first sweet thing Kunal had ever said to her, on his first call. Kunal touched her cheek. "I meant it."

"You didn't. You can't lie."

"I did. No matter why I wanted to marry, I wouldn't have married you if you weren't beautiful, or weren't good to talk to. I have a reputation to maintain socially." He grinned cheekily. "But you know, you look much prettier now." He pause. "And today, you are dressed to kill."

He brought her closer to him. And when they were just about to make contact, Shreya slid her hands down from his shoulders to his chest; she felt hesitant about her breasts touching his chest.

"Just a gentle hug, Shreya." She moved her head in refusal.

"You are being too hard on me," Kunal said.

"Can I buy some more time? I am not over my trauma yet. A night every girl waits for all her growing years was snatched away from me brutally." Her pain reappeared in her eyes.

"We need to get over that. You need to move on."

"It's easier said than done."

Kunal was deeply disappointed with that answer from Shreya. He was disheartened.

This is very confusing. Please say something; give me another piece of my puzzle if nothing else. I need to solve it quick. It's not easy for me, either.

One Two, Mumma Loves You

Shreya's parents returned from Shirdi and were scheduled to leave for Nasik, but as Sandhya had developed a bad stomach, she couldn't travel. Shreya asked her to stay with them rather than be alone.

Sandhya reached the Kharbanda home at 4:15 in the afternoon and was told that Shreya and Anuradha had just left for the NGO and would be back by six. Only Kunal was home, it being a Saturday. She was happy that she could speak to Kunal alone.

Kunal welcomed her and ordered tea in the rear garden. He was also glad that they could finally talk one-on-one.

"So, Mumma, how was your Shirdi trip?"

"Very nice. I am not much into temples but Maheshji wanted to go there so I joined him."

"You don't believe in God?"

"I strongly and deeply do, but not in temples. However, going once a while is pleasant. Making a wish at times should be alright."

"That's a nice thought. Most people, including my mom, who strongly believe in God, believe in temples too."

"Yes, but not me. I taught my children the same thing—believe in yourself and be nice to everyone. God doesn't really mean anything else."

"Beautiful thought, again."

"Our duties towards our family and society are equivalent to serving our god. I take care of the house, have brought up my kids righteously, ensured my family's respect in society; and I remember to thank God for a good life. I am doing what my god expects me to do. But few things are beyond our control and that's exactly what I wished for my kids.

"For Madhav, all I wished was that God continues to shower his blessings on him so that he always maintains a balance in everything."

"And Shreya?"

"I am totally confused," Sandhya said, looking troubled. "In fact, I asked God to take away some patience from her. She's too tolerant, that's why I think God keeps putting her to the test. I would want her to fail so that God can start treating her like a child again."

Kunal was dumbfounded. "She's alright, Mumma." He paused. "I know, for some reason you don't like me. But I am not that bad."

"Honestly speaking, Kunal, I shouldn't be complaining. I always thought Shreya's married life would be very average. She didn't have many dreams and desires like girls her age do. I am sure you know of her past—she had stopped believing in love after that. Not because her feelings were very deep, but because of the way they split. She always felt that if it takes such a small misunderstanding to call it off, then it's probably not worth it." Sandhya's voice choked.

"When Madhav was getting married, we all wanted Shreya to get married first. She refused and then we couldn't keep Aastha's parents waiting any longer. And when Madhav asked her what kind of guy she wanted, her demands were simple. I know my daughter didn't expect much out of life." Tears rolled down her cheeks.

"But then you happened to her. Despite such major odds, she gave you a genuine consideration. You had an effect on her, right from your first call." Kunal got emotional as Sandhya said that.

"My daughter was very happy; she really liked you. I saw her being excited about her marriage. She would wait from 6 o'clock for your 10 o'clock call; she was looking forward to starting a new life with you. After years, she talked about a guy with a twinkle in her eyes.

"I don't see that happiness in her eyes now. I see the eyes she had for five years, fearing love. I just wish God would weaken her; she doesn't need to stand so strong always. She's just 27, her courage disturbs me." Sandhya's eyes overflowed with her emotions.

Kunal was crestfallen. He realised that his actions had had a more severe fallout than he had thought.

That's the centre piece of my puzzle. My journey is not to her heart; it's a journey back to her heart. Sorry Shreya!

Sandhya requested Shreya to sleep with her that night. Shreya was preparing to leave her room when Kunal said. "Shreya. Can I have a hug please?"

"We've talked about this Kunal. The status doesn't change daily."

"Please. I beg of you."

"Are you alright?"

"Maybe, no. Maybe your hug can do wonders for me."

"Good marketing strategy. The answer is still a no." Shreya shunned the topic playfully and moved to her mother's room.

Kunal also went to see his mother. She was sitting on a chair. Kunal sat on the floor and rested his head on her lap. Anuradha gently massaged his head.

"Mumma, I have a confession to make." He paused. "I am an asshole."

She slapped his head gently but soon realised that Kunal was very emotional. "What happened, Kunal? You should be in your room at this time."

"She has moved to her mother's room for today. My room doesn't feel the same."

"You miss her?"

"Mumma, you know, I would have never even dated a girl like Shreya. I am too incapable of that. I have her because of you. I must be thankful."

"You need to tell her, not me."

"She won't believe me. I haven't done enough for her to trust me."

"I shouldn't be speaking between a husband and wife. You both need to sort it out."

"Isn't that weird Mumma? My wife entered my life, to give me everything my life ever wanted. And I just broke her heart and trashed her dreams." Kunal was crying now. "And she still is around, being a pillar of my life. She surely has stepped down from heaven for me." He wet his mother's lap with tears. She gently ruffled his hair and wiped the tears from his face.

"Mumma, can I ask for a favour?" He paused. "I swear, it's the last one for my entire life."

"Tell me, my son."

"Can you please get me married again?"

Anuradha's fingers froze. Kunal touched her fingers to bring them to life.

"Again. To the same girl. I promise I won't bug your darling daughter-in-law this time."

"Sure. You need to ask her though. If she's fine with it, we can do that the first thing tomorrow morning."

"Why do I need to ask her? You did it last time; just arrange it again."

"It won't be an arranged marriage this time. So you need to pop the question to her."

"Let it be, then. I know her answer; I won't take that chance." She smiled warmly at Kunal's love confession.

"Can I say something, Kunal, now that you've mentioned this?"

"Yes, Mumma, please do."

"You are very much like your dad, but there's one thing that he possessed that you terribly miss."

"Good looks?" Kunal was getting back to normal.

"Farsightedness," she said. "He always kept the end in mind when he initiated anything. You are too impulsive. You need to evaluate the end you are looking for even before you start." She kissed his forehead to soothe him. "And about good looks; again you need to ask your wife."

"I did, she isn't impressed."

"What?" Anuradha exclaimed.

"Yeah, I tried my luck on that ground. She turned it down, saying my looks are below average."

Anuradha burst out laughing. Kunal too smiled, wiping his tears.

Upstairs Shreya and Sandhya talked about her Shirdi trip.

"So, you wished that Madhav and Aastha should be parents soon?" Shreya asked. She was lying on her side, facing her mother.

"Yes, he's 31 now. I may be orthodox, but I think their child should happen now." Sandhya replied.

"What did you wish for me?"

"From what you show me, you have everything. " Shreya got emotional; she knew her mother was worried about her. "Talk to me, my child, I am not your enemy. I am not here to take you away from your husband."

Shreya said slowly. "It's not that bad, Mumma. We have an arranged marriage; we are not lovebirds."

"You know Shreya, I am very proud of you." Sandhya said. "I am extremely happy with your bond with Anuradhaji. Though the credit largely goes to her. Your generation is incapable of handling delicate relationships so gracefully. It's because of her maturity that you all live happily under one roof. But you deserve a compliment too, that you respect her always. Keep it up, dear."

Shreya pulled her mother's hand towards her and kissed it gently. "She has earned it. She's another you."

"What's up with you and Kunal? Tell me, I'll try to help you make it better," Sandhya said.

Shreya replied chokingly. "Things are much better now, Mumma. It's just that Kunal didn't start his marriage on the right note. He was very disturbed then; he messed up our beginning horribly." She wept softly. "I had no clue how to deal with it."

"What did you do then?" Sandhya wiped her daughter's tears.

"I was completely devastated; all I knew was that I had to keep trying. I had to give it my best shot without making it very evident."

"You did exactly what you were required to do." Sandhya kissed Shreya's hand. "And from what I see, all your attempts have borne fruit."

"I don't know that. He's so unpredictable."

"You mean he never says, 'I love you'?" Sandhya sighed in exasperation. "What is it with your generation? Why are words so important? Men haven't changed; your father was the same. The first time your father said that to me was the day you were born. And I am sure it was an emotional accident." She smiled. "But that doesn't mean it was the first time he felt that."

Shreya was quiet.

"What do you think he means when he says good tea is the one which you make for him? When he comes back home from work, I've noticed his eyes looking for you. He fought with his mother on *chowki* because her silly mistake caused you tension; he does so many little things to put a smile on your face. And it's very evident that he's doing some repair work. He's really sorry; I could read his eyes today. You need to go easy on him; you are tantalizing him." Sandhya said stroking Shreya's arm.

"And you? You fought with me over him. Each time I targeted him, you stood on his side. You make such a wonderful wife." Sandhya asked, "What's stopping you from starting afresh with him?"

Shreya choked with emotion. "He owes me an apology. He gave me a tough time for no good reason. He should say sorry." She cried harder.

Sandhya smiled sarcastically. "Words again! You know what I asked for you at Shirdi?" She paused. "To grant you what your heart desires the most."

Shreya looked into her mother's eyes. "Mumma, how does

this intuition system of yours work? It's a wonder."

"It's no wonder. And you'll have an answer to that when you become a mother yourself," Sandhya said. "And one more thing, Shreya, Kunal blabbers a lot, it seems. You should just accept him as he is, like it or not."

"I have no issues about how Kunal is. I enjoy his blabbering. He is a marketing genius; if he won't be good at blabbering, we would run out of business. Secondly, it's his defense mechanism to cover up what's going on inside him."

"You know him pretty well. That's a good sign." She paused and looked at Shreya thoughtfully. "Your feelings for him are so changed ever since your marriage."

Shreya took a deep breath. "My feelings for him change almost every week, and at times every hour." She choked. "He has literally played an orchestra with my emotions; striking each one of them and bringing them to life. He has broken the spell of my emotional slumber." A tear dropped. "And it's not a five-year slumber, it's a 27 years old slumber. I've never felt so emotional in my entire life. My marriage has made me emotionally active."

Sandhya held her daughter, her chin resting on Shreya's head. "On that note, I think you also owe him something; a big thanks." She patted Shreya's head. "Don't be so surprised, true love does that to us. He's the closest to your heart and that's the final feeling."

Sandhya kissed her forehead. "Let your emotions flow now; you are holding them back too tightly; you need to let them loose. He's had all his lessons, he needs to have your rewards now. Stop it. Get over it."

Shreya raised her hand to wipe her tears. Sandhya stopped her. "Let them flow, dear. One tearful night is worth a great deal if it can assure a beautiful morning henceforth."

Shreya sobbed out the loneliness, the frustration, the grief of the last few months in her mother's arms. She finally quietened down.

"You didn't answer my question. Be completely honest with me when you answer this; what's that desire your heart is seeking?"

Shreya's emotions were at their peak. "It has to be the man I can love completely."

"Then my dear child, it should be him you want and not his apology."

A Dirty Secret

Shreya woke up even earlier than normal despite the emotional night she'd had. She hurried to her room to see him.

He wasn't there. She hunted all over and finally found him sleeping in Anuradha's room. She smiled and did her daily chores.

Kunal didn't wake up until nine and that too only after Shreya sent Raju to wake him up. Raju came back in a few seconds. "Charaya madam. Sir is calling you," he said.

She hurried to meet him. "Good morning." Her eyes were smiling.

"Why did you send Raju?" Kunal grumbled. "Do you think he should be the first face I see in the morning?"

Shreya grinned. "No. It was just that it's pretty late for office."

"I don't care, Shreya. I should be your top priority."

"I am sorry. You are right, I should have come myself." She smiled broadly to soothe him.

He didn't say anything and walked out of the room. Shreya went to the kitchen to make tea and asked the cook to pack the breakfast along.

When she reached upstairs Kunal was getting ready.

"Tea, please." Shreya smiled.

"Now you are not getting late?"

"I thought we'll leave together."

"Why?"

"To be together."

Kunal was pleasantly surprised with that answer. He always feared to ask that question. She had finally so simply conveyed what he had hesitated to say all these days. Maybe things were finally looking up, he thought joyfully. He also noticed a new softness in her.

It was afternoon; the two of them were seated in the board room with Vineet discussing a vendor evaluation, when Kunal's phone rang with an unknown number.

"Hello."

"Hello, Kunal." A female voice answered.

"Who's this?"

"It's me."

"That doesn't help. Who's calling, please?" Kunal was distracted because of the meeting.

"Please, don't pretend that you don't recognize my voice."

Kunal suddenly looked up, shocked. It was Saloni. He walked out of the room to take the call.

"Why are you calling me?" He asked softly.

"I need to talk to you."

"Why?"

"Please just give me 15 minutes. I won't take long." She said weeping.

"Listen, I don't even have 15 seconds for you. And for heaven's sake, don't call again." He hung up and returned to the meeting.

"Is everything alright?" asked a concerned Shreya reading his nervousness.

"Oh yes. Just an old friend, didn't expect her call. Err... his call." Shreya noticed his discomfort, but ignored it.

Saloni called up again after two hours. Shreya guessed it was the same caller—she could see Kunal's uneasiness through the glass partition. She left office early, so as to drop her mother to her uncle's place.

Saloni called up again at 6:30. "I am in the coffee shop next to your office. Please come for just 15 minutes, I beg of you."

Kunal decided to get it over with. He looked at her, and was very relieved to realize that he had no feelings left for her. She was just another girl to him now.

"I am so glad you came over." Saloni said.

"You need to be quick. I need to head back home."

"I just came over to say sorry. I've been very unfair always. I was chasing a dream, but I didn't realize that such happiness is short-lived; true happiness lies in true love. I now realize what I lost when I broke up with you." Her eyes filled up with tears.

"Don't you think this topic is irrelevant? We both moved on long back."

"But you didn't. I know you still love me."

Kunal freaked out. "What is this crap? Listen, I am not sitting here to hear your nonsense."

"Don't be so hard. We can start afresh."

"Just to let you know, in case you don't, I am a married man. And I have always nurtured my relationship with fidelity. And my marriage is surely my final destiny. I am still middle-class at heart and will always be."

"What the hell! I know you don't love that Shreya K."

It's the name she uses for official references. How come Saloni knows that?

"I am not even answering that," Kunal said sternly.

"How could you love her, when she's the reason we aren't together anymore. She created our misunderstanding in the Bangalore hotel room."

Kunal was shocked. "How the hell do you know that? There are only three people on the planet who know that."

"Your wife herself told me," Saloni smirked. "She came to see me a month back telling me that you still love me and can never accept her."

Kunal was furious at Shreya. Saloni gently touched his hand but he swiftly pulled it back. "Please, Kunal, let's chuck her out of our lives." She smiled slyly. "By the way, I've heard she takes a keen interest in Vineet. You should also help her."

Kunal said wrathfully, "Saloni, you know, you've just made me feel great. I've done a big shameful deed in my life for which I considered myself to be the most disgusting person I know." He said. "But I've just realised it's actually you. You are pathetic."

"How could you say that? You love me. My pictures are still on your wall."

Kunal dug the final nail in the coffin. "I don't hate anyone more than I hate you."

"You'll repent your words."

"You can't make me repent more than I already do. And I repeat, I hope this is our last meeting in this life or in any other life to follow." He paused. "Though you don't deserve to know this, my wife is an amazing person. You should meet her someday and try learning what womanhood is all about. It may help you."

"Great womanhood and a meaningless marriage; isn't that a weird combination?" Saloni spat out. "So great she is, yet she couldn't make it to her husband's bed," she said sarcastically.

Kunal stood up and smiled at her scornfully. "I forgive you for your petty thinking. Maybe someday someone will make you feel what true love is all about. Maybe someday you will be as lucky as me, to find it or for it to find you. Good bye!"

He drove back home wildly furious. He wanted to break Shreya's neck for what she had done, and then kept it a secret. He then remembered Shreya's sweet words in the morning and her complaint over his anger management. He managed to cool down before reaching home and decided to ignore her blunder. Nothing should disturb the peace of their bond now.

Shreya had his favourite dish prepared. He treated it as just another nice evening.

Trouble doesn't seem to come singly in our couple's life.

It was Thursday of the same week when the third person who knew one of their secrets reappeared in their lives; an unexpected, unwanted page of the past. A tawdry secret Kunal never even intended to share with Shreya. Even on the night when Kunal brutally slaughtered Shreya's dreams; he had been humane enough to withhold this dirty secret from her.

His secretary gave him a buzz at four in the afternoon. "A gentleman is here, Sir, wanting to meet you. He says he's your old college friend. He's from out-station…"

"Name please." Kunal asked.

"Gurdip Varma."

Kunal stood up in shock. He peeped through the glass partition into Shreya's room; she wasn't there. Every afternoon at around that time, she and Vineet usually took a coffee break at the café nearby.

"Please send him in immediately," Kunal said hastily.

He quickly pulled down the blinds of his office in case Shreya looked in when she returned. He was standing at the door when Gurdip walked out of the elevator.

"Come in, quick." Kunal said.

"Hey man, look at you. You are getting better with age like wine." Gurdip joked.

"What are you doing here?" Kunal said abruptly.

"Just thought I'd catch up with you. The last time you called me was two-and-a-half years back, looking for my ex-girlfriend. After the Bangalore episode."

"We were never great friends that we should call each other regularly."

"Are you troubled to see me?"

"No, nothing like that. I was about to leave for an important meeting, so just wanted to be quick. Is there anything urgent I can help you with?" Kunal tried to cover his nervousness.

"Well, it is kind of urgent." Gurdip's voice became serious. "Did you ever find Shreya? I am looking for her."

"Well, you told me you had no contact with her."

"I lied. I had one contact. I knew her old address, and the girl next door was her brother's girlfriend. But they refused to give any details about the Kohli family."

"Why did you lie to me?"

"You were too mad at her. She's a nice girl."

"And why the hell are you here asking for her?"

"I wanted to apologize. I made up false stories about her."

Kunal was perplexed. "Are you a psycho?"

"I was a psycho. That long distance relationship was unmanageable. I wanted to have fun with girls in Australia, but always had this guilt since I was engaged. I wanted to explore more options; I thought I'd made an impulsive decision to get engaged."

"Why didn't you have courage to walk up to Shreya and tell her that? Do you realize we both actually hurt a nice soul? For what, your urge for sex?"

"I know," Gurdip said heavily. "But I blame it on my age and immaturity. I wasn't ready for commitment then."

"Well, the answer is no. I never found her." Kunal thought it was entirely unnecessary for Gurdip to know his part in the later drama. "And I have a request to make." Kunal looked out of the office, the other two weren't back yet. "Please leave the office right away. Don't speak to anyone on the way. I hope you have no other questions for me."

Gurdip passed Kunal his visiting card. "I am in Mumbai for the next three days; call me." Kunal flung the card on his desk. Gurdip looked at it sadly and then up at Kunal. "I'm really sorry for defaming her all those years ago."

Kunal was rude. "See, Gurdip. You need to leave my office now. And I don't think we need to meet or call each other."

"Fine, fine! Take it easy. Good bye." Gurdip was offended; he left right away.

While walking outside the building, he saw Shreya near the coffee shop. He was elated to see her; he ran towards her. She was standing and cracking jokes with Vineet.

"Shreya." She turned hearing her name. She was shocked to see Gurdip. Vineet noticed her uneasy reaction. It was then that Gurdip noticed her diamond *mangalsutra*. He assumed Vineet was her husband.

"Sorry, I didn't mean to interrupt," Gurdip said, coming to a halt next to them.

Shreya recovered from her shock. "Vineet, I'll catch up with you later."

"Are you sure?" Vineet asked. He was concerned—he had seen her turn pale when the stranger called her name. But when she nodded, he went back to the office.

"How are you?" Gurdip asked.

"Great."

"You got married?"

"Yes, it's been around seven months."

"Do you work around here?"

"Yes."

"Oh my God!" He pointed at the tower that housed Kunal's office. "Don't go near that tower. In fact, for the sake of your marriage just avoid this area."

"What are you talking about?" Shreya asked.

"There's someone hunting for you; someone powerful enough to destroy you."

"Please, can you just stop making this up. Your concern for me is quite unnecessary now."

"Just trust me. I am still a well-wisher."

"Really?" She paused. "Then please let me know the name and reason too."

"The reason you know. He's the guy who had to get divorced because you made him pay for his prank." Shreya was crestfallen. "Name is Kunal Kharbanda."

"How... do you... know that?" Shreya asked assertively.

"You don't need to know that."

"I need to," she said urgently. "Tell me."

"Ok, fine. He's my engineering college friend. He didn't appear from anywhere in your room, I brought him along. I was tired of our long distance relationship and wanted to move on. But since we were engaged and our families were involved, I had to come up with a legitimate reason to break up with you. You would have never doubted me, so I had no other option but to come up with a plan where I could accuse you of infidelity." He paused, having the grace to look ashamed. "I am sorry. It was highly foolish of me to do that."

Shreya was thunderstruck. Gurdip continued, "And he's the best prankster I could think of. You punished him harshly."

Shreya looked at Gurdip one last time and, without saying anything to him, turned around and walked off. She didn't return to the office.

Kunal reached home at 8 pm. "Where's Shreya?" Anuradha asked him.

"She must be home."

"No, she isn't here. I thought she'd be back with you."

Kunal tried calling her number; it rang on, unanswered. He tried few times but with no response.

He called her father, in case she had gone to meet her parents. She wasn't there. Kunal told his father-in-law not to worry; she must be stuck in traffic. But Kunal himself grew apprehensive. He decided to check with Vineet.

"No, Kunal," Vineet said. "The last I saw her was around 4:30 pm for coffee."

"Didn't she return to the office with you?" Kunal asked.

"No, some slightly chubby, short guy came over to meet her. She wasn't very happy to see him. He wore a blue checked shirt."

Kunal plopped into a chair in shock. *Shreya met Gurdip!*

Shreya walked in just then. Her eyes were red, as if she had been crying.

"Where were you, my dear?" Anuradha was so relieved to see her, she ran to hug her.

Shreya held her tight. "I was in hospital. My friend fell ill suddenly, so I had to rush. I couldn't answer the phone as I had to switch it off in hospital."

Anuradha could make out something was terribly wrong—Shreya's voice sounded so sad. Shreya walked towards Kunal and looked him in the eye. He looked at her but soon lowered his head in shame. She then turned and moved towards the stairs.

Kunal turned to join her upstairs, when his mother shouted, "Kunal. Stop!" She assumed Kunal was giving her a tough time again.

"Mumma, I need to speak to her. "

"You need to spare her," Anuradha blasted.

"Mumma, I have a bigger issue at hand. I'll speak to you later." Kunal was irritated.

"No, I need to speak to you right now." She was disappointed with Kunal. "The divorce papers are lying in my left drawer. I want Shreya out of my house by tomorrow."

Kunal sighed in frustration. "Can't you see she's in pain?"

"I know what the cause of her pain is. I want her to feel better forever now." She paused. "Tomorrow morning, that's it."

"She isn't going anywhere. She's my wife; she'll live where I live. And next time you ask me to let her go, she won't go alone; I'll go along. No matter how much I love you."

"Oh really! She's your wife? Just for you to make her cry every second day. Just get those papers signed."

"Mumma, you are getting on my nerves. I read documents

from that legal advisor daily at my office; I can make out where your documents are coming from. Maybe she doesn't know, but I do know what divorce papers look like.

"So just relax and let me handle the situation. I know how much you love her, and what you actually wished when you asked me to leave her." Kunal ran up the stairs. Anuradha smiled, hoping this was the couple's last fight.

Shreya was standing in one corner of the balcony. Kunal walked up slowly to her.

"Shreya, it's an old story. I hope you meant it when you said you are not mad at me anymore." Kunal made an attempt to pacify her.

She cried, "My problem is not over, Kunal. I am hurt that you never told me this."

"There was nothing in it to be told. It was just kiddish on my part, and immature on his. We don't really understand how much something like this can hurt unless it happens to us. It's the worst feeling in the world to know someone is looking for a reason to breakup with you."

"I always wondered what you meant when you said, 'You deserved it' on our wedding night. I just learnt today." She turned to him in anguish. "So you married me thinking I was characterless, which is why my fiancé wanted to get rid of me. And you thought the 14th vow of our marriage was a done thing. That sleeping around was an everyday affair for me." Her eyes blazed.

"Please calm down," Kunal said desperately. "I can't allow you to use such words for yourself."

"Really? Then you tell me—why did you marry me? When you wrote down your vows what were you thinking?" She choked. "And do you really know what's the worst feeling in the world? It is when your husband tells you that he doesn't even want to see your face, as the first thing after marriage. You have no idea how painful that is."

Kunal stood still, humbled and ashamed. Because Shreya was right. He couldn't meet his wife's eyes.

I know that I committed a sin. I hurt a beautiful soul twice in my life. I deserve her punishment; she has all the right to be mad at me.

She walked into my hotel room without letting me know; I walked into her life without letting her know. Then she crept into my heart without letting me know. You don't fall when you are in love with a woman like her; you rise in her love.

The next day, after Kunal went to office, Shreya walked to Anuradha's room and expressed a desire to go to Delhi with her parents who were leaving that night.

"No, my dear, it's not right to leave your house over a fight," Anuradha tried to calm her down.

"Mumma, I am too tired. Please let me go."

"Try to understand, dear. You are making it worse."

"I cannot make the worst any worse." Tears ran down her cheeks.

Anuradha tried a different way, "You won't get a ticket so soon."

"It's a train. I'll go sitting. I've had many sleepless nights; one more won't make much of a difference."

"Ok! At least let Kunal know."

"I see no reason to tell him."

"He's your husband, Shreya."

"Why the hell is everyone telling me that he's my husband.

Someone needs to tell him that I am his wife." Shreya freaked out. "Somebody needed to tell him what marriage is all about." She realised she was shouting at her mother-in-law. "I am sorry, Mumma, I am just out of my mind."

Anuradha tried pacifying her. Shreya broke down weeping hard, hugging Anuradha tight.

"When will you be back, dear? I'll be waiting."

"I don't know Mumma. But I'll miss you."

Love Expressed

Kunal was too distracted at work and decided to leave office early, to discover that both ladies were out.

"Where are they?" Kunal asked Raju.

"Charaya madam had to catch the train to Delhi today; your Mumma went to drop her off," Raju said.

"My wife's parents are travelling, not her."

"No, she's going too. She packed her suitcase. She said she's leaving tonight, and that I should clean the room regularly."

Kunal panicked as he heard that. He turned towards the clock: he still had time before the train left.

"Hurry up, Sir. You can't have a better wife than Charaya madam," Raju added his two cents to Kunal's hundred dollar determination.

He drove dangerously fast to reach the nearest local train station, where he boarded a local train to reach the railway station. He managed to reach the railway station 40 minutes before the train's departure.

All of them were seated in the train. Anuradha's phone was ringing but Shreya asked her not to answer if it was Kunal. She had switched off her own phone. Sandhya's throat was getting dry now and Shreya got down the train to buy a water bottle.

Kunal saw Shreya from the top of the staircase. He hurried down, bumping into porters carrying luggage and people walking slowly down the stairs. His white shirt had all the flavours of Mumbai city by then.

The train still had 35 minutes to depart, but for him every second mattered. He caught up with Shreya and grabbed the hem of her *dupatta* to stop her. She felt the jerk around her neck, and turned to see what held it. Her eyes filled up when she saw her husband standing in front of her.

Mahesh got up to greet Kunal, but Anuradha folded her hands, begging him to let the couple talk. Sandhya held her husband back. The young couple were at a distance from where they could be seen, but couldn't be heard.

Kunal was breathless; Shreya realised he had come running hard. She wordlessly offered him the bottle of water she'd just bought. Kunal was moved to the depth of his heart. *She cares, even when she's mad at me.* Kunal grabbed the bottle and drank it all in one go.

"Where are you going, Shreya?" Kunal was still breathing hard, his face red with the exertion of running through the station.

"I am going home," Shreya replied in a choked voice.

"No, you are going away from home."

"Home is where the heart is. I am going home."

"Are you really sure? Your heart may miss you here."

"Please, let me go. Don't make me weak."

"How can I let you go?" He paused. "You know my office doesn't run without you; my dinner isn't great if it isn't cooked by you; I don't get a good night's sleep unless I've spoken with you; it's not a good morning for me if you are not the first face I see." He choked. "Do I need to tell you explicitly what you mean to me?"

"Kunal, you need to sympathize with me. I am going through an emotional trauma. I never made any mistake, but was punished severely, always."

"You made a terrible mistake too, which I avoided speaking about because it didn't matter. It was devastating to get a call from Saloni that my wife had walked up to her to say that I still loved her; to speak out every single secret of our marriage. With whose permission did you do that? You are no one to decide whom I love or who should get into our personal life. I don't get it. What difference does it make if it was a plan and not a prank in your room six years back. How is it relevant today?" Kunal said desperately. "If I have this serious issue with anger management, you have an equally serious issue of not moving on."

"Not moving on? I did get married to move on, Mr Kunal Kharbanda. I didn't get married to go through the hell you threw me into. I tied the knot to be with you till the last day of my life. I took my seven vows of marriage seriously. But that too was either a prank or a plan for you. Do you even realize that you broke my heart into pieces? Do you realize that you almost killed me too?" She was weeping like a child now, rubbing her nose with the back of her hand.

"We need to move past the night of April 14. You need to absolve me. And I owe you something," Kunal said, nearly in tears. He fell down on his knees and Shreya ran to him, begging him to get up.

"Just stop and listen."

She pulled at his arms. "We can talk, please get up, everyone around is watching."

"I don't give a shit. Just hear me out." He held her hands. "I deeply apologise for my prank. I had no right to ruin your life; I had no right to crush your dreams." Shreya could see he was full of remorse. "I am your culprit. I deserve your punishment. Your anger is justified."

Tears fell from his eyes. "But on second thoughts, I didn't really ruin it. I am here, to give you all that you ever desired; there's just a little delay. I know I am a difficult man to handle, but someone has to do it. You have to bear with me. I am sorry, but the match was probably made in heaven. You can sue God when you meet him.

"But, for this life, don't even dare to think of leaving me. I have no courage to see you going. I thought I've been in love before, but you have shown me what selfless and pure love means. Please be around always, you are the best thing that has ever happened to me."

Shreya was also crying by now; she now gestured him to stand up.

I know you want to hear that from me loud and clear.

"Mrs Shreya Kunal Kharbanda," Kunal smiled through his tears, "I Love You."

She raised her eyes to meet his. She wiped her tears. Shreya was standing four steps away from Kunal. She walked the first step, and ran the next three to put her arms around Kunal's neck; standing on her toes, she snuggled up to him endearingly, crying her heart out as her anger perished. Kunal instantly clasped her closer with his arms around her. He too dropped a few tears on her cheeks as her love reached his grief-stricken heart.

The journey that started seven months ago, finally reached its first destination that day. The world around came to a rest when Kunal and Shreya expressed their love for each other. A long affectionate hug, alleviating their pain and unwinding the emotions that had been seething since long.

His white shirt finally had an immortal flavour of the city, rather of the whole of India—of love.

Sandhya and Anuradha were crying tears of joy. They walked towards them.

Shreya composed herself and looked at Kunal. "Mr Kharbanda, your wife is crazy about you."

Kunal gently moved his fingers through his wife's hair. "Then why the hell was she acting so pricey?" Laughter flashed out through the tears. Kunal held her face and kissed her forehead tenderly.

"Now that's what is called a happy ending," Sandhya exclaimed.

"No, Mumma, it's called a new beginning," Kunal said. "I am sorry for troubling everyone." He felt so much stronger with Shreya's hand in his.

"No one is troubled," Sandhya said, smiling happily now. "Every love story has its own journey. Reaching the destination is important."

"I am sorry, Sandhyaji," Anuradha looked at her. "I should have talked this out with you, but I always thought they'd sort it out soon."

"It's alright, Anuradhaji. Even I would have done the same. I am so glad we'll be travelling back to Delhi lighter and carefree," she said. She turned to Kunal. "You are wonderful, Kunal. We all make mistakes but most of us fail to even acknowledge them. You are so brave to not only acknowledge them but also to repair the damage. It's no surprise Shreya loves you so much."

She gently kissed Shreya's cheek. "Stay happy, my child. And two things you should always remember. Firstly, as Anuradhaji also mentioned, don't leave your house over a fight. Everything is amicably solvable if it's not infidelity.

"Secondly, you need to talk clearly to Kunal always. You should express what you want unambiguously. You keep things to yourself too much; it isn't really required."

"Don't mention that, Sandhyaji," Anuradha said. "Shreya's very mature. Praise goes to her patience that issues stand resolved today. I don't care what the issues were; all I care is that they are solved."

"You can't take praise away from Kunal," Mahesh now spoke up. "What he did today takes lot of courage for a man to do."

"Mumma, you are amazing," Kunal looked at Sandhya. "I owe this to you more than anyone else." He bent down to touch her feet. He touched his mother's next and then Mahesh's. "I think we really need your blessings as we start our new life today," he said.

Shreya looked at him with surprise. He had never done that to anyone before. The train whistle blew and the passengers to Delhi climbed onto the train.

Shreya gently whispered to Kunal. "Let's go home."

Kunal sat down on his bed, emotionally drained and almost motionless; Shreya sat beside him, gently resting her hand on his shoulder. Kunal's dam of self-control shattered again; he broke out crying. She held his face and wiped his tears.

"I am sorry, Shreya, I made you so miserable. I am such a loser," he said emotionally.

Shreya caressed his face. "You just gave me the world's most beautiful feeling, and that's what matters to me. That's all I want to keep and wash out all the sour memories."

Kunal placed his head on her lap and Shreya gently massaged his head till he fell asleep. With a little effort, she moved his head to the pillow and then she lay next to him, holding his hand all night long.

Kunal's sleep broke at early dawn. His happiness soared to find Shreya sleeping next to him, still holding his hand loosely. It was a new dawn indeed; it deserved celebration. Kunal decided what should follow next.

Right after breakfast, he went out of the house. He had picked up Shreya's passport from her closet without asking her. He returned after three hours, and found Shreya standing in front of the portrait in their room.

He held her from behind, resting his chin on her shoulder and holding her hands over her stomach, looking at the portrait with her.

"You know how to make somebody's day." She lifted a hand and placed it on his cheek.

He lightly kissed her shoulder. "I have something for you." He pulled out the air tickets and their passports from an envelope. "We are leaving tonight, so we have lots of packing to do. And I also want to take you shopping. We just have nine hours to go."

Shreya turned to face him, her eyes shining. "Where are we going?"

"I chose a beautiful place for you. I've heard great things about it; let's go and see it ourselves."

"Where?"

"Sshhh. Get ready. I'll go and tell Mumma now; come down soon."

"I'm curious," she said excitedly.

"Trust me and *HappyTrips*." He winked.

"Mumma, I am taking Shreya away for a week. Please take care of yourself." Kunal gave a warm hug to his mother.

"That's wonderful," she exclaimed. "Honeymoon, finally."

He chuckled. "Yes, a much awaited. Much deserved too."

"Take good care of my daughter-in-law."

"I am taking your *bahu*, but I plan to return with my wife."

Kunal took her shopping to his favourite shops, and chose loads of clothes and accessories for her including a stylish *Scavin Aviator* for her to match his. On her insistence, he also picked a few articles of her choice for himself.

Next, he took Shreya to a jewellery shop. At the counter, he pulled out a receipt from his wallet and handed it to the shopkeeper.

"Sir," the shopkeeper said, 'This has been waiting for you for over a month."

"I was not sure if she would like it," Kunal said. "So I brought her along to choose." Shreya was confused.

"Shall I bring the one you selected?"

"Yes, please, to start with."

Shreya whispered to Kunal. "What are you guys talking about? I am lost."

The shopkeeper returned with a glittering diamond necklace. Shreya was thrilled; her eyes sparkled.

"Do you like it?" Kunal asked. "Usually people don't like my gifts."

"This is beautiful." Shreya was emotional.

"You may want to see a few others before we buy."

"No, I don't want to. This is perfect; simply majestic.

I love your gift."

He asked the shopkeeper to pack it.

"When did you order it?"

Kunal showed her the slip. It was the seventh of October, *Karvachauth* day. Her eyes filled with tears. Kunal gave her a hug.

"Then why didn't you give it to me that day?" She asked.

"I was scared. You were too mad at me those days. You might have flung it out of window."

"You cared enough to buy me a gift on a special day, and I just offered weird attitude. I gave you a tough time too."

"Tough times are over dear. Come on, we just have six hours to go and we need to pack as well. Good times await us."

Happy Trip to Jeju

Jeju is a volcanic island, one of the nine provinces of South Korea. The island is blessed with pristine natural beauty, and the volcanic island and the Lava tubes are a world heritage site. Mandarin oranges grow all over the island. The spectacular natural scenery, soothing breeze and early winter climate made it a perfect honeymoon location for the couple.

They reached Jeju late in the morning. The drive to Seogwipo city was about an hour. Kunal had booked an ocean facing room, so that he and his lady love could see the sun rise out of the ocean.

Shreya, however, turned a spoiler—she was airsick through the flight and slept like a baby for hours as soon as they reached the hotel. While she was sleeping, Kunal made arrangements for sightseeing, before he also had a nap. He was looking forward to the evening and the night.

Shreya had recovered by the evening and they walked around the hotel premises before dinner. She marvelled at the view; the lights on the boats and the beam from a distant lighthouse made the dark night ocean look magnificent. They had a quick dinner and headed back to the room.

Kunal took a shower and Shreya stood on the balcony, lost in the view. There was a knock at the door—the bearer had brought complimentary wine, a plate of oranges and chocolates. Kunal couldn't ask for a better atmosphere to woo his wife. "Have a great evening, sir." *I will. I will. We will. We will.*

Kunal poured wine into the glasses and walked up behind her. He brought his hand forward, offering her the wine. He held her around the waist and gently kissed her shoulder. "Cheers."

"This is just so beautiful. I have never seen anything more serene than this. Thank you so much for bringing me here," Shreya said softly.

"You are welcome." He rubbed his nose behind her ear. "But that's not what I brought you here for."

She giggled. "I know. I can sense your desires."

"But before that, I want to get you talking. You give annoying one-liners to my two-page questions." He turned her and put the glasses on a side table. He trapped her between his body and the railings. "Look up. I've had enough of you looking down always." Kunal raised her chin with his fingers.

"Do you plan to interrogate me?" Shreya pretended nervousness.

"Of course." Kunal playfully bared his teeth. "So, first question. What does it mean to be crazy?"

"Being crazy is being crazy. It means what it states," Shreya replied coyly.

He tickled her waist, and stopped only when she agreed to give a proper answer.

"So, being crazy means," Shreya said shyly, "I find you good looking, attractive and an absolute charmer."

"So I'm not actually below average?" She shook her head; she was breathing faster. "And the way you talk, you sweep me off my feet."

"Really? Yet it took so long to get you in my arms. It seemed to have a slow effect on you."

"It had an effect on me from Day One. I find your voice hypnotic." She lowered her head in shyness. He raised her chin again. "No looking down today. By the way, where are you looking? We'll get there too." She gently slapped his arm.

They laughed lightly. "Just make a wish, and allow me to make it happen," he said.

"You are quite a romantic."

"You are just starting to know me." He winked.

Shreya smiled and then looked at him flirtatiously. "Let me think," she said thoughtfully. "How about proposing to me?"

"Ok." He held her hands romantically. "With your sharp brain, you hold my office. You run it efficiently and it's in its best form ever. With your responsible hands, you hold my house. You cook, you decorate, you spread joy around; and it's in its happiest phase ever. Now allow your heart,that is sitting idle to engage with mine. So that we can be in love forever and ever."

Shreya was enraptured. "Had I not been married, I would have married you for this right away."

"Will you marry me?" Kunal said. "Again." He paused. "Let's start all over again. "

He tucked her hair, which was blowing in the sea breeze, behind her ears. "By the way, did someone tell you that you have beautiful eyes?"

"No," she beamed. "At least not the way you did."

"And a radiant face, a stunning figure; and when you do your award winning dance performance, even your enemy would melt away."

She grinned, remembering her 'floor show'.

"And one more thing." He kissed her eyes gently and placed her hands on his shoulders, resting his own on her waist. Moving his face closer to hers, he whispered, "Rosy pink lips."

He locked her upper lip gently between his lips, electrifying her. Her hand moved up to his neck and she held his collar tightly. He released her lip, just to return and absorb it deeper. She loosened her hold gradually, surrendering inch by inch. Soon her fingers moved up to his hair in total submission. They both relished the first kiss, each giving in to the other.

It took a while for them to let the moment go; but he released her lips finally to look up—Shreya's eyes were still closed and her face was glowing. He fell in love again with the simplicity of his wife.

He whispered, "Mrs Shreya Kunal Kharbanda, your husband is craving for more."

She smiled shakily; the glow on her face was more illuminating than the lighthouse behind her. She held him close and whispered in his ear, "You are not the only one craving."

He lifted her in his arms and walked to their bridal bed.

Later in the night, they finished the bottle of wine, lying on the floor under a blanket and enjoying the beautiful night of Jeju.

They served the 14th vow of their marriage with grace, love and passion.

PS Kunal brought in the new pack of condoms, trashing his preserved one along with the left-over debris of the past.

Shreya was yawning as they walked up the Seongsan Ilchulbong Peak to look at the volcanic crater. The peak rose from under the sea in a volcanic eruption over 100,000 years ago. The crater was about 600 metres in diameter and 90 metres high. With the 99 sharp rocks encircling the crater, it appeared like a gigantic crown.

Kunal had pulled out his SLR camera to capture the natural beauty of the place. His own beauty was a bit sleepy though that day.

"You are yawning since we got up," Kunal teased her.

"I don't know, but I have this heavy head."

"It's called a hangover." He laughed. "You are quite a boozer."

"I see. So if one glass of wine is boozing; what's gulping the rest of the bottle called?"

"Giving company to a boozer," he joked.

"Well, I need a full night's sleep today." She yawned again.

"We'll head to the hotel after this spot, and you can relax the rest of the afternoon."

"No, it's okay. A good night's sleep will do."

"My dear wife, couples don't come on a honeymoon to sleep all night. What kind of stupid girl did my mom choose for me," Kunal said in good humour.

"By the way, your mother just facilitated the marriage; you chose me." She smiled naughtily.

"Right! So it's my duty to ensure that you get the right education." He paused. "Champagne tonight?"

At midnight, cake and champagne arrived at their room on Shreya's orders.

"Happy Birthday!" Shreya exclaimed.

Kunal was truly thrilled as he cut the cake.

"Where's my gift?" He asked.

"Gift?" She paused. "Don't be materialistic." She winked.

"Did I say I want a materialistic gift?"

"Then what? How can I make your day special?" She put her

hands on his shoulders. He kissed her gently on her lips.

"You need to think about that?"

"Please tell me. Your wish will be my command."

"You shouldn't have said that. God save you now." He paused. "How about an award winning performance?"

Shreya tried to shy away, but he caught her wrist. "And that's a command."

She danced shyly to begin with, then her gestures got bolder. Soon they were both dancing together, in perfect rhythm.

The days passed by in a blur. Kunal insisted on sightseeing during the day and Shreya agreed happily, even though she was tired after the unaccustomed activities of the night. They visited the world heritage site of Manjanggul Cave; a tunnel that was formed when the lava that was deep in the ground, spouted from the peak and flowed to the surface.

"This is so amazing. I never even imagined volcanic eruptions could lead to such a transcending site centuries later," Shreya said admiringly.

"Maybe the volcano was guilty of erupting, so it cooled down strategically to leave behind a pleasant signature," Kunal replied, tongue-in-cheek.

"Yeah, some volcanoes do realize that in time." She looked at him pointedly, laughing at his rueful expression when he realised she was teasing him. "You are much smarter than I assumed." She grinned and held his arm. Kunal passed the camera to another tourist and got the moment captured.

On their last day they visited another wonder of nature—the Jungmun-Daepo Coast, with pillar rocks of nearly perfect hexagonal shape, as if carved by a master craftsman. The waves of the high tide crash into the side of the cliff, providing an exhilarating view of the ocean surrounding the pillars.

"Wow, there couldn't be a better end to the holiday," Kunal said, inhaling the sea wind deeply.

"I don't want to go back," Shreya said giving him a hug.

He gently kissed her forehead. "I promise, we'll go for a vacation every quarter now."

"Work will not allow us."

"Trust me. I've awaited for these moments for years; I want to live my life to its fullest with you. You just made it so beautiful, and it's heaven when you smile."

She was floored. "Did someone ever tell you, your words are intoxicating?"

He chuckled. He held her face and kissed her lips. PDA accidentally or intentionally?

Together We Stand

They returned in a euphoric state of mind. Life had changed blissfully and there was love in every corner of their hearts. Anuradha was thrilled to see her son happy again.

"Mumma," Kunal whispered at the dinner table. "I asked her and she's okay to marry me again."

Anuradha chuckled. "So, when do we need to get it done?" she whispered back.

"I was thinking it will be an unnecessary expense. What say you? Maybe we should let this one be."

"Yes, right. Otherwise I will have to give her another lavish gift next *Karvachauth,* as it will effectively become her first one again." They laughed and Shreya wanted to know the joke, but they kept this their secret. Shreya smiled, happy to see the mother and son bonding together again.

Dinners at the Kharbanda house henceforth were the liveliest moments for the family.

Vineet was also super-excited to see both of them. He had managed everything flawlessly in their absence.

"This is wonderful, Vineet. I am so proud of you." Kunal exclaimed in the conference room. Shreya stood up and clapped.

"You are embarrassing me, Shreya," Vineet said shyly.

"No, I mean it. See, when you trusted in your potential, everything else just simply followed."

"I owe this to you. You injected confidence in me, both professionally and personally." Vineet said admiringly. "Thank you, *Bhabhi*." He winked.

Shreya blushed. "What does that mean?"

"It means brother's wife."

"I know, but you never addressed me like that before."

"Well, you just returned as my brother's wife." He gave a naughty smile.

Shreya's face flushed; she pulled his ear. They all had a huge laugh. Kunal showed a few pictures to Vineet of their vacation.

Life was getting beautiful with each passing day. The emotional bond between Shreya and Kunal was getting stronger. They knew each other's likes and dislikes pretty clearly by now; they were pleasantly surprised that they both thought alike in many aspects. And to their total surprise, they both were diehard romantics. Romance was flowing in everyday tasks.

Shreya now took total charge of all his belongings; she wasn't scared to touch his things any more. She even started accompanying him to the club on weekends, registering for swimming classes and watching him play squash.

He always kept her busy with himself. His office, his food, his closet, his hobbies and most importantly his tantrums; he just engaged her round the clock. He still did mischievous things to trouble her and grab her attention. He was enjoying being pampered, and wanted to be spoiled by his wife. He rewarded her with his flirtatious and cheesy conversations; he knew that's what drew her to him. *She didn't marry any face, she actually married a voice.*

Shreya discovered another of Kunal's secrets, this time a nice one. Kunal had a good voice, not just to whisper sweet nothings to her but also to sing. He learnt to woo Shreya at times by singing romantic songs for her. "You need to sing me my song first; else you are not getting anything tonight," Shreya would teasingly push Kunal away when he came to her in the night.

She would love those moments and Kunal was clever enough to capitalize on her excitement.

He pulled Shreya closer with force. "Unless I get it, your ears need to wait."

"And I am blamed for dragging things." Shreya slid away from him.

He turned on his side and slid in same direction.

He moved his fingers on her hair, rubbing his body to hers. She exclaimed. "Stop. Don't try to be smart." She slid further away.

"I don't have to try it. Few things flow through me naturally." He slid along.

"Good try." She slid again. "You are uselessly prolonging it. All I need is my song." She slid to the corner of the bed, almost about to fall off. He locked her with his arm and one leg to avoid her rolling down.

He moved his nose to tickle her ears and then whispered two lines of her favourite song. She was lost in his voice.

He turned her over him.

"I was wondering what is more rewarding, your charm or my voice? Latter didn't even qualify to compete." Kunal said smiling amorously, his fingers reaching for her body.

He kissed her on her lips. Shreya was breathless and hot. "It's been quite many times, but you are still shivering and hesitating," Kunal said.

"It's called melting, sweetheart." Shreya moved her fingers to his hair.

"How can someone melt each night?"

"Can't help it. Your fingers move a bit too erotically," Shreya replied in a seductive tone.

Kunal unknotted the straps of her dress playfully. "Impressive?"

"You bet." She kissed him in style.

It was Christmas Eve and the couple were seated in a restaurant of a five star hotel, after a movie date.

"Movie was good," she said.

"Nothing great," he said.

"The company was great, so movie was great naturally." She winked.

"Impressive! Someone is learning really fast," he teased.

"Learning to be a flirt, you mean. I am sure you must have been a big flirt in your growing years."

"On that note, I think I am still growing." He winked.

"No, I think you are an expert at flirting. It's in its ripened state."

"Enjoy the ripened fruit my love. Why are you bothered how and where it grew?" He said flirtatiously.

On the 12th floor of the same hotel trouble was brewing. Saloni and her mother were in conversation with a representative of an international modelling agency.

"See ma'am, you have to bear the expenses. The payment will

be done by my client at the end of the assignment. If that suits you, I can finalise the details. Don't bother me otherwise."

"I don't have the money you are asking for," Saloni said smoking hard.

"That's not my problem. You should consider marrying then and producing babies, for all I care." He was tired of dealing with Saloni and her idiosyncrasies.

Saloni's mother, Bhoomi, tried to mollify him. "Maybe you can lend us some money and when the client makes the payment we'll return yours with interest."

"You ladies are wasting my time. Let me know by next week if I need to find another model." He stormed out of the room.

"What the hell is going on in my life? Where do I get the money he's asking?" Saloni got up angrily and walked to the window.

"Cool down, Saloni. The ups and downs of a career should be handled maturely. You've never taken any right decision in your life, anyway," Bhoomi said sternly.

"Is that so?" Sonali asked rudely. "Tell me one wrong decision I've made. I even married because you asked me to, and then got divorced on your orders. You manage all my work, where did I go wrong?" Saloni shrieked.

"You made a terrible mistake of walking out of the marriage without a hefty alimony."

"Give me a break."

"Just shut up and listen. Make another attempt to woo him. Even his wife had offered him to you when she came to see you that day, almost colliding with me. Maybe all is not lost yet."

"No way! I'm not going to him. He was very disrespectful last time."

"Fine, then. Just continue sobbing and live with your financial miseries. You've lost all the brands to newcomers, and as the agent also said, your career is over."

Saloni wiped her tears and continued smoking. She had to meet Kunal. She picked up the phone and made a few calls.

The Christmas Night Dance was being held at the club. Most of the couples were dressed in the green and red colours of Christmas, Kunal and Shreya among them. Also on the dance floor were Jyothsna and Vineet. Shreya was surprising Kunal with her dancing skills. During a break in the music, Kunal walked towards the restroom. As he got out of the disco area, someone put their arms around him. He assumed it was Shreya.

"Hang on darling. Let's go home if you are so despo."

"Take me home, please," Saloni's voice whispered back.

Kunal was flabbergasted and turned around, pushing Saloni's hand away. "What the hell do you think you're doing?"

"You looked so uneasy throughout the party, so I thought to make it better for you," she said amorously.

He turned to walk back to the party but she hurried to stand in front of him. "Please, stop being so rude. It's not suiting you." She tried hugging him.

"Please behave yourself." He freed himself.

She was adamant though and kept trying to put her arms around him. "I think you are drunk, you need help," he said angrily.

"Yes, please, help me out." She brought her lips closer to his.

Kunal pushed her away. It was then that he noticed Shreya. She and Vineet had come looking for him and had seen the whole scene. Vineet was furious, but she held his arm to hold him back. Saloni also saw Shreya.

"She knows it all, Kunal," she said. "She too wants the same; you both have to stop pretending now."

Vineet was seething, but Shreya held his arm harder. Saloni raised her eyebrows at Shreya holding Vineet's arm.

"I told you, Kunal. Let her be happy with Vineet. You always belonged to me." Shreya closed her eyes in disgust.

Kunal turned to Saloni with extreme hate and raised his hand to slap her. Shreya ran to him and held his wrist just in time.

"Leave me, Shreya,' he said, his eyes bloodshot with rage. "I am going to kill her today. How dare she?"

"No, Kunal, don't!" Shreya begged, holding his arm with both hands now. "It's the way she thinks. According to her, that's the only relation between a guy and a girl."

Kunal looked into Shreya's eyes. The look in them made him calm the demons in his head. "Let's go home," Shreya said. Kunal was quiet all the way back home.

He had changed and was lying on the bed with his arm over his eyes when she joined him. She gently massaged his head. He looked at her.

"Don't be too happy, it's just me," she said, with a gentle smile.

"I am glad it's you. And trust me, it's just you."

"You don't even have to say that. It will be shameful on my part to doubt you now." She held his face and kissed his cheek. "You really need to work on your anger management. She didn't deserve the attention you gave her today."

He felt better. "She tested me beyond tolerance. I couldn't help myself after her nasty remark at you."

"Again, it's the way she thinks. Please, next time, don't behave the way you did today. It's not your job to punish anyone. And trust me, ignoring somebody is at times the best way to punish."

"Like you ignored me." Kunal pushed himself closer to her.

"I just did what you wanted me to."

"Really? Yet you saved my foot from the broken glass."

"I would have done that for anyone."

"And yet, you stole glances at me, to see my reaction, when you made initial attempts with cooking," Kunal said caressing her face.

"I didn't!"

"Please be honest." He winked.

"Ok! Yes I did."

"Why?"

"Hoping that you liked it," she said smiling.

He looked at her with intense love and kissed her eyes. "Did someone tell you that you excel in the art of stealing the heart?" He moved down to her lips.

"It's 3 am my dear husband," she said against his lips.

"Just the right time."

The Kohli family had just sat down to watch the 7 o'clock news. The next news item made them all sit up. The newsreader was reading out a spicy breaking news.

"*Saloni Gupta, one of India's super models, attempted suicide this afternoon. Her mother spoke to our news correspondent and informed us that she was going through bad times. She said her life turned upside down when she recently discovered that the woman who broke her marriage had now got married to her ex-husband. She played a dirty game to break them apart and to make her way in his life. She said Saloni was devastated and undergoing mental trauma.*"

"My god, these Page 3 people are so dramatic." Aastha was dismissive of the news item.

The newsreader continued. *"Just for our viewers information, Saloni Gupta was briefly married about two-and-a-half years back to Kunal Kharbanda, owner of Kharbanda Textiles of Mumbai."*

They all stood, thunderstruck. Aastha was the first one to freak out, crying, "Let's call Shreya."

"I am going to Mumbai right away," Madhav said, in deep shock.

"Will everyone please relax?" Sandhya said. "We need to let Kunal fix it." Everyone looked to her with amazement.

Sandhya and Mahesh had decided not to disclose the event at CST station to Maddy and Aastha. Sandhya chose being perceived as apprehensive over flaunting rightness of her intuitions; to save Shreya any unforeseen awkwardness.

"Mumma, what's up with you? We need to call Shreya and calm her down," Aastha said worrying.

"The phone is right there, put it on speaker. I am sure she won't be reacting the way you guys are." Sandhya maintained a cool head.

Aastha rang Shreya. Shreya tried calming them down but Madhav was adamant. He landed in Mumbai at 8:30 am the next day. Kunal dealt with him with utmost courtesy and patience.

"I've issued her a legal notice; she needs to prove her allegation in court," Kunal explained his plan.

Kunal's phone rang a couple of hours later, but he kept hanging up. This continued for a few times, and finally Shreya's phone rang.

"Hello," Shreya said.

"Saloni here, I want to speak to Kunal." She sounded hysterical.

Shreya was calm. "I don't see any reason for that, Saloni," she said. The men's heads jerked up at the sound of the name. Shreya continued. "Maintain a distance from my family, else this time it could be me teaching you the hard way."

"I am impressed at the sudden change in tone. Looks like the gold has dazzled your eyes."

"It sure has. But what you call gold is different from what I consider gold." Shreya took a deep breath. "I heard you attempted suicide. Do you know it's a punishable offence?"

"Do you know breaking into somebody's room is also an offence?"

"Prove it."

"Listen. I don't want to waste my time talking to you. I want to speak to him."

"You listen. You are indeed wasting your time; you should invest this time in trying to trap some other gold mine. I have seen enough of the world to know your intentions. Emotions and love are the last things on your mind."

"Cut the crap."

"We'll see you in court. We have hired the best lawyer of the city; you should also hire some top notch legal person. I think the penalty for defamation is about 50 lakhs, I'm not sure though. Kunal might have even doubled it; he was really furious," Shreya said confidently.

Saloni put the phone down, her hands shaking from the confrontation.

Three hours later, Saloni spoke to the press and offered an apology:

"My mom misheard me. I was under the influence of medicines and blabbered rubbish. I have never even met his wife, leave alone blaming her for my divorce. I deeply apologize for the confusion. It was entirely unintentional."

There was much relief in the Kharbanda household that evening. Kunal, however, sat motionless until Shreya sat next to him and held his hand firmly.

"It's all over now." At last he returned her smile and hugged her tight.

Madhav was delighted. "Shreya, why don't you come with me to Delhi for a few days?"

Shreya shook her head. "New Year is around the corner. I'll come a few days later. And anyway, you guys are coming for Prateek's marriage on the 15th of January."

"Yes, you can come back to Mumbai with us then. It will be a good change for you."

"I don't need any change. My life is perfect."

"Sorry for the interruption," Kunal held up a hand. "But Madhav, does Aastha's family also only invite her?"

Madhav looked like a child caught doing something naughty. "Well, no." He paused and turned sheepishly to Kunal. "I think it will be a great idea if all of you come over to Delhi for the New Year."

"That sounds better, even if it was half-hearted," Kunal said with good humour. Madhav laughed and insisted on repeating the invitation, this time seriously.

They reached Delhi late evening on the thirtieth. Shreya was elated: she would be spending her New Year with all the people she loved. Anuradha wasn't with them—she had already planned on being with her sister in Pune. The delicious dinner they received was very welcoming; and most importantly Sandhya's attitude towards Kunal was transformed. Shreya was enchanted to see this new warmth between the two.

Madhav offered Kunal a drink and the two brothers-in-law drank till late in the night. Everyone else retired. Aastha had offered the guests their bedroom as it had an attached bathroom, but Shreya chose her old one.

The next morning Shreya was unpacking the suitcase. Her family was sitting at the dining table; the dining room was very close to Shreya's room. They could hear the whole conversation between Shreya and Kunal.

"Where's my brush, Shreya?" Kunal asked.

"How would I know?"

"You did all the packing, who else would know?"

"I only packed what you kept on the bed to take along."

"Wasn't a toothbrush obvious?"

"This is weird. Next you'll ask me, 'where's my underwear'."

"Wait a minute," he said. "Are you trying to tell me you didn't pack that either?" He paused. "This is not done."

"Don't you think you are overreacting?"

"No, infact I am underreacting. "

"You need to give me a break here."

"Yes, indeed. Take a break, rush to the market and get all that you forgot to pack."

"Are you serious?" she was shocked. "You really need to keep your booze under check."

"I don't booze," Kunal said with mild irritation. "Don't give me any unnecessary shit early in the morning."

"Excuse me?" Shreya pulled out his brush from the bag. "Take it." She threw it at him. "Your shampoo, your deo, shaving cream, razor and your precious underwear." She scowled at him. "Is that good enough, Mr Kharbanda?"

"You are amazing, Mrs Kharbanda." Kunal now smiled smugly.

"Now you don't give me any of this shit early in the morning." She pretended anger.

Everyone at table laughed mutely. Sandhya was particularly very happy hearing a perfect husband-wife conversation.

Kunal pulled her close with one hand. "Do I need to shave?" he asked, rubbing his stubbled cheek on hers.

"Ouch!" she screamed lightly. "You must."

Mahesh and Madhav walked onto the balcony to avoid listening to this intimacy. Sandhya and Aastha shamelessly got more attentive.

Kunal was rubbing her other cheek. "Stop," Shreya squealed.

"By the way, when you had packed it all, why didn't you tell me?"

"So that you know when I say all your stuff; you should check."

"Well I did keep the most important commodity."

"You need a toothbrush first thing in the morning."

"That doesn't mean the last thing you need at night is not important."

"Drop it. I think one of my new resolutions will be to give up arguing with you," Shreya said, shaking her head.

"No please. Don't take the fun away from my life. I'll tell you better resolutions."

"Really? For instance..."

He replied thoughtfully, "I'll stop faking."

Aastha banged her head laughing. Sandhya was embarrassed.

"I think you need tea." Shreya freed herself and walked out of the room, to come to a dead halt seeing Sandhya and Aastha sitting at the dining table, grinning.

The day passed in fun and frolic. They took Kunal on a tour of the city and loved his company. The Kohli family was very satisfied to see both of them so happy and so much in love.

Later that night, in the privacy of their room, Kunal rested his head on his wife's lap; Shreya was enjoying moving her fingers through his hair. They listed a few New Year resolutions: a vacation every quarter, Salsa dance classes for both and the bedroom makeover on his list. She expressed the desire to start a family by the middle of next year, which Kunal rejected outright, deferring it to be discussed at a later date.

The clock ticked 12. 2010 was welcomed with open arms.

To Sum It Up

As one of her New Year resolutions, Shreya finally created a Facebook account. She chose a picture of her and Kunal at Jeju as her profile picture. She now reached out to all her school and college friends. She found that most of her friends were settled with people other than the ones they were going out with five years ago. She regretted taking her break-off so gloomily; she now understood that all she had gone through was part of growing up and the transformation from adolescence to adulthood.

She uploaded pictures of all the major events of her life of the last year—wedding reception, Diwali *puja*, *chowki*, honeymoon—they all mirrored her pride in her marriage. She received calls and mails from her old friends. Shreya broke out of her shell gradually.

Kunal was very pleasantly surprised, and amused, to get a relationship request from Shreya Kunal Kharbanda. He tagged himself to her pictures to avoid the work of uploading them. He, however, chose the reception picture as his profile picture, a copy of the portrait in their room. For him, it was then when his life was blessed.

It was the first working day of 2010, and after Kunal gave the New Year speech to the entire office, the next level managers were invited to the board room for a short meeting. Post- meeting, they were all chatting informally. Vikas Pradhan, the Accounting head pulled out a box of sweets. He had got engaged during his winter vacations. Everyone congratulated him.

"Love or arranged," one of their colleagues, Nivedita, enquired.

"Arranged."

"That's quite a risk for your generation," Mohit teased.

"Well, the risk is for the girl, Vikas you shouldn't be worried." Kunal joked, giving Shreya a naughty look. Laughter followed.

"Are you serious? Yours surely wasn't arranged." Nivedita was surprised.

Shreya nodded in answer to her query. "In fact through *BharatMatrimony.com.*"

"And it worked magically, thanks to my wife," Kunal said, grinning.

"I think the only difference is that, in an arranged marriage the relationship begins post ceremony. It's just a matter of initial comfort," Shreya said to Vikas.

"Very well said," Vineet said.

"As always." Kunal added proudly. Everyone smiled.

"Trust plays an important role," Nivedita added.

"Agreed. But respect is slightly more important. I mean, if you don't respect your partner in front of the world, others will have all the reason to disrespect him or her; and chiefly the relationship," Shreya said assertively.

Kunal held Shreya's hand lovingly under the table.

"Very true," Kunal said thoughtfully. "But Love would still stand as the most critical element; everything else follows only if love blossoms in the relationship. Eventually, every marriage has to prove its worth and mettle. Finally it's two individuals who need to deal with it maturely and earn respect for their bond."

"Wow. Someone sounded like a marriage counsellor," Shreya said with pride.

"Impressive?" Kunal jumped to his favourite question.

"As always," was Shreya's honest confession.

"Well guys, you must share this success story for *BharatMatrimony.com* to put on their website."

The Kohlis were invited to the Kharbanda residence for *Lohri* celebrations. It was a celebration with close family and friends.

Kunal threw the scroll of his seven vows of marriage into the holy fire of *Lohri*. While dancing around the fire, he whispered in Shreya's ears. "Let's revise our seven vows of marriage. Let's get married again around this holy fire."

"Which ones? Yours or the old priest's?" she teased.

"The ones you followed so dedicatedly." He smiled affectionately.

She smiled. "You don't remember any one of them?"

"Honestly speaking, they all appeared redundant; they all mean the same thing."

"No, they all mean different things, the final one being the most important."

"Absolutely right. How do you manage to be so right always?" He smiled. "Let's just revise the last one. The rest will all follow naturally. You first."

Shreya took a deep breath and looked into his eyes.

"I belong to you and only you henceforth. I promise to stand by you in all turbulent weathers and assimilate all your negativity.

I swear to keep my character high and deeds right so that your reputation in society is never questioned. With my angels watching today, I leave everything behind for you. My heart, my mind, my body and my karma will now always be ruled by my husband."

She smiled blissfully. Kunal was enthralled. It took him a while to recite his vow.

"You are my best friend for life. A friend for all seasons and journeys. I offer my patience, my love and my understanding for life, today. Together we shall fight all difficult times, and create a beautiful world full of compassion and laughter. You are welcome to my life, it's been longing for you to arrive."

Shreya was overwhelmed by his sincerity and she threw herself into his arms, ignoring the public around. He completed the moment by putting his arms around her.

The public display of affection received all possible reactions, from 'Awww' to 'Huh'.

It was the day after Prateek's wedding; the younger generation had driven to the beach for ice-cream. The women wandered off to inspect some interesting stalls nearby, leaving the men sitting on the rocks.

"Isn't today's Indian woman a bit too amazing." Kunal said thoughtfully, looking at his wife. Madhav and Vineet nodded.

"I know, the criterion of a good match has changed radically," Madhav said.

"You stole the words out of my mouth. Being rich, good looking or qualified are obsolete qualities," Kunal said.

Vineet agreed ruefully. "Yeah, women are so capable, educated and self-sustained that they really don't need a guy to support their shopping bills anymore."

Kunal patted his back. "Somebody is growing up fast." They shared a warm smile.

"I don't mean to get personal. But Shreya had very simple demands. 'I want to keep my job. Don't keep telling me that I am too qualified'," Madhav said.

Kunal smiled. "She told me once that her parents got furious over yet another hike in her pay."

"Yes. They were so worried about her independence. They thought she was getting too ambitious. She replied back stating she was happy being single in that case."

"It's so unfortunate, though, that many successful Indian women have stopped believing in the idea of marriage. They either fail to find a compatible match or just don't want a man in their lives. Men actually make their life difficult," Kunal said.

"But why do those few men think like that? What's really wrong with a smarter partner?" Vineet quizzed. "She can really help you get even better. Why be insecure?"

"And even if you consider her as competition, it should be healthy and constructive," Kunal added.

"I think it's just male chauvinism—a few confused souls who enjoy disdaining women power," Vineet said.

"We really need to keep life simple. We men really need to relax and realize that it's our responsibility to maintain a harmonious balance. I understand that being a partner you tend to vent out your frustration on her at times, but a line needs to be drawn," Madhav said.

"Women power is actually driving this world," Kunal said assertively. "And I am not ashamed of acknowledging that. Today's woman has struck perfection in all spheres; she's flawless at work and an impeccable homemaker. We worship goddess Durga who has many arms; today's woman is a perfect depiction of that image." He paused.

Madhav was emotional. Vineet had pride in his eyes for his friend.

"I would always like to remember my journey. It was full of surprises and soul ablution," Kunal said.

"Can I say something I never did?" Vineet asked.

Kunal nodded.

"It was also because you too were a firm believer of love." He paused. "There are many wonderful girls like Shreya, but still marriages fail miserably because their men keep belittling their efforts. You realised her value well in time." He grinned. "Now you can celebrate Valentine's Day happily!"

Madhav appeared confused for a while as he suddenly realised, his mother had been correct. Kunal turned towards him and read his mind. "I gave her a very tough time. Feel free to blast me."

Madhav smiled warmly. "She says her life is perfect. I know she means it. You are the kind of man she's always wished for."

"I think so too." Vineet added. "She did mention that once. Had Kunal been in Delhi and in close proximity, she would also have had an eight-year-long relationship as Aastha did."

"You never told me that." Kunal narrowed his eyes at Vineet.

"She's my best friend. I am supposed to keep her secrets. But then I thought for a change I should let you fly," Vineet said. They all laughed lightly.

"All a woman really wants is some understanding and love. She's a friend; she's a companion. She's strong; she's fearless. Don't try to beat them, join them!"

In their circle, Kunal and Shreya are known as marriage experts. Each friend considers them as the first ones to speak to if there's any problem in their own relationship. They are considered the most romantic and spirited couple around.

When Vineet expressed his love to Jyothsna, she wanted to get married immediately and in January 2011 they tied the knot. Shreya collapsed dancing at their *sangeet* ceremony to discover the ultimate happiness of womanhood was on its way.

Joy also came in pairs. On July 19, Shreya delivered twins. She wanted to keep her family tradition to have the daughter take the first letter from the mother and the son from the father. Kunal liked the concept, but twisted it a little.

Their babies are named Sarthak and Kuhika. The Pujari's Ramayana joke however, still runs in the family—Vineet and Madhav and their families call the twins Luv and Kusha.

And if my efforts to make you reach under the skin of my character are successful, this shouldn't come as a surprise. Kunal is spoiling the kids and Shreya's a strict mom.

Kunal didn't replace Shreya in office during her maternity leaves. He dissolved the position temporarily, increasing his own workload. Her cabin still awaits her return to work and is occasionally used as a meeting room.

Happiness lives with such couples forever.

God's a perfect match-maker; but yes he does work in mysterious ways!!